FINDING *Mercy*

FINDING *Mercy*

MICHAEL LANDON JR.
& CINDY KELLEY

transforming lives together

FINDING MERCY
Published by David C Cook
4050 Lee Vance View
Colorado Springs, CO 80918 U.S.A.

David C Cook Distribution Canada
55 Woodslee Avenue, Paris, Ontario, Canada N3L 3E5

David C Cook U.K., Kingsway Communications
Eastbourne, East Sussex BN23 6NT, England

The graphic circle C logo is a registered trademark of David C Cook.

This story is a work of fiction. All characters and events are the product of the author's
imagination. Any resemblance to any person, living or dead, is coincidental.

LCCN 2014943147
ISBN 978-0-7814-0870-7
eISBN 978-0-7814-1241-4

© 2014 Michael Landon Jr. and Cindy Kelley

The Team: Alex Field, Jamie Chavez, Amy Konyndyk,
Nick Lee, Helen Macdonald, Karen Athen
Cover Design: DogEared Design, Kirk DouPonce

Printed in the United States of America
First Edition 2014

1 2 3 4 5 6 7 8 9 10

072814

CHAPTER ONE

May 1866

The sky was as dark as pitch except for the streaks of lightning skittering across the heavens. Fat drops of rain pelted the top of Mercy's head as she hid from the world inside a vertical tomb. The muscles in her legs, pressed against brick on either side, trembled, and she tried to shift positions even as she listened for noise unrelated to the storm. Faceless men had been chasing her; now it seemed they had found her. She felt the rain run down the back of her neck and shivered. *Maybe this is my punishment for leaving the protection of Elijah and Isaac.* At the moment, wedged into a brick chimney on the second story of a boardinghouse, she regretted that action greatly.

The wind ripped down around her, causing her to look up. Something wasn't right. She squinted hard at another layer in the darkness—grayer, moving, closer than it should be. She had only a few seconds to think of the possibilities before a surge of lightning backlit a man leering down at her. Thunder followed, and her scream dissolved into the vortex of night noises.

"Come out, come out wherever you are, Miss Mercy." The sing-song tone of his voice mocked her, and her heart hammered. The sheer speed of what happened next took her off guard. A hand shot out and strong fingers wrapped around her arm. She tried to pull free as he tugged and yanked, moving her inch by inch toward the opening. His face was so close at one point she could smell alcohol on his breath as his other hand grappled for purchase any place on her body. But still she had the crazy thought that in other circumstances she would think him a nice-looking young man. Not at all like the bounty hunters she'd conjured up in her imagination.

She resisted with all her weight as he tugged, but it wasn't enough and she could feel the end of her journey coming at her with ferocious haste. Thunder cracked overhead—so close it felt as if it were sitting right on top of them—and the young man seemed startled by it. Mercy seized the opportunity. She pushed upward, giving slack to the man's grip on her arm, and catching him off guard. For a second, his hold loosened, and she yanked her arm back with all her might. Without the tension and her weight, he lost his balance, staggered for a moment, tried to grab the edge of the brick, but missed. The angle of the roof lent itself to his swift tumble down the shingles and off the edge. She could hear his scream over the sound of a brief lull in the storm. More telling than the scream from his fall was the way it abruptly ended. An alarmed voice from below yelled out, "Hell's bells, he's down!"

Mercy swallowed big gulps of the wet air just before she felt herself slip down the brick toward an even darker place. She struggled against the fall, knees bent, twisting and turning until she thwarted gravity by wedging herself sideways in the chimney. She tried to still her escalating panic and told herself she was safe for the moment. At least, she thought, if anyone else came out on the roof and looked into the chimney, they'd not be able to see her. Now, if they looked *up* the chimney from the fireplace in the parlor, that might prove to be a problem. She had no idea how far she'd fallen—only that the sky above seemed farther away. She wondered about the man who'd fallen from the roof, and wondered how many were left. She'd heard two men whispering in the hall outside her rented room, seen another standing thirty feet below as she'd stood barefoot on slippery shingles and contemplated her escape. *Did the man survive his fall from the roof? What kind of people hunt someone for money? How long will they wait to catch me?*

A soft but steady shower of rain hit the young man lying on the wet grass behind the boardinghouse. A man called Gus knelt beside him. Behind them, three other men stood in an uncomfortable semicircle. Luther and Newt, two ex–Union soldiers who had saved one another on the battlefield more than once, traded sad glances. The third man,

Harland, had spent the last four months of the war confined to an army hospital for two bullet wounds. Vengeance for the Confederate who'd shot him had gone unmeted. It was Harland who finally broke the silence.

"He's gone, Gus," Harland said. "Let's get him outta the rain."

But Gus didn't move. Harland traded looks with the other men, who shrugged. Luther looked up at the pitched roof and shook his head. "I swear that vixen is half witch. Disappeared is what she did."

"We need a new plan," Newt said.

Gus never took his eyes from the man on the grass. "You keep after her," he said. "I'm taking my boy home to his mother."

It was the sound of garbled voices that made Mercy open her eyes again. She stared at a triangle of light on her arm and then looked up. Daylight. Broad daylight overhead that left her wondering how on earth she'd passed the rest of the night in the chimney. Her head throbbed, her joints ached, and her back felt as if she'd never be able to straighten it again. She shivered in her damp dress and, ironically, wished she were *sitting* next to a warm fire. Had she really fallen asleep in such nightmarish conditions?

The sounds below her floated up the flue, which magnified people's voices. She pictured the interior of the boardinghouse, specifically the parlor with the large fireplace and the worn velvet chairs placed in close proximity to the hearth.

"Really, Mr. Douglas, that is most unkind!"

Mercy recognized the voice of Mrs. Douglas. She and her husband of fifty years had a strange way of addressing each other so formally; Mercy wondered if the two even remembered each other's first name.

"I am not being unkind, Mrs. Douglas." The old man's voice was querulous. "I am simply stating the truth. That young woman was too beautiful for her own good. Beauty like that gets a woman in all kinds of trouble."

"I liked her," his wife said. "She was sweet and didn't gossip."

"We knew her all of three days. Not nearly enough time to form a suitable opinion of her."

"You just said she was beautiful," Mrs. Douglas responded tartly.

"That is not an opinion," Mr. Douglas said. "It is a fact." His tone said he regarded the subject closed. "I don't remember a spring as cool as the one we're in now, do you?"

If Mrs. Douglas was miffed at being dismissed, the pleasant modulation of her voice gave no evidence of it. "I don't believe I do," she said. "Well, maybe the spring of '32. Remember how cold it was the day Joseph was born? Positively frosty in April."

"Yes, you're quite right. That was a cold spring. And right now, it feels rather frosty in here," he answered.

From her perch in the chimney, Mercy tried to shift her weight. She tried not to think of her thirst. Then she tried not to think about her other basic needs that needed to be met.

Below her, she could hear Mr. Douglas moving very close to the fireplace. More sounds carried up the shaft. Someone seemed to be stacking kindling as if intending to start a fire.

Mercy looked up at a sky that seemed miles away while she wriggled and turned to get her feet wedged in a better position on the brick. She'd have to climb up. Her legs quivered, muscles protesting every move she tried to make, as gravity seemed to grab hold of her ankles and pull her back down. She heard Mr. Douglas ask Mrs. Douglas for a match. Her nerves frayed to a breaking point, Mercy had a quick mental picture of a fire below her. The thought was so frightening her urgent need for the outhouse vanished and was replaced by sheer panic.

"Don't light the fire!" Mercy yelled.

Silence from below, then, "Did you hear that, Mrs. Douglas?"

"I think it came from the stairs, Mr. Douglas."

Mercy yelled again. "It came from in here. Don't light the—"

She slipped and the hearth of the fireplace came quickly at her. She clawed at the creosote-covered brick to slow her descent, but it didn't help—she dropped like a rock into the wide opening of the hearth in the parlor. She landed on the stack of kindling feetfirst, but her legs buckled and she found herself on her backside staring at the astonished faces of Mr. and Mrs. Douglas.

"Good day," Mercy said.

Mrs. Douglas, holding a teacup, opened her mouth as if to scream, but no sound came out. Mr. Douglas stood rooted to the spot, a box of matches in hand, his jaw dropped in shocked surprise.

"I'm sorry if I startled you," Mercy said, struggling to get out of the hearth.

"What the blazes is this?" Mr. Douglas demanded. "Where did you come from?"

Mercy tried to dust the chimney soot from her dress but then noticed her arms were as black as her dress.

Mercy looked around nervously. "Who else is here?"

"No one," Mr. Douglas said. He went to the fireplace, braced his hands on his knees and bent to look up the chimney.

"How in the world …?"

"Where is Mrs. Kline?"

Mrs. Douglas seemed to have found her voice. "Bess hasn't been down yet. It was a late night here. Lots of commotion."

"She knows it was a late night, Mrs. Douglas," Mr. Douglas said. "I believe we can surmise the commotion was about her."

"I'm sorry about that," Mercy said.

Mrs. Douglas swallowed hard, then pointed a trembling hand at Mercy's chest. "You … you appear to have a gun in your bosom."

Mercy pressed a soot-covered hand against the pistol tucked into the bodice of her dress, more to reassure herself it was safe than to apologize for it. "Yes," she said. "I don't have pockets."

Mr. Douglas glanced at her pistol, then caught himself and looked away. "It seems you're in a tight spot," he said. He looked at the chimney. "No pun intended, my dear. Let's get Bess and maybe we can help you figure this out."

"Thank you for your kind offer, but I'll be fine," Mercy said. "No need to wake Mrs. Kline. I'll just get my things and leave you all in peace."

Mercy hurried out of the parlor. She tread lightly on the steps, carefully avoiding the two she knew creaked, and made her way toward her room. The door stood open and she could see the splintered wood of the doorjamb where the lock had been kicked in. She should probably pay Bess, the landlady, for damages, but she'd spent her last dollar securing the room.

Mercy entered and went straight to the bed, got down on her knees and did a sweep with her hand to feel for her saddlebags and shoes. Nothing. She tried again, pressing herself even closer to the floor so she could extend her arm farther—but again, her hand came in contact with nothing at all. She lifted the bed skirt, pressed her cheek to the floor and looked under the bed. She had little in this world—just her pistol, the clothes on her back, a pair of shoes, and the saddlebags. She might have been able to leave without the shoes, but the saddlebags were another matter. She didn't know if the men had taken them or if they were still in the house. She stood and thought of what to do next, and that's when it dawned on her—the bed was made. Neat as a pin. Quilt pulled up, pillow fluffed. It certainly didn't look like the rumpled bed she'd deserted in the middle of the night. It *looked* like someone had done some housekeeping in the wee hours. Mercy had never been in her landlady's room, but she knew where it was. She padded barefoot down the hall.

CHAPTER TWO

The door to the bedroom was ajar. Mercy pushed tentatively and it opened a little farther; she could see inside. The bed was made, just as neatly as Mercy's bed had been. She didn't see anyone, but the saddlebags she sought lay across a padded bench at the end of the bed.

Mercy entered the room, which smelled of mothballs and stale perfume, single-minded of purpose, but a gasp stopped her cold. She turned to see Bess Kline in a rocking chair tucked into an alcove in the corner of the room.

"Mrs. Kline!"

"I thought you were gone," Mrs. Kline said.

"Not yet," Mercy said. "I apologize for coming into your room like this, but I was looking for my things. As soon as I get them, I'll be on my way."

Now that she was closer, she could see her shoes were beside the saddlebags. Mrs. Kline was silent as Mercy picked them up, opened the pouch, and felt around inside.

"It's not in there," Mrs. Kline said.

"Where is it?"

Mrs. Kline pushed up from the rocking chair. What she lacked in height she more than made up for in weight. The landlady raised her left hand and held aloft a leather-bound book. "Right here."

Mercy went toward her. "Thank you."

Mrs. Kline kept a grip on the book. "I was stunned when those men told me they were searching for a woman wanted for war crimes."

"Mrs. Kline …"

"I wouldn't normally read someone else's private thoughts, but when you disappeared last night, I assumed I'd never see you again, and honestly, you can probably understand my curiosity—can't you?"

"Yes, I suppose …"

Mrs. Kline smiled stiffly. "You know, I'm one of those terrible types who read the last page of a book first. No patience, I suppose." She opened Mercy's journal and read aloud from the page.

"I am building a fortress of lies. The worries involved with this are so great I can't list them all; suffice to say I will spend the rest of my life living with guilt that can be buried only by time—and more lies. I wish only to fulfill my duty. Finish my task. End the battle with a different outcome. Construct a plan so carefully thought through that there is no chance of error. It is my only chance at happiness with Rand."

She looked up from the journal. "Of course, your latest entry on that page didn't come as quite a big as shock to me as the rest. I already knew that information from the men who were here."

Mercy held out her hand. "May I have it, please?"

"Is it safe to say you never married the man you were engaged to? Rand, was it?"

"I didn't marry Rand. Now I really must be going …"

"The men are long gone," Mrs. Kline said.

"How can you be sure?"

"The one that fell off the roof—you *were* up there, weren't you? In the chimney from the looks of you."

"Yes …"

Mrs. Kline shook her head. Mercy couldn't tell if it was admiration or disgust.

"They had to leave to tend to the young man who fell off the roof. He died."

Mercy's mind flashed to the man peering down the chimney flue at her—his hand gripping her wrist, the frightening smile. She shivered.

"There's a basin of water on my dressing table," the landlady said. "You're a dirty mess."

Mercy went to the dressing table, where the oval mirror attached to the back provided a view from her neck down. The damage to her dress—black soot, creosote, and ash—could never be repaired. There was a tear in the skirt and a ribbon that had gone around her waist had torn and lay forlornly against her side.

Mercy was so tired; her body felt as if any minute it might betray her and she'd drop. She started to tremble from sheer exhaustion.

Mrs. Kline must have had the same thought because she reached for a flannel gown hanging on the wall and spread it across the ivory brocade seat of the vanity to protect it.

"Sit," she said.

Mercy sank gratefully onto the stool. When she raised her eyes to the mirror, a black face stared back at her. The whites of her eyes widened—her reflection was startling. *I look like a Negro in this light. Black skin, but still me underneath ... Would the old me hate me looking this way?*

Mrs. Kline handed Mercy a rag. "I'd start with your face."

"All right."

"Were you in the chimney the whole night?"

Mercy nodded, dipped the rag in the water, and then scrubbed at her cheeks, forehead, and chin. "I climbed in after I heard you in the hall with those men."

"I can't believe you were able to do that."

Mercy kept her eyes on her own reflection. Her skin was now a pasty gray. She swished the rag in the water again and squeezed out the excess.

"You'd be surprised what you can manage when you fear for your life," Mercy said.

Mrs. Kline sat on the edge of the bed, Mercy's journal pressed into her middle. "The last page of this book sounds quite damning," she said. "Are you guilty of their accusations?"

"No. The truth is, I was tried and convicted for a crime I didn't commit. A judge overturned the ruling and I was set free. Those men ... didn't agree with the judge."

"They aren't lawmen, then."

Mercy shook her head. "Bounty hunters." She dipped the rag into the murky water and gingerly washed the soot from her arm. She winced when she passed the rag over the places skinned by the brick.

"What were the charges against you?"

Mercy hesitated. "Treason."

Mrs. Kline frowned. "Those men broke into my home in the dead of night, then ruined a bedroom door by kicking it in."

"I'm sorry about the damage," Mercy said.

"You knew they were chasing you?"

"I knew it was a possibility."

"You wrote of being a soldier in the war," Mrs. Kline said. "I've heard of that. Women who dressed themselves as men so they could fight."

Even though the black was mostly gone from Mercy's face and arms, her skin still had a gray pallor. "You probably also read that I have amnesia. No memory of my motives for doing that."

"My husband, Wendell, fought for the cause." Mrs. Kline shook her head. "Shocked me to the core when he told me he'd enlisted. He wasn't a young man, but he wouldn't listen to my arguments. He left the summer of '62. I was glad we'd never had children. I couldn't have stood watching a son go off to fight too.

"He came back to me twice. The first time I could see the war was taking its toll, but he was still my Wendell. The second time he came back I barely recognized him. He was bitter, angry, resentful—spoke of nothing but his hatred of the enemy. I pleaded with him not to go back, but he didn't hear me. I don't think he even *saw* me. He left and I didn't see him again until July of 1864."

Mercy felt a rush of relief. "So he lived? He wasn't killed in the war?"

"He was captured. He was allowed to send me a single letter telling me where he was. It was short and emotionless. And it made my heart stop. I knew of the prison and the high mortality rate of its inmates."

"Prison is a horrible place," Mercy said quietly.

"I went there and bribed the guards to let me see him. It was a nightmare. There were men—walking skeletons covered in filth—and vermin inhabiting nearly every inch of space. I would not have known my husband if not for the cocky soldier who led me to him. Wendell was in a corner on the hard ground. A pile of bones, really. Cheeks so sunken he looked as if he'd been long dead, but yet he was breathing. It was scurvy, they said. Nothing to be done by that point. I sat and put my husband's head in my lap. He woke for a minute or two, whispered he regretted his decision to fight and was sorry to leave me. He died a few hours later."

"I'm so sorry," Mercy said.

Mrs. Kline's eyes hardened. "Please spare me your pity. I know you were a Confederate soldier. My Wendell fought for the Union— the side of the just and the right. He was condemned to die by Southern soldiers at Andersonville Prison who treated him worse than an animal. I'd like you to get out of my house now."

Mercy stood. "Wait, Mrs. Kline, please ..."

"I'm sorry they didn't catch you. Sorry they didn't make you pay for whatever it is that you've done—yet. They *will* find you again because now they have a new reason to hate you. The father of the young man who died was right here to see it."

"I'm sorry he died. That wasn't my intention. And I will leave—but not without my things." She held out her hand. "Can I have my journal back, please?"

"Can I have my life back before my husband died fighting against a cause you defended?"

"I'm just asking for my property and then I'll go," Mercy said.

Mrs. Kline sneered at her. "You don't get to ask for anything. I look at you and see all the evil of the South. My husband's death is on your head."

"I didn't kill your husband," Mercy said. "And I want my book." She drew the pistol from deep in the bodice of her dress and leveled it at her landlady. "Now."

"Once a low-life dirty rebel, always a dirty rebel," Mrs. Kline said, not without some satisfaction.

Mercy sighed. She was so tired. "So it seems." She kept her gun trained on the landlady until she threw the journal back onto the bed. Without taking her eyes from the older woman, Mercy grabbed her journal and stuffed it into a saddlebag. Clutching her shoes and saddlebags with one hand, she backed out of the room.

"I hope they catch you!" Mrs. Kline's voice followed her down the stairs. "I hope they catch you and hang you!"

CHAPTER THREE

The white man and the Negro boy had a system in each town they came to. The man entered every established business he could find with a carte de visite photograph of Mercy. The boy questioned every colored person on the street. But each time, they received a shake of the head, a frown, a shrug. It seemed no one had seen the lovely young woman they sought.

They galloped out of the latest small town on their path, taking their disappointment with them. When they rode through southern Illinois, the man finally slowed his horse to a walk. The boy did the same and for nearly an hour there was comfortable silence. But finally, the boy, being a natural-born conversationalist, broke the quiet.

"What'choo thinkin' on, Cap'n?"

Captain Elijah Hale looked over at fourteen-year-old Isaac and said the first thing that came to mind. "I'm wishing I could go back six months in time."

Isaac frowned and shook his head. "Not me. Nassuh. I've had me more good months since I knowed Miss Mercy dan I did before."

"Isaac, you're basically homeless because of Mercy," Elijah said.

The boy shook his head again, more adamantly this time. "She made me feel like a 'portant person. Treated me nice. Tol' me I can do things with my life. She stand up to Ezra and tell him quit beatin' on me." Isaac flexed his jaw and sat up a little straighter in the saddle. "She didn't ask me to come lookin' fo' her, Cap'n. This be my doin'. I ain't ever gonna be sorry I met Miss Mercy. Nassuh. I ain't."

Isaac was getting warmed up to the conversation. "First time I laid eyes on Miss Mercy be on my birfday. What 'bout you? When was da first time you say hello to her?"

"That's a little … complicated," Elijah said.

"What'cha mean?"

"The first time I saw her, she was dressed as a man—as a soldier."

Isaac let the information sink in. "Did you know I be in the courtroom when Miss Mercy be on trial?"

"No. You never told me that."

"I sit up in da top seats where da colored folks could be. And I hear da man ask Miss Mercy if she remember being a soldier—and she say no."

"I believe she was being truthful. She doesn't remember it," Elijah said.

"But den she tells da man dat even though she *don't* 'member being a rebel, she *do* believe she was," Isaac said. He looked pointedly at Elijah. "Somebody must a' told her."

"Yes."

"Dat somebody be you?"

Elijah sighed. "Yes, Isaac. It was me."

"Can't even get my head to think on Miss Mercy lookin' like a man."

"It sounds impossible, but she fooled everyone with her disguise … including me."

The face of that young Confederate sergeant came to mind as it often did when Elijah thought back to that day a year earlier. The sergeant had chased him down during the heat of battle to kill him but had instead stood quietly while Elijah prayed over his younger brother, Jed, who lay dying from a bullet wound sustained in a Tennessee field. That had been one of two days in Elijah's twenty-seven years when grief had driven him to his knees—the first being the day his father died. He had felt both helpless and numb when he said good-bye to the brother he'd grown up with, raced through meadows, climbed trees, and wrestled to burn off the steam that builds in boys. As an officer in the same company, Elijah felt he had failed to protect his brother, but because of the mercy of the sergeant, he'd been able to have a last few moments with him. His hand went to the mercy medallion around his neck that his own mother had given him as a reminder to pray daily for safety. *Should have prayed hourly,* Elijah thought. *Or maybe minute by minute because that's how quick life changed for Jed—and for me. Minute by minute …*

There had been very few words between Elijah and his rebel counterpart that April day. Elijah had met the sergeant's brown eyes when he uttered his thanks, and then he'd hung his medallion on the end of the soldier's knife and walked away.

"So—den you see her again," Isaac said. "Bet dat be a big surprise."

Elijah nodded. "But when I saw her again, I didn't know we'd met before."

It was several months later, when he attended an engagement party with some friends in St. Louis, that he'd been introduced to the bride-to-be and looked into those same brown eyes he'd seen on that battlefield.

"She was all dressed up at a party with Mr. Rand," Elijah said. "There was just something familiar about her. Her eyes … I don't know. But I spoke without thinking and asked her if we'd met."

"But she don't remember you."

"No. I was quickly reminded she had lost her memory. And by then I had told myself I was being foolish," Elijah said. "I tried to let it go … but I couldn't. I had to find out the truth."

Elijah had asked around about the mysterious woman and learned she'd been found wounded and alone with a head injury that had caused her amnesia. She'd taken her name from a mercy medallion she wore around her neck and could shoot a rifle with stunning accuracy. He *knew*. He knew Mercy, now engaged to be married to a proud and vocal supporter of the Union cause, had been that sergeant who had fought for the Confederacy—the one to whom he'd given his mercy medallion. He believed her amnesia to be real—that she really couldn't remember her time in the war. But he also believed she needed to know about it—and needed to tell her intended before their wedding day. She had argued at first and saw no point in dredging up a past she couldn't even remember. But Elijah had been adamant. *"What happens someday when your memory returns—and along with it, all the hatred that you felt for the North? It's possible if your memory returns you will be in the thick of the emotions that propelled you to fight for the South. You could wake up one morning and literally be sleeping with your enemy. He has to be told before you marry him."*

He remembered the look on her face and knew he was asking her to do something that seemed impossible. But it was the truth and he couldn't let it go. Elijah gave her a few weeks to tell her fiancé, Rand Prescott, what she'd learned about her past, and promised her if she didn't tell him, then he would.

It had seemed so simple. Mercy just needed to tell Rand the truth about her past. But the cascade of events that transpired while Mercy tried to come to terms with telling the man she loved about her Southern affinities had taken Elijah by surprise. When the story finally came out, it was a version of the truth manipulated by lies, anger, and hurt. Mercy was caught in a rolling tide that couldn't be stopped and by the time Elijah learned she was found guilty of a crime he knew she didn't commit, he barely made it in time to stop her hanging. She was released into his custody on a technicality of law others didn't agree with. Others that included a group of bounty hunters who still hated anyone or anything that had to do with the Confederacy. Mercy had every reason to hate Elijah, but he remembered the look of gratitude on her face when he told her he'd escort her safely out of Missouri. Gratitude, wonder, fear. He wondered how one woman could look so innocent and beguiling one moment, then steadfast and convicted the next.

"Miss Mercy be a lady full of surprises," Isaac observed.

Mercy *was* an enigma, but he'd had no reason to believe she'd run when they stopped to rest a few hours from Gratiot Street Prison in St. Louis. She took the first watch, and he gave her a pistol for her own protection. But it turned out she'd had one more surprise for him. He'd memorized the note she'd left for them while he and Isaac foolishly slept; it was folded neatly in his pocket along with a photograph of the woman herself the night of her engagement party—the night Elijah had seen her again. *"Elijah and Isaac—I'm sorry, but I'm going on alone. I have done enough damage, disrupted enough lives—and I won't have the two of you endangered because of me. You have a post to get back to, Elijah, and Isaac, it's time you thought about your own life for a change. Go north and find those opportunities you spoke of. You have a big heart and a great capacity for compassion. I know you will find the happiness you deserve. I left you the medallion, Elijah. It seems only fitting that you have it—especially considering it is your family heirloom, not mine. I need to find my family. My name. I know that I can't go forward with my life until I go back. After all, what are we if not the sum of our memories? Thank you for saving me. Mercy."*

It was the last line of the note that haunted Elijah. *"Thank you for saving me."* He may have saved her from a hangman's noose, but without his insistence on the truth, the events that transpired would have never happened. He saved her from one fate, only to catapult her into running from another. If the men who hunted people for money found her, then it seemed to Elijah that hanging would have been kinder for her. At least it would have been quick. He didn't believe the same would be true if bounty hunters found Mercy before he did. She had been released into his custody and he'd failed in his commitment to keep her safe. Elijah needed to find her, see her home, and only then could he get on with his own life. Each day on her trail felt as if she were slipping farther and farther away. Elijah pressed his heels into the horse, and they picked up speed.

"My belly is rumbling," Isaac said.

"Your belly is always rumbling," Elijah said. "We're running low on food. There's a fort south of here—two or three days' ride. We'll get more provisions there, and I need to send a telegram back to Fort Wallace to ask permission to extend my leave."

"What if you ain't able to stay gone?"

"I'll be able," Elijah said. "I've got more time coming."

"Seems kinda peculiar to hafta send a wire tellin' folks who *know* you ain't there, that you ain't there," Isaac reasoned.

"Not so peculiar," Elijah said. "The army is supposed to know where I am. I took an oath and it's part of that oath."

"Oath?"

"It's like a promise."

"Like your promise to da court to help Miss Mercy get to the state line?"

"Something like that."

He looked over at the boy, who'd already taught him more about what it meant to be a Negro in post–Civil War America than he would ever learn from books or newsprint. He knew finding Mercy was the thing in Isaac's mind that would set everything right—but the longer they went without a trace of her, the more pessimistic

Elijah became. He could only hope that the bounty hunters on her trail had come up as short at finding her as he had.

"Guess we better stop and fill that empty belly of yours," Elijah said.

"I think you is a born problem solver," Isaac said. "An' I kin think of one more problem you can take care of."

"What's that?" Elijah asked.

"Learnin' me to shoot that pistol o' yours," Isaac said. "What if someone overtakes you and I be the only one around? If I don't know how to shoot, how am I gonna save you?"

"Isaac, even though I believe they are wrong, there are still laws on the books in some states that make it illegal for a Negro to fire a gun. I don't want there to be any reason at all for someone to lock you up."

Isaac looked resigned. "Yassuh, Cap'n. I guess I'll just hafta save you by my own wits if you get in some kinda trouble."

"All right. I'll take that help because I believe your 'wits' are nearly as lethal as any weapon," Elijah said.

CHAPTER FOUR

Bess and the town of Salem were twenty-four hours behind her. Mercy had gone straight to the livery from the boardinghouse and, when she was sure no one was waiting for her, had collected her horse, Lucky. He was the only living thing in the world that she could say with any certainty loved her. Lucky meant the world to her. She knew he would run forever if she asked it of him. So when he stumbled over a large tree root on the outskirts of Cairo, Illinois, she knew they had to stop.

The town was situated between two large rivers that were busy ports for traffic moving along the water. She gravitated west where she followed the banks of the Mississippi. She'd been vaguely aware of people in the area, some sitting on the river's edge, some lounging under trees. But it wasn't until she actually stopped and dismounted that she realized every face around her was black. Lucky immediately began munching on clumps of tall, reedy grass. Nervous, she tried to pretend there weren't hundreds of eyes upon her, and opened her saddlebags while her stomach growled in protest. But there was nothing, not even a morsel of food. She would let Lucky get his fill of grass, get some water from the river, and move on. She thought about the pistol she had tucked under the saddle blanket and wondered how quickly she'd be able to grab it if one of the Negroes surrounding her got aggressive. *Not quickly enough,* she decided. One of her and probably two hundred of them. She needed to go. Just get back in the saddle and find Lucky another patch of delicious grass.

"I kin see it on yo' face, missus."

Mercy looked around for the source of the voice and saw an old woman sitting under a tree a few feet away. She had a red kerchief tied around her head, and a dark, serviceable dress was stretched out like a blanket over her legs, and on top of that, a colorful apron. Her bare feet poked out past the hem of the skirt.

"Excuse me?" Mercy said.

"It is your first time seein' so many black folks in one spot," the woman said. "The look on yo' face say I'm right."

"Oh. No. I … I …"

"Don't fret. Ain't no one here gonna hurt you."

Mercy glanced around, then looked back at the woman. "So many people. Why here?"

The woman offered a smile missing several teeth. "So many a' *my* people."

"Well, yes."

"Most all of us was slaves. Union Army tell lots of newly freed Negroes to come to Cairo ... mostly 'cause they don't know what else to do with us. Some left; some stayed. Ain't 'nuff work to go round. We gots no money and no place to live."

"I didn't think about what would happen when everyone was freed," Mercy said.

"It's a mess. Dat's a fact. Good Lord knows slavery is wrong, but freedom come with its own set of troubles."

Mercy looked at the faces of the men, women, and children— eyes filled with uncertainty and jaws slack with resignation. Their shoulders were slumped in defeat. She knew how they felt.

"You should sit," the old woman said. "You ain't lookin' so good."

"I need food," Mercy said.

The old woman looked at Lucky. "Is too bad we cain't eat grass like da pony."

"Yes."

"You got money?"

Mercy shook her head. "No."

The old woman frowned. "I think all pretty white woman's got money."

"Not me."

The old woman shrugged. "Den you wait."

"Wait for what?"

The woman struggled to her feet and pointed toward a barge steaming toward them. "Fish."

Mercy watched the barge slow enough near the dock so crewmen could jump out and tie up to the moorings. The old woman was lame in one leg, but she managed to make it to the river at the same time dozens of others streamed into the water. Crew hands dumped baskets of fish off the sides of the barge into the river. The people descended on the bounty. In less than five minutes, the old woman was back by Mercy's side. She unceremoniously turned the pockets of her apron so that fish fell onto the grass.

"It's food," she said. "And it be free."

"Why do they throw it back into the river?"

Another shrug from the old woman. "Too much. Wrong kind. Not good 'nuff. I dunno and I ain't carin'. It's food." The woman squatted, pulled a knife from her pocket and slit the belly of one of the fish. In another swift movement, she peeled back the skin and then held it out to Mercy.

"Don't you cook it?" Mercy asked.

"I gots no pan. No fire. No place to fix fancy fish," she said. "My belly used to da raw fish." She cocked her head to one side. "You ain't too hungry, den?"

Mercy looked around at dozens of others who were devouring the fish the same way. She knew she needed something in her stomach to go on. *It's food.* She accepted the fish, pushed down the revulsion she felt, and took a tentative bite. After the first bite, it got easier. She gratefully finished off the first fish, and then one more.

The old woman's name was Magda, and she told Mercy she'd had a son named Hector who fought at the battle of Fort Henry.

"The Confederates win da battle, but my Hector lost his war."

"I'm sorry," Mercy said.

"Me, too, missus. Me, too."

"I'm sure you're very proud of your son," Mercy said.

"Proud. Yes. He helped build Fort Henry for da South. And Fort Donelson. He was a good son. A good soldier."

Mercy's search lay heavy on her heart. "I need to go. But thank you …"

"I wanted to go dere, see his last place on dis earth," Magda said. "But I hear tell da river took it away"

"What about the other one, Fort Donelson?"

"Still there," Magda said. "Someone say dey gots records there. Pictures and letters and things a mama would wanna have."

"Maybe you'll go someday," Mercy said. "How far is it?"

"Gotta be a hundred miles downriver," Magda said. "Wit dis bad leg a' mine, might as well be a million."

Mercy looked at the faraway look in Magda's eyes, then gathered Lucky's reins. "Thank you for the fish." She led Lucky down to a swiftly moving spot in the river to drink his fill, quenched her own thirst, and finally had a plan. She knew where her next stop would be.

It started with cramping in her stomach after she'd been in the saddle for about eight hours. Mercy told herself it was just new hunger pains. The fish had satisfied her for a while, but she couldn't survive on two fish alone. And then she quickly changed her mind when the first wave of nausea hit her. The fish came up violently. She'd been following the river, and now in the full moon, she could see the water shining to her left. Lucky kept walking, and she felt a wave of heat start in her core and radiate out, and wondered if it were possible for a person to burst into flame from a fever. By the time she saw garrisons of artillery on the bank of the river, she was shivering violently. Cannons rose up from the water's edge like ghostly images in the moonlight. When she saw hundreds of flowers that seemed to be lying across the ground, she was sure she was hallucinating. By the time the outline of the fort came into view, she was lying over Lucky's neck. Everything in her vision swam, and she held tight to Lucky's mane. *Please, God—help me see this through. Maybe they have answers about me.*

A flare suddenly appeared and illuminated double doors of a building. Mercy vaguely wondered what people had against death. The way she felt, it seemed like a good option. But she told herself to hang on. Maybe here she would find a sympathetic ear. She'd tell them her history and how she'd fought for the South. Surely they would do what they could to help her find clues to her past. A fellow soldier; a fellow Confederate. She told herself she was among friends. It might be all right. All she wanted was a place to lie down, some hay for Lucky.

A soldier stepped into view. Mercy frowned. Even with just the moon for light, she could see something wasn't right. His uniform. His hat. The color. All wrong. The soldier yelled something at her, but it didn't make sense. He came toward her and she knew she should go—ride away from the stranger who was asking her name. But then he yelled for help. *That's good, get help,* she thought. *Just let me sleep. Please. Just a little sleep and some food for my horse.*

Strong arms went around her and helped her from the saddle. She frowned at him, wanted to thank him, but the bile rose in her throat again and instead of issuing a thank-you, she vomited all over him. Her knees buckled and she felt herself lifted off her feet. She felt him heft her weight and settle her more securely as another man finally arrived.

The man carrying her called out to the other. "Get the door!"

"Ma'am?" he said. "Can you tell me your name?"

"Is this Fort Donelson?" She wondered why her voice sounded so far away.

"Yes, ma'am. Home of the bravest soldiers that ever fought for the Union."

Chapter Five

There were five of them. Soldiers still in the army assigned to be glorified caretakers of Fort Donelson. After the horrors of the war—the fighting, killing, disease, and malaise—the duty was easy. They had trickled into what used to be the headquarters of the place, one by one, four privates and a second lieutenant.

Eventually, the trickling of new personnel stopped and the five men were prepared to call the fort home indefinitely. They lived in the four-thousand-square-foot building constructed of ten-foot walls made of rough-hewn logs caulked with mud. Double doors from outside led into a twenty-by-twenty-foot room they referred to as the "receiving room." It held a long counter, a few battered desks, and stacks of supplies that had seen better days after years of war. At the far end of the receiving room, another door led into a huge anteroom called the common area, housing a makeshift kitchen, a long wooden table, several chairs, and a wood-burning stove with a stack that shot right through the flat roof. On the north side of the common area was a row of doors that led into former officer quarters that the men now claimed for their own. Their duties were light. They were to keep the place tidy, see after the half dozen horses in the corral, and maintain the cemetery filled with brave Union men who had died there. Once a month, women from the closest town of Dover arrived with flowers to tuck next to the simple grave markers lined up in the cemetery near the river.

The fort had been built by the Confederates to help them hold the South, but then they'd lost it to the Union—just like the rest of their Southern cause. The soldiers had light duty and wages the first of every month. It was a dream posting for those with no ambition; all five men fit the bill to a T.

Lieutenant Harry Brewer found the arrival of the mystery woman unsettling. The minute he'd picked her up in his arms and looked into her pale face, he knew she was going to be trouble. Women were *always* trouble in some form or fashion. She'd been incoherent most of the twenty-four hours she'd been in their care, but cleaned up and in the light of day, she presented a pretty picture. He saw the way the men looked at her. He had looked at her the same way.

In fact, as he sat next to her cot, he found it impossible *not* to look at her. Long, wavy hair fanned across her pillow and framed her beautiful face; her slim arms and long legs, and … He tried to stop his runaway thoughts. He'd heard all the crude comments about her, he'd even made a few of his own. There was a reason the men had taken to arguing among themselves over who got "bedside duty." The appeal of sitting next to the cot to gaze on her without reprimand or reproach was a draw too great to forgo. In fact, he was staring at her so hard, it almost took him by surprise when her eyes fluttered open. He watched her try to focus, then turn her head and look at him—eyes filled with questions. He watched as she took in his face, then his blue uniform. The look in her eyes changed to fear. Without saying anything, she scooted closer to the rough log wall and tried to push herself up.

"Better take it easy," Brewer said. He couldn't help the way his eyes dipped to her bare shoulders. She caught his gaze and looked down to see a coarse blanket had puddled around her waist, leaving her thin cotton chemise exposed. She snatched the blanket back up to her chin, and her cheeks flamed red. It was the first color he'd seen in her face since her arrival.

"Where's my dress?" Her voice was hoarse and tentative.

He nodded at material folded over the back of a chair.

"It was awfully dirty," he said. "We washed it as best we could. Took your pistol for safekeeping."

She swallowed at that. Then her gaze swept over the room.

"What's your name?" he asked.

"Where am I?"

"Fort Donelson."

"My horse. Where …"

"He's been fed and watered. Got him in the corral," Brewer said.

She looked relieved, and relaxed against the pillow. Her eyes fluttered closed.

"At least tell me your name? Can we contact someone about you?"

But she didn't answer, and he could see she'd slipped back into sleep. He studied her, then reached for the blanket to pull it higher across her shoulders.

"I like to adjust that blanket too." The voice startled Brewer, and he turned guiltily toward the man standing in the doorway. It was Dwight Westland—West to his fellow soldiers.

Brewer got to his feet and tried to ignore the smirk on West's face.

"She woke up for a few minutes," Brewer said.

"Say anything?"

"Not really. Wanted to know about her dress and her horse."

"Didn't get a name, huh?"

Brewer shook his head. "No. She was back to sleep too fast."

West walked over to the cot and looked down at her. Brewer could practically read his mind. It had been a long time since any of them had been with a woman.

"I just can't figure it," West said. "You gotta wonder where she was going. And why? You don't see ladies like this traveling alone."

"Ladies like what? She wasn't exactly dressed to the nines when she arrived."

"Doesn't matter what she had on. She's a beauty. Even a flour sack would look good on her." As if he couldn't help himself, West reached out and touched her hair. "I'm telling you, a woman that looks like this belongs to someone."

Brewer agreed, but he didn't say anything. West plunked himself down in the chair next to the bed and looked up at Brewer with a grin. "If you need me, Lieutenant, you know where to find me."

Four of the five men posted at the fort gathered around the makeshift poker table in the common room, their card game all but forgotten as they discussed the guest sleeping in a room just fifteen feet away.

"I say she's like our own personal Briar Rose." A hand-rolled cigarette rode up and down on Jake Stern's bottom lip when he spoke. He grinned at his own notion.

"Who?" West asked.

"You know—*Briar Rose*. Didn't your moms ever read you fairy tales? She's the beautiful girl the evil fairy cursed to sleep for a hundred years."

Ed Marvin, short, stocky and homely as the day was long, spoke up. "Hey—I remember that one. Some prince has to kiss her to wake her up."

"I volunteer," West said.

"You ain't no prince," Stern said.

"That's all right, 'cause she's not a princess." They turned toward the door, where Lieutenant Brewer stood with Mercy's journal in his hand. "She's a rebel—and one on the run at that."

Brewer walked into the room and held up the journal. "I found this in her saddlebags about an hour ago. It's some kind of diary. Says her name is Mercy. I wasn't going to read it. Had sisters who wrote in books like this. You know, private kind a' stuff. But then I thought it might give us a clue to who she is."

"You said she's a rebel—meaning she's from the South?"

"No—she fought in the war. She was an actual Confederate sharpshooter."

Brewer opened the leather cover and flipped to the back page. "Listen to this. It's dated three weeks ago." He cleared his throat, then began to read aloud. *"I've left them behind. I can't risk their safety in exchange of my own. I'm alone now. Alone again with no idea of where to go—or who I'm looking for. The only thing I do know is to head south. Back to the place I suppose it all started—where I took up arms in defense of things I can't remember. It's best this way—unless the men find me. Then ... I don't even think God can help me.'*

Brewer looked up from the page. "There's more. She's got something called amnesia."

"What does that mean?" West asked.

"She's got no memories. Doesn't know who she is or where she's from—but somehow she knows she fought for the South."

The men traded looks. It was Stern who said what was probably on everyone else's mind. "So if she's got no memory—no family ... no plan of where she's going ..."

"No one knows she's here," West said. They let that sink in.

"She said men were looking for her," Stern said. "Why?"

"You only run if you're guilty," Marvin said.

"We're basically our own government here. They don't care what we do as long as the proper requisitions orders are filed and the place remains standing. We can offer our own brand of justice for beautiful lady soldiers. Shouldn't be fighting anyway."

"What kind of justice?" Stern asked.

A slow smile spread across West's face. The others stared at him, shocked, but also intrigued.

"Cripes' sake, West," Stern said quietly.

"What? You guys saying I'm the only one who's thought about having a rebel woman?"

No one contradicted him. Another knowing smile from West. "You know we're all thinkin' it."

CHAPTER SIX

The bright May day had gone from pleasantly warm to unusually hot by the time Elijah and Isaac made their way onto the post. There they planned to pick up more supplies and wire Elijah's superior officer at Fort Wallace.

Elijah had heard about the battle of Fort Donelson. Hundreds of lives had been given to secure it to ensure that the Union could use the Cumberland River to move supplies farther into the South. Garrisoned artillery still stood pointing at the river, the cannons a testament to military plans that went awry. More than once he'd heard when the Confederacy lost the river, they lost the war. The infamous fort seemed almost deserted as they rode toward the front of the building. They dismounted, and Isaac took Elijah's reins.

"What you wantin' me to do, Cap'n?"

Elijah pointed at the corral some fifty yards away. "See what you can find in the way of food for the horses. If anyone asks, give them my name and tell them they can check with me if there's a problem."

Isaac led both horses toward the corral while Elijah pulled open the double doors and entered the building.

A soldier behind a long counter frowned at him. "This is a military post, mister. No civilians. You'll have to move along."

Elijah pulled some papers from his pocket and put them on the counter. He unfolded the top paper, then spun it around for the soldier to see.

"I'm Captain Hale from Fort Wallace, Kansas." He pointed to something scrawled across the paper. "My leave papers from Company M, Second Cavalry."

"Sorry, sir. Private Westland. Since you're not in uniform I didn't know …"

Elijah waved away the apology. "I need to send a telegram to my commander. Can you do that?"

"Yes, sir. Right away."

Westland rummaged under the counter for some paper and a pencil. "Ready."

"Put it to the attention of Post Commander James J. Gordon. 'Request to extend my leave by one month. Stop. Present location Fort Donelson, Tennessee. Stop. Captain Elijah Hale. Stop.'"

"I'll send it right away, sir," Westland said.

Elijah looked around. "The place seems pretty quiet. How many men are here?"

"Five of us, sir," he replied. "Lieutenant Brewer is our ranking officer. Would you like me to get him?"

Elijah shook his head. "Not necessary, Private. Just send the message."

Westland turned from the counter, but Elijah stopped him. "Before you go, I'm wondering if you can provide me with a map of this part of Tennessee and the north part of Kentucky."

"I believe we've got some maps here somewhere." West ducked under the counter. "They're a couple of years old, though." He brought out three maps and put them on the counter, shoving Elijah's papers aside.

"Here you are, sir. I'll just go send that—"

Something of Elijah's seemed to have caught Westland's eye. Elijah followed the private's gaze to the photograph of Mercy.

"Private?"

Westland looked stricken. "She's beautiful."

"She's missing," Elijah said.

"Excuse the impertinence, sir, but is she your wife?"

Elijah shook his head. "No. She's a young woman who has been acquitted of a crime. But she's still in danger from some unscrupulous men who want to see her pay for her allegiance during the war."

The young private's eyes were still glued to Mercy's image.

"Do you recognize her?"

Westland finally looked up. "No," he said quickly. "Never seen her before. What'd she do anyway?"

"It doesn't matter now. As I said, she was acquitted."

"Yes, sir. Let me send that wire for you," West said. "The telegraph is in the next room. Be right back."

West closed the door behind himself and tried not to panic. He was headed to the telegraph machine when he ran into Stern.

"Hey! There's a captain out there who has a photograph of Mercy. He's looking for her—and it sounds like he ain't the only one."

"Did he say what she did?"

"No."

"You didn't tell him she's here, did you?" Stern demanded.

"Of course not. Give me some credit, will ya?" West arched a brow. "The little lady is finally getting well enough to be a decent companion. Nobody's taking her away from us. Who's got the watch right now?"

"Brewer," Stern said. "The lieutenant never misses his turn."

"Keep her quiet and out of sight," West said.

Stern hustled away and West made his way to the telegraph. In just a few minutes, he was pushing back into the receiving room, where the captain stood perusing the maps.

"All set, sir. Telegram's been sent to Fort Wallace." West smiled. "Safe travels."

"I need to see the requisitions clerk, Private," Captain Hale said.

West fought the urge to curse. "You're looking at him, sir."

"I could use some fresh jerky, hardtack ... wouldn't mind some potatoes if you can spare them," Captain Hale said. "Any fruit you might have on the post would be appreciated."

West shook his head. "No fruit at all, sir. But I can get the other items for you and have Private Stern bring them out."

The captain made his way back out the door, and West felt his heart rate slow to nearly normal. He needed to get the supplies and get the captain on his way. And the sooner, the better.

While their horses ate, Isaac stood against the corral fence and watched as a private curried one horse after another. He moved next to a chestnut, but the horse didn't want any part of the grooming. He snorted, bucked, tossed his head in a manner that had the private backing up and moving on to another horse.

Isaac walked toward them. "Guessing he don't like attention."

The private snorted. "He don't like nothing. Ornery cuss."

The private turned back to his task and Isaac made his way closer to the obstinate horse. "He take a saddle?"

"What's it to ya?"

Isaac shook his head. "Nothin'."

Isaac approached the restless horse from the side. When he got to within an arm's reach, the chestnut turned and eyed him. He flared his nostrils, snorted, then turned his head to shove his nose right into Isaac's outstretched hand. Isaac moved closer and stroked his nose. When he spoke, it was in a voice meant only for the horse.

"It *is* you," Isaac said. He trailed his fingers over the white markings on the bay's nose. "Hello, boy. Hello, Lucky. Where be your lady?"

Lucky nickered softly under Isaac's caresses.

"Hey … step back from that horse." The private frowned at Isaac. "He's unpredictable."

"He be fine wit' me," Isaac said. "Maybe he don't know you too good."

"Don't be sassy with me, boy," the private said. "Just step away from him."

Isaac did as he asked but was happy to see Elijah striding toward them. He hurried out of the corral and rushed to his side.

"I can't believe it, Cap'n," Isaac said excitedly. "We done found Miss Mercy."

Elijah stopped. "What are you talking about?"

Isaac nodded in the direction of the horses. "Dat dark chestnut over there. Dat her horse, Lucky. If he here, den I figure she here. You didn't see her?"

"No." Elijah cut his gaze to the private who seemed to be watching the two of them. He lowered his voice. "Are you sure about this?"

"Yassuh, I am. I be the one who took care of Lucky when Miss Mercy stayed at da cottage. He was a mean cuss to ever'one but me and Miss Mercy. Lucky was dat color with da black mane and one white sock. You look at his nose and you see he got a star 'tween his eyes and a stripe that got a break in it halfway down. That *is* Lucky. And he knowed me."

Isaac followed Elijah into the corral. The private working in the corral crossed the fifteen feet it took to join them.

"I'm Captain Hale," Elijah said.

The private snapped off a salute. "Private Stanley Mitchell, sir."

Elijah returned the salute. "I appreciate the food and water for our horses."

"No problem, sir. Plenty of oats here to go around," Mitchell said.

Elijah nodded. "Good. Too many animals suffered the effects of the war."

"Darn shame," Mitchell said.

"That chestnut looks like he could use a little fattening up, though," Elijah said, pointing to Lucky.

"He's only been on post about a week or so," Mitchell said. "Cantankerous cuss, but he's learning where the food comes from."

"Got your supplies here, Captain."

Another private came toward them with his arms full of supplies. "Private Westland said you were ready to head out, so I'll get these packed up for you, sir."

Mitchell hurried toward him. "Lemme give you a hand, Jake."

Mitchell grabbed some of the supplies and headed toward Elijah's horse.

Elijah stepped in front of the new private before he could follow. "How long have you been assigned here at the fort, Private?"

"It's Private Stern, sir. About eight months."

"I was wondering how long that horse has been on post. The chestnut."

"I, uh … couldn't tell you, sir. This is Private Mitchell's domain."

Elijah nodded. "Handsome horse."

"Yes, sir," Stern said. "Let me help get you packed up …"

MICHAEL LANDON JR. & CINDY KELLEY

"I've had a change of heart, Private," Elijah said. "I could use a bed and a good night's sleep. I assume you have room?"

"Let me go find Lieutenant Brewer for you, Captain."

Mitchell was back. He looked at Stern. "You're holding up the captain with all this chitchat, Stern. I'm sure he wants to get on his way …"

"Actually, he's staying," Stern said. "I was just going to find the lieutenant and let him know."

"I don't know that we have a room for your … for the … Wouldn't be right to put a colored boy in the officer's quarters, sir," Private Mitchell said.

Elijah looked at Isaac. "That does pose a problem, Isaac."

"I'm sure you figure it out, Cap'n," Isaac said. "After all you is a problem solver."

Elijah nodded. "I'll see about where we can put you. In the meantime, stay here with the horses. This gives you some time to check on their saddles, their shoes. We want them in great condition to ride. I like to be prepared. You understand?"

"Yassuh. I believe I do," Isaac said.

Isaac watched as Elijah led the way back to the building with the two privates right on his heels.

CHAPTER SEVEN

Mercy knew two things when the private called West came to get her. First, he seemed agitated, worried about something. And second, she could see he was carrying her journal. The latter took the air right out of her lungs and made her feel even weaker than she already felt.

She had been out of bed a few times to take care of basic needs, but she was dismayed at her lack of strength. She had no choice but to lean heavily on West as he hurried her along.

"What's happening?" she asked.

"Just moving you for safekeeping."

"Safekeeping from who?"

"Never mind."

But suddenly she knew. They'd found her. The bounty hunters

had somehow tracked her down—and the soldiers had read her journal. They knew she was running.

They stopped at a locked room, and West produced a key from his pocket. He unlocked the door and brought her inside.

Late afternoon sun poured into the room from a single window. There were boxes and crates, papers, and large portraits leaning against the wall. A Confederate flag draped over a chair caught her eye.

"What is this?"

"Losers' room," West said.

He turned one of the crates over, dumping the contents unceremoniously out onto the floor.

"Sit here."

He plunked her down on the crate, and she was happy to be off her feet. She hated feeling so weak and dependent, but was grateful that the men were obviously trying to keep her safe from the bounty hunters by hiding her away.

"Thank you for—" Her words were cut off when he suddenly put a piece of cloth across her mouth. The action was so surprising, she didn't have time to react before he tied it tightly behind her head. She shook her head, tried to speak, but he had already moved on to binding her wrists together.

"You'll stay quiet and still until I come back for you," he said, leaning down to her face. "Understand?"

She shook her head, but he just smiled and tossed her journal at her feet. "Great reading, by the way."

He left her alone, and she heard the lock of the door engage. Why would they feel the need to bind and gag her when she didn't want the bounty hunters to find her any more than they did? West's actions made no sense.

She worked the gag from her mouth, but the knot in the rope around her wrists was too tight to free. Trying to tamp down her rising fear, she let her gaze roam over the room. *The Losers' Room.* She had come to the fort looking for something—records—anything that might jog her memory or help her on the path toward home, and now it seemed she was steeped in all things Confederate.

She struggled to her feet and made her way toward the crates of files. There seemed to be no rhyme or reason to the piles. She began to rifle through the stacks of paper, not an easy task with her tightly bound wrists. She read name after name, but in just a few minutes, she realized the idea that some name or date would jog her memory was a long shot at best. Her hope gave out at the same time her legs did, and she sank to the floor.

She had no idea what was happening outside the door. What if the soldiers who'd seemed so kind and nursed her back to health had thrown in their lot with the bounty hunters for the money? Scooting along the floor, she made her way back to the place where her journal lay and put her back against the wall. At least she would see them coming if they burst through the door. She wondered what she could use for a weapon if it came to that, and she took another longer look around the room. And that's when she saw it. The thing she'd been waiting to find; the moment that made her feel as if she *had* existed before the day her memory left. She stared at a portrait leaning against the opposite wall. He was a handsome man in full colonel's uniform. Dark hair, strong chin—midforties, maybe. But it was his eyes that drew Mercy in and made her feel as if she knew this man. For the first time in over a year, she was gazing on a familiar face.

Elijah, who'd been left waiting at the counter in the receiving room, was just about to go touring the place on his own when a young lieutenant entered.

"Captain Hale? I'm Lieutenant Brewer. My men tell me we're going to have the pleasure of your company here tonight."

"I've waited so long I was beginning to believe it might be a problem for you," Elijah said.

"Not at all. I'm sorry about the wait. Private Westland is making up a room for you. Our visitors are few and far between. In fact, you're the first unfamiliar face we've seen in more than two months."

"Is that right?"

"Yes. And usually when someone comes through they're in a hurry to get to Dover, or wherever they're headed."

"I'm in no hurry," Elijah said. "Got a month of leave coming to me and I intend to use every last day."

Brewer smiled. "Lucky you."

"If you don't mind, I'd like to see my quarters now," Elijah said.

Brewer hesitated. "I'm not sure that Westland has it ready …"

"I've seen my share of bare mattresses, Lieutenant."

"Of course. This way," Brewer said. He turned and Elijah

followed him through the door on the opposite wall and stepped into the common area.

Private Westland was halfway across the room when Brewer stopped him.

"Did you take care of everything … for the captain?"

West nodded. "All taken care of, Lieutenant. The quarters are ready."

They moved toward the row of rooms on the other side of the common area. Brewer led him to a closed door.

"Here we are, Captain," he said. He opened the door and gestured for Elijah to enter first. But Elijah barely stuck his head in the door.

"It's fine, Lieutenant," he said.

"Good. Now, the men tell me you're traveling with a Negro boy? If you're not opposed, we've got a small barn on the property. It would keep him warm and—"

Elijah interrupted him. "I'd like a tour of the place. Maybe we'll find a more suitable place for Isaac."

"I assure you, Captain, the rest of the rooms are in use, and—"

Elijah walked to the door next to the officer's quarters. "Let's start here."

He opened the door to reveal Private Stern and another man he'd never seen before. "Can we help you, sir?" Stern asked.

"The captain is just having a look around the place," Brewer said. "Private Marvin? Go tell Westland that he'll need to make a little more chow tonight."

"Sure thing, Lieutenant," Marvin said, hustling past Elijah into the common room.

Elijah walked to the next closed door. "More enlisted quarters?"

Brewer shook his head. "No. That would be mine." He reached past Elijah and opened the door. "Please. Have a look."

Elijah stuck his head into the sparely furnished room. A cot with a wool blanket spread over the top. A desk with several books, the makings for cigarettes, and a single window with heavy wooden shutters.

They continued down the row of doors with Elijah opening each one until they reached the end. Brewer smiled. "End of the tour. Nothing too exciting."

Elijah looked down a long hallway, then started that direction, leaving the common room behind. "What about down here?"

Brewer hurried after him. "Nothing of interest."

Elijah arrived at another door. "And this is?"

"Just a storage room," Brewer said. "I've never been in there, but I'm told it's filled with old Confederate papers ... service records, portraits, a few diaries from some generals who we now know couldn't fight their way out of a schoolyard brawl. We call it the losers' room."

"I'd like to see inside," Elijah said.

"Sorry. Door's locked and we don't have the key," Brewer said.

"I want the key to that door, Lieutenant."

"I don't have it."

"I suppose I don't have to have a key." Elijah drew his pistol from the holster and leveled it at the door lock.

"Wait!" Brewer said. "I'm responsible for any damage that's done here. Let me see if I can find the key."

Elijah nodded. "I'd appreciate that."

Brewer scurried back down the hall. Elijah watched until he disappeared from view, then shot the lock off the door.

Mercy sat against the wall, eyes wide, knees drawn up defensively when he came through the door. He could see the conflicting emotions playing out in her eyes as he crossed the room toward her.

He knelt. "Mercy. Are you all right?"

She stared at him and he realized he looked quite different from the last time she'd seen him. His hair was long, he was bearded, and he wasn't in uniform.

"Elijah?" she finally sputtered. "What are you doing here?"

"You first." He untied her wrists and helped her to stand. Her journal fell to the floor and he retrieved it.

"I was ill when I arrived. The men have been taking care of me … helping me get my strength back."

"By tying you up and locking the door?"

She frowned and shook her head. "I don't know. They had my journal … brought me in here. I don't understand …"

"We stopped for supplies. Been looking for you."

"I thought maybe the bounty hunters had tracked me down again," she said.

"Isaac saw Lucky in the corral," he said. "They denied ever seeing you."

She frowned. "Why?"

"We need to get you out of here."

"Yes. All right. But first, look at that man." She pointed to the portrait leaning against the wall. "Is he someone famous? Someone I should know?"

"No. Never seen him before."

"I'm almost sure I have. It's the first face I can ever remember feeling as if *I know him.*"

Elijah handed her the journal and his gun. "Keep it trained on the door."

"I don't think I need to—"

"Just do it."

She did as he directed while he pulled a knife from his pocket and hurried to the portrait. He slipped the blade under the brass nameplate on the bottom of the frame and popped it off. Then after tucking it into his pocket, he took the revolver back. He could see how unsteady she was—and how weak.

"Can you make it?"

She nodded. "I think so."

"Stay behind me and stick close," he said.

They made their way along the deserted hallway outside the storage room. The only noise in the place was from their footsteps.

When they arrived in the common room, Elijah thumbed back the hammer of his revolver.

"They've been nothing but nice to me until just a bit ago," she whispered.

"And yet no one came to check on you when they heard a gunshot?"

She frowned. He motioned for her to keep following him across the room, which was just as devoid of people as the hallway.

Elijah led the way to the door that would take them into the reception room and then outdoors. He pushed through with Mercy on his heels—and came face to face with Lieutenant Brewer and his four men. Elijah wasn't the only one who was armed.

Brewer gestured with his own gun. "Put down your weapon, Captain."

"I don't think so."

Mercy shook her head. "What's going on here? Why the guns? Why tie me up?"

"Do you know this man, Mercy?" The question came from West, who also had a gun trained on Elijah.

"Yes. His name is Captain Elijah Hale."

"He could be forcing you to say that," Brewer told her.

Mercy frowned. "No, he's not. I know him."

"You looked right at the image I have of her and said you'd never seen her before," Elijah said to West.

"That's right," West said. "I was protecting her."

"You saw my orders. Could see I was an officer in the army," Elijah said.

"There *are* unscrupulous officers," West said.

"We know she has men after her. And we had no idea what your intentions were," Brewer said.

Elijah looked at him. "I think I can guess yours."

"She arrived in bad shape." This from Stern. "We've been nursing her back to health."

"That's right," Marvin said. "That's all we were doing."

"No ulterior motives here," Mitchell said.

"Shut up, Mitchell," Brewer said. "No one said anything about …"

"We're leaving now," Elijah said.

"You got nothing on us, Captain," Brewer said. "This little incident is exactly what we said."

Elijah nodded. "You were just protecting her."

"That's right."

"Do you tie up every woman you protect?"

Brewer lowered his gun. "Just go."

"They have my gun," Mercy said to Elijah.

"The lady would like her weapon back," Elijah said.

West lowered his gun but didn't move. It was Stern who hustled around the counter and retrieved the pistol.

Mercy swayed on her feet, then braced herself with a hand on the counter.

"You all right?"

"I'm … fine."

"Any fool can sees she's not fully recovered yet," Brewer said. "As I said, we were taking care of her …"

Elijah slipped an arm around her waist. "Real heroes. You should be proud."

They didn't move a muscle as Elijah helped her from the room. Outside, he whistled shrilly, and Isaac came from the direction of the corral, riding one horse and leading two others. He grinned when he saw Mercy.

"I am mighty happy to see you, Miss Mercy," Isaac said.

"I'm happy to see you, too, Isaac," she said.

She took a moment to run her hand down Lucky's nose, then leaned close as if she could get strength just by being near him. She held the journal out for Elijah. "Could you put this in my saddlebag?"

Elijah opened the bag, shoved the book inside.

Her countenance was of relief and extreme weariness. "If someone will just help me into the saddle …"

"You'll ride with me," Elijah said.

"No," she said. "I'm perfectly capable of riding my own horse."

"You're not in any shape to ride," he said. "You'll ride with me."

"I think I should know if I'm strong enough," she said, even as she grabbed Lucky's bridle.

Elijah led his horse next to Mercy and unceremoniously took her arm. "You're coming up. I wouldn't fight it."

In spite of her pride, Mercy couldn't help but lean against Elijah as they rode away from the fort, past artillery that sat like silent sentries, and away from acres of grave markers that told of lost love and lost lives.

CHAPTER EIGHT

It was just before sunset when they rode into Dover, Tennessee. In spite of her objections to riding with Elijah, Mercy knew she wouldn't have been able to hang on in the saddle alone. She was physically done in, and all she could think of was sleep.

Elijah led the way to the Dover Hotel in the center of town. He dismounted, then helped Mercy from the horse. Isaac, holding fast to Lucky's reins, stayed in his own saddle.

"What'choo want me to do, Cap'n?" Isaac asked.

"Let me get Miss Mercy settled in a room and I'll be back to help with the horses," he said.

"I don't have money to pay for a room," Mercy said.

"I do," Elijah said.

"I'm not going to take your—"

She swayed on her feet and Elijah slipped an arm around her. "Quit talking."

He led her to a wooden bench in front of the white clapboard two-story hotel. "Sit here," he admonished. "Don't move."

He shot a glance at Isaac. "Watch her." Then he disappeared inside.

Isaac dismounted, tied the horses to a post, and went to sit down beside Mercy. "S'cuze me fo' sayin' so, Miss Mercy, but you ain't lookin' so good."

"I feel about how I look," she said. She put her head back against the wood of the building and closed her eyes.

"It's been a rough couple weeks, Isaac."

"You ain't gonna run again, are you?"

"No," Mercy said. "Even walking sounds like too much right now."

Just a few minutes later, Elijah was leading her past the interior desk of the hotel, up a flight of stairs and depositing her in a room for the night. She said only two words as she crossed over the threshold into the room. "Thank you."

"Lock it," he said.

The door closed and she started toward the bed when she heard his gruff voice from outside.

"I said lock it."

She turned the lock, crawled into bed, and was asleep almost before her head hit the pillow.

Mercy was awake when she heard a knock on the door the next morning. She felt much more rested, a little stronger, and she was rehearsing her "Thank you for your help, but I'm perfectly capable of going on alone" speech to Elijah when she opened the door and found him standing there with breakfast.

"I brought food," he said.

She stepped back into the room. "You didn't have to do that."

He walked in with a brown bag, and she could smell the aroma of cinnamon buns. "You're not hungry?"

"That smells delicious."

"They taste even better."

She sat down on the edge of the bed and tucked into the breakfast. She could feel him watching, and though she knew it shouldn't, it irritated her. She looked up. "What?"

He shook his head. "Just thinking that you look a sight better this morning than you did yesterday."

"I feel better," she said. "I'm not sure if I thanked you for coming to get me."

"You did."

"Those men weren't going to stay gentlemen toward me, were they?"

"I don't think so."

She shuddered with the thought. "I wonder if I'll ever be a proper judge of people."

He didn't answer her question, but instead, he asked one of his own. "Why did you say you thought it was the bounty hunters—again?"

"They nearly caught me in Salem," she said, stuffing the last morsel of the bun into her mouth. "I was at a boardinghouse. I needed to rest, so I took a room."

"That was taking quite a chance," he said.

"Honestly, I was so tired I didn't have a choice. And I hadn't actually *seen* them in the two weeks since … since—"

"Since you snuck away while Isaac and I slept?"

"I left a note."

"So you did. Tell me about the bounty hunters," he said.

"I think there were three or four men. They broke into the boardinghouse in the middle of the night. I heard them and managed to crawl out the window and onto the roof before they got into my room."

"Obviously they didn't find you."

"One of them did. But he … slipped off the roof. He must have died before he could tell the others I was in the chimney."

He raised his brows, as if he hadn't heard her correctly. "Where?"

"Inside the chimney," she said. "I stayed there the rest of the night. When I came out, they were gone."

"Seems strange they left—even if they lost a man."

"It was a young man. And I found out later he was the son of one of the others."

Elijah rubbed his knuckles against the stubble on his chin. "You haven't seen them since?"

"No. But then again, I was busy trying not to die from food poisoning."

"You were foolish to leave us behind and strike out on your own."

"You're the one who told me I was in the war. If I managed that, I can take care of myself."

"Clearly," he said. The sarcastic tone wasn't lost on her.

"We aren't in Missouri anymore. Why are you still following me?"

"I made a commitment to the court."

She crossed her arms over her chest. "A man of high principles."

"How soon can you be ready to go?"

"I think I'm fine to go on alone," she said.

"Is that right?"

She nodded. "Yes. I … appreciate your help, but I'm fine now. If I hadn't been so sick, I would have never gotten myself into that situation at the fort."

He studied her. "I didn't come all this way and spend all this time looking for you to ride away now. We're going with you."

"I don't want you to." She was aware that she was almost shouting now, but she couldn't seem to help herself.

"Why not?"

"I look at you and see all I've lost. It makes me hate you a little …"

"How soon can you be ready to go?"

"It might even make me hate you a lot!"

"Once we check out, we can go to the livery for Isaac and—"

"*Where* is Isaac?"

"Isaac is with the horses."

"But I thought he stayed here last night?"

Elijah shook his head. "Haven't found a place yet that will rent to a Negro."

"So he slept in the livery with the horses?"

Elijah drew his brows together. "Yes. He was fine—"

"You and I slept in our rooms, in soft comfortable beds, while you made that boy sleep with the animals?" She was incensed and strangely happy about her indignation. "Isaac has sacrificed to come and find me and this is how he's repaid?"

"I'm giving the hotel manager back the key. We're leaving now," he said.

He turned, and she followed him out of the room. They started down the stairs.

"I don't know why I expected more from you," she said.

She stumbled. He caught her, kept a hand on her elbow as they continued down the steps and stopped at the front desk. Elijah addressed the clerk.

"Can you tell me where the county courthouse is?"

"Why the courthouse?" Mercy asked.

"It's a half mile down the road on your left, sir," the clerk said.

"Thank you." Elijah slid a key across the counter. "The key to number seven."

The clerk smiled. "Thank you, sir." He looked at Mercy. "I trust you were comfortable, ma'am?"

She nodded, distractedly. "Yes."

Elijah turned to go. "Wait," she said. "What about *your* room key?"

"Doesn't require a key or a fee to sit in a chair outside a room all night," the clerk said.

She looked toward Elijah, who had already walked out the door, then turned her attention back to the clerk.

"Can I ask you something?"

He smiled. "Yes, of course."

"Do you rent rooms to Negroes?"

"No, ma'am, we do not. Nor, for that matter, does any hotel in Dover."

CHAPTER NINE

Mercy's head of steam and all her righteous anger left her flat. She made her way to the door of the hotel and stepped outside. Elijah was leaning against a post waiting for her.

"We *are* going with you," he said.

"Fine. But I hate the thought that you see me as incompetent."

"I thought you hated the thought of me."

"Sometimes."

"Fair enough," he said.

"And just so you know, I was told Fort Donelson was a Confederate fort. I thought they might have records or something to jog my memory."

"The South built it, but the North took it in '62," he said.

"I know that *now*," she said. "I believed those men wanted nothing more than to help me."

"Things aren't always what they seem," he said. "Nor are people."

"Does that include bounty hunters?" she asked.

"Yes, I would say so," he said. "You'd be hard pressed to figure out who might be a bounty hunter in a roomful of people."

"Do you know who put the bounty on my head?"

"No, but it was obviously someone who didn't believe your sentence to hang should have been commuted. Someone who had the connections to put a posse together within a few hours of hearing you were to be freed."

"I still don't have any idea where to go," she admitted. "I had hoped to find something at the fort. Something that might trigger a memory."

He dug into his pocket and produced the brass nameplate he took from the portrait in the storage room. "You did." He studied it. "Does the name John Chapman mean anything to you?"

"John Chapman," she murmured. She sighed and shook her head. "Not the name—but his face. Those eyes. I could swear I've seen him before."

"It's common to have portraits painted of commanding officers who served the post. Perhaps he was *your* commanding officer at one time."

"How do we find out?"

"We'll go to the courthouse and see what they have on John Chapman. It might not be much—or it may turn out to be everything. At any rate, it's a place to start."

"You spent the night sitting in a chair outside my room?" she asked.

"I've slept in worse places," he said.

"Isaac was happy to stay with the horses?"

"He's slept in worse places too."

"Should we bring Isaac some breakfast before we go to the courthouse?"

"He's already enjoyed two cinnamon buns and some hot tea."

"Do you enjoy seeing me squirm like this?"

"I won't deny it's been the better part of my morning so far," he said. "Let's go to the courthouse."

The Stewart County courthouse was a short walk from the Dover Hotel. Though Elijah offered to go and get the horses, Mercy insisted she was all right. The exercise and the sunshine would do her good.

They made their way up the wide steps of the red brick building and Mercy noticed a sign tacked up outside the door: *Whites only.* She looked at Elijah.

"This is why Isaac isn't with us?"

He nodded. "Let's go see about John Chapman."

The clerk at the counter ran a finger down columns of names, then shook his head. "Nope. Sorry. No John Chapman mentioned here."

"Colonel Chapman," Elijah said.

"Yes, yes. Colonel Chapman," the clerk said.

"Those are records from the commanders at the fort?" Elijah asked.

"Not just the commanders. The enlisted and officers alike. We wanted an accurate count for our county records. Figured someday it might matter what the population of this area swelled to during the war."

"Good thinking," Elijah said. "I'm just a little confused, then, as to why the name we're looking for isn't there."

The clerk sighed impatiently. "These are all the names of all the Federals that were in a twenty-mile radius of Dover from '62 through '65."

"We think John Chapman was a Confederate," Elijah said.

The clerk raised his brows. "That right? Well that makes a difference, yes sir. That makes a big difference." He slammed the book closed, reached under the counter and pulled out another book. This one was treated a little more reverently as he gently turned to a section that was bound with a ribbon.

"These are names of the Confederate war heroes that served at Donelson before General Buckner surrendered to General Grant."

He started at the top of one column and went down row after row of names. "You know they say when we lost Donelson, we lost the war, yes sir. Gave the Yanks the darn rivers to move supplies and whatnot. Brave men tried to hold 'em off—did it, too, for a while, but they were just outrationed. Yankees had twice as many men and twice as much ammunition.

"Here he is!" the clerk said. He turned the book around so that Elijah and Mercy could see for themselves. "Says right there, John Chapman, September, 1861. He was there, all right."

"Is there any other information about him?" Mercy asked, leaning closer to look at the page.

"It should show the age and the military man's home of record," the clerk answered. "And in some cases it gives the profession before they were soldiers. Some men answered the question, but some felt like we were snooping into something that was none of our affair."

Elijah followed the line from Chapman's name across the page. "Doesn't have his age … but it does list his home of record as McIntosh County, Georgia."

"Does it give his profession?" Mercy asked.

Elijah traced his finger down to the next row where the words *rice plantation owner* had been scribbled into the small space. Mercy turned to look up at Elijah.

"A plantation in Georgia," she said. "All along I've been thinking Tennessee."

"So now, we think Georgia." He said it with conviction, but prayed this was the lead they needed to get her home. He turned to the clerk and asked the next logical question.

"Do you have a map?"

CHAPTER TEN

Elijah waited with Isaac in front of the Dover train depot. Isaac paced and Elijah kept an eye peeled for Mercy.

"Maybe she run again," Isaac said.

"Not without Lucky," Elijah said.

Isaac nodded. "That be true, Cap'n."

Finally, Mercy came from the general direction of the station and headed straight for them. Isaac beamed.

"You be right, Cap'n. Here she comes."

"You all right?" Elijah asked her.

She flushed. "Yes."

"Good. The stationmaster says the tracks are intact as far as Savannah."

"I know we talked about taking the train, but I've been thinking about it and I say we ride the horses the rest of the way," she said.

"It's five hundred miles. That'll take us a week," Elijah said. "It would be hard on the horses and on us."

"You hear that, Miss Mercy?" Isaac asked. "It be hard on us."

She ignored him, looking at Elijah, and frowned. "I thought you were in the cavalry."

"I am," he said.

She raised her brows. "Getting soft, Captain?"

"You've been through a lot physically," he said. "The train would be for your benefit."

"I don't want you to spend any more of your money on my account," she said.

"The tickets have already been purchased."

Her jaw dropped. "Then return them and get your money back."

"I can't. Besides, the horses have already been loaded into the freight car," he said.

"Get them off! Get Lucky off that train. I can't believe you did all of this without consulting me!"

"Cap'n had to decide on account a' da train leaving soon, and you was in dat outhouse a terrible long time," Isaac said.

The blush started at her neck and worked its way up. Elijah lifted a brow at Isaac, who suddenly found the ground fascinating.

Elijah broke the uncomfortable silence. "If we take the train, we can be in Savannah in two days. The plantation is a day's ride from there. If it's the wrong place, at least we'll know quickly and I won't be burning through all my military leave."

"That make sense," Isaac said. "Don'tcha think that make sense, Miss Mercy?"

"That does make sense," she conceded.

"Besides, I would think you'd be in a hurry to get there," Elijah said. "It could be the answer to all your questions."

She nodded, but didn't feel sure at all. "I know. It could be."

Isaac grinned. "Glory be, we takin' the train!"

Since Isaac wasn't permitted to ride as a passenger in the white's only car, Mercy and Elijah rode with him in the colored car. Once they were under way, the conductor came through to collect their tickets. "You turn your eyes out those windows," he told them, "and you'll see things that'll make your heart bleed for the towns we pass through. It's a pitiful sight to behold what war does to everything."

The conductor had been right. In the passing scenery, over the next two days, they saw indelible scars across the land General Sherman and his army had left in the wake of their devastating march to the sea. Rolling through the town of Marietta, Georgia, they saw burned-out skeletal remains of buildings that spoke of a previously thriving town. Brick chimneys, once the heartbeats of family homes, stood like abandoned sentries against the otherwise beautifully green countryside. But over and over again, they witnessed teams of people wielding hammer against nail, frames being erected over charred ground and piles of rubble. Towns were being reborn.

It was the middle of the morning when they arrived in Savannah, leaving them plenty of time to begin the ride toward their final destination. At the end of the line, Isaac was even more enthralled with traveling by rail than he had been when they started.

"Was plannin' on being a sheriff when I'm all growed up, but maybe I might get me a conductor job," Isaac told Mercy as they waited for the horses to be unloaded from the freight car.

"I think that's a fine idea," Mercy said. "You might even want to be the engineer. Be the man who drives the train down the tracks."

Isaac grinned. "I just might do that. Or I just might be a train-ridin' engineer who is a lawman too. I could see me the whole country that way and keep da peace besides."

Mercy smiled. "It sounds ambitious, but I think you could do it, Isaac."

"I been pesterin' da Cap'n for some shootin' lessons, but he says no on account of da laws 'bout Negroes and guns."

"Someday those laws will change," Mercy said. "But until then, Elijah's right. You can't break the law—even when it's an unfair law."

Elijah joined them. "I spoke to the stationmaster. He knows the Chapman Plantation," he said. "We head south from here."

Mercy had been vaguely aware of the change in landscape since she left St. Louis, the different types of trees, grass, and spring flowers, but now, riding through Georgia, she couldn't help but appreciate the scent of pine and the perfume of yellow jasmine. Above them, gray moss hung like a gossamer veil from the branches of cypress and magnolia trees. When they arrived at the mouth of the Altamaha River, she could smell the water and feel the slick humidity of the air across her skin. She felt … content. How could that be? Mercy looked around her with heightened senses. It wasn't familiar. But it was comfortable.

They skirted the edge of Darien in the late afternoon. According to their map, the town was the last stepping-stone to the Chapman Plantation. Even from the fringes of the place, they could see ruin and devastation everywhere. But people here were rebuilding too. Mercy could hear the monotonous sound of hammer hitting nail after nail somewhere in the bowels of the town. The harbor to the Altamaha Sound boasted a few small fishing boats tied to the dock.

The road to the Chapman Plantation was as fragrant as it was beautiful. Ten-foot-high walls of wild myrtle lined the road, and white dogwoods and a bright spectacle of magnolia blossoms spilled across the dark green foliage and onto the red clay soil of the path. The perfumed scent of the flowers, the earth, and the nearby water teased Mercy's memory. At least she thought it did, but she worried it was more a hopeful mind-set than anything else—hope that someone from the Chapman Plantation could give her some clue to her identity; hope that there would be a moment when life wouldn't be such a mystery. They rounded a bend in the road and finally saw a large white house in the distance. Even from her vantage point of a quarter mile away, she could see how imposing the structure was. Twin chimneys stood at either end, tall white columns lined the front, and wide matching verandas on the first and second floor looked out upon lush green grass. To the side of the house, she could just make out the edge of the rice fields.

"Whoa!" Elijah called out to his horse. Mercy and Isaac stopped on either side of him. They all stared at the house.

"At least it's still standing," Mercy said.

"I think there's something we need to talk about before we go any farther," Elijah said.

"What?" Mercy asked.

"I'm wondering if you want me and Isaac to wait here while you go the rest of the way alone. If the people in that house know you, it might be a moment you want to keep private."

She didn't hesitate. "No. You've come this far with me. I think you should be there whether this is the place or not."

"All right. But if we spend any time here, then I think it's prudent we don't say much about my ... Northern background," Elijah said. He turned and looked at Isaac. "While we're here, you need to call me Elijah, Isaac. Not Captain, all right?"

"All right, Cap'n ... Elijah," Isaac said.

He turned back toward Mercy. "The wounds in the country after the war—particularly here in the South, are fresh and painful. If these people *do* know you, then they'll have enough to adjust to with your sudden appearance without adding a Yankee to the mix."

Mercy nodded. "Agreed. But surely they'll ask who you are to me."

"We'll tell them the truth. I'm the man who escorted you home," Elijah said. "Best case, they turn out to be your family. Then I'm sure they'll be so happy to see you, it won't matter who I am in the short time I'll be with them."

"What do you mean?"

"If this is the right place, the last thing you need is for me to stay," he said.

"It's late in the day. You can't just turn around and leave. You will at least spend the night?"

He nodded. "All right. Are you ready to knock on the door?"

Mercy's thoughts flew back to that awful day over a year ago when she awoke in Doc Abe's clinic. *Your mind is most likely protecting you from what was certainly a traumatic experience. I can hear a trace of the South in your speech. Where are you from?* Her answer that day had been "I don't know," but now she might be on the precipice of finding out—or not. The entire thing might be a mistake. A very expensive, time-consuming mistake.

She didn't immediately answer him. She just stared at the house in the distance.

"Mercy?"

"What if I just *wanted* to believe I knew the man in that portrait?"

"I think you need to trust your instincts," Elijah said.

"My instincts say to turn around and ride away as fast as I can."

"That's not instinct. That's fear. What are you afraid of?"

"The truth!" She turned and looked at him. "I'm not sure what scares me more though—that someone in that house may have those answers or that they won't know me at all."

Mercy gave Lucky a nudge and they started forward again.

CHAPTER ELEVEN

They'd barely traveled ten feet down the long road toward the house when a Negro boy came crashing out of the tall green wall of wild myrtle, his bare feet digging into the road and nearly catapulting him right into the path of Mercy and her horse.

Lucky stopped before she even gave him the signal. Elijah and Isaac did the same. The boy's eyes widened. "Sorry, missus."

"It's all right," Mercy said. She dismounted. "Can you tell us if we're at the Chapman Plantation?"

The boy took a look behind him at the wall of green, then looked at her. "Yassum. This be da Chapman Plantation."

A man on horseback came down the road toward them. The boy seemed to shrink and stepped closer to be in Lucky's shadow—then glanced at the green hedge again. Mercy looked toward the greenery and nearly gasped when she saw the black face of a man peering out.

The rider stopped, and even from her vantage point on the other side of Lucky, Mercy could see he was handsome and fair skinned, with light blond hair. He didn't acknowledge anyone but the boy.

"What are you doing out here, Moby? Aren't you supposed to be working?"

Moby bobbed his head. "Yassuh, Mista' Beau. Sorry, sir."

The green wall rustled and the head in the bushes became a large Negro man, who glared at the boy. The man on horseback looked at him. "Bram? Is there a problem?"

"Caught Moby napping, suh. He say he sick but he don't run like he sick," Bram answered.

"Get yourself on back to work then, Moby. You're not paid to sleep in the fields."

"Yassuh," Moby said. "Sorry, Mista' Beau."

Mercy felt sorry for the boy as he made his way back toward the hedge and the angry-looking man called Bram. The two of them went back through the bushes and disappeared.

Mercy stepped out from beside Lucky, and the man put a hand across his forehead to shield his eyes from the late afternoon sun.

"We don't mean to be trespassing," Mercy said, "but we're hoping to see someone ..."

"I don't believe it ..." He quickly dismounted and came toward her.

Mercy's heartbeat picked up speed. She didn't know him, but the slight tilt of his head, his eyes that never left her face, the way his hands clenched at his sides as he walked toward her, all spoke of a man who recognized her.

Mercy sensed, rather than saw, Elijah dismount as the man closed the distance toward her. He was young, his face unlined and nose slightly reddened from the sun. He started to say something, then stopped. He opened his mouth to speak again, but then just ran his tongue over his bottom lip as he stared at her.

Mercy squirmed under his gaze. She finally broke the silence. "I don't know if I'm in the right place ..."

"It *is* really you," the man said, quickly crossing the last few steps between them. He wrapped his arms around her and held her close. Mercy stiffened from the intimate contact with the stranger. He was only a few inches taller than she was, allowing her to look over his shoulder at Elijah, whom she noted looked simultaneously concerned, relieved—and a little sad. Though it seemed like a long time, the embrace lasted only a few seconds before the man stepped back and frowned.

"I truly thought you were dead!" he said. "Where the devil have you *been*, Charlotte?"

For a moment, it seemed as though time stopped. *Charlotte? He called me Charlotte. Is this possible? Could I have finally found someone who knew me before the war?* Now it was her turn to be tongue-tied.

She'd often thought about the moment when she might finally meet someone from her past—and here it was. But she had no idea what to say. In fact, she couldn't force words out even when she tried. The man's frown deepened, and he turned from her and stuck out his hand toward Elijah.

"It seems the proverbial cat's got Charlotte's tongue." He spoke with a pronounced Southern drawl. "I'm Beauregard Chapman. People call me Beau. And you are …?"

"Elijah Hale."

Mercy watched the two of them shake hands and had the most jarring thought. *What if he's my husband? Oh, please, God … don't let that be true. Don't let me be married. A husband I can't remember would be too much right now. Too much …*

Beau turned to regard Mercy once again. "I can't believe you're here."

She finally found her voice. "Neither can I."

"It's astonishing. Have you been to the house yet?"

She shook her head. "Umm … no. Not yet. We were on the way. But there's something I should tell you. I don't re—"

"I know, I know. You don't regret your actions," he said. Then he threw his arm across her shoulders and grinned. "Some things never change, big sister. Some things never change."

She nearly buckled with relief. *Sister? He's my brother. Not my husband. My brother! He's family … my family.*

She automatically looked at Elijah with wide eyes. "I have a brother."

Elijah smiled in response. "So it seems."

Beau dropped his arm from around Mercy's shoulders and looked at Elijah. "My apologies. I didn't make that clear when I introduced myself." He tilted his head again and studied Elijah, then Isaac, who had yet to say a word.

"In fact, I didn't ask what *your* relationship is to my sister," Beauregard said. He turned to Mercy. "Did you go and get yourself married while you've been gone, Char?"

"What? No," she stammered.

"We just escorted her home," Elijah said. "A lady shouldn't travel alone these days."

Beau frowned. "Hmm. I never knew Charlotte not to be able to take care of herself. But I suppose you're right. In any case, thank you for bringing her back to us."

Mercy studied the young man who had called her *sister* and tried to will into being a modicum of recognition for him. Something like she'd felt when she'd seen the portrait of John Chapman. But there was nothing. Nothing but a friendly, handsome young man who was mounting his horse.

"I was on my way to town," he said, "but now, wild horses couldn't drag me away from seeing Mother's reaction when she sees you, Char."

The thought that she was about to see her mother made Mercy weak in the knees. But in spite of that, she stuck her foot in the stirrup and hoisted herself up into the saddle. She tossed a look at Elijah and Isaac, and they all followed her brother down the drive toward the house. As they got closer, she could see it wasn't in the pristine shape it had seemed from a distance. The white paint was scarred and faded. The entire place had a general feeling of neglect and apathy about it. Acres and acres of rice fields abutted the land where the house sat and Mercy could see there were at least two dozen Negroes working in those fields—some appeared to be wearing bits and pieces of Confederate uniforms. Beau brought his horse to a stop in front of the steps of a wide veranda. They all dismounted.

Elijah reached out for her reins. "Why don't Isaac and I wait here while you have your reunion with your family?"

"Nonsense," Beau said. "Come inside. Mother will think I'm infernally rude if I leave you standing here in the hot sun. Your boy there can take the horses to the stable on the other side of the yard."

"He's not our 'boy,'" Mercy said. "That is Isaac. He is a friend of mine."

Beau stared at her. "I'm sorry?"

"Isaac is my friend," Mercy repeated.

"I be happy to take da horses to da stable," Isaac said.

Mercy looked at his earnest expression and knew he was trying not to cause any trouble for her. "Are you sure, Isaac?"

He nodded. "Yassum. I'm sure. Dey be needin' food an' water and a good brushing. Ain't trustin' nobody else wit da animals but me."

Elijah caught her eye and nodded.

Beau ran a hand through his hair as he looked from one to the other of them, then turned to climb the stairs. He looked back at her. "Coming?"

Mercy nodded. "Yes."

"Watch your step," Beau said. "We've sustained some … damage since you left."

Mercy climbed the wide front steps after him, carefully avoiding boards that were sunken or split. The massive columns, though impressive in their height and girth, bore big pockmarks as if chains had beaten against them. They crossed the deep veranda, and Beau opened one-half of the double oak doors and entered.

Mercy realized she was glad for Elijah's presence, and she took the arm he offered her. Then she took a deep breath and walked straight into a past she couldn't remember.

Chapter Twelve

Beau stood in the middle of the foyer and yelled into the depths of the house.

"Mother! Mother! Come here! Can you hear me? Come. Here!"

He looked at Mercy. "Let me just find her," he said. "Don't go away."

As he rushed out of the foyer, Mercy cast a glance up at Elijah. "Why do people keep telling me that?"

He lifted the corner of his mouth in acknowledgment. "This is quite a place."

Mercy nodded and looked at her surroundings. It had all the earmarks of a very grand residence, but with some distinct differences. The floor beneath their feet was highly polished but scarred, expensive-looking wallpaper had tears, and some of the wainscoting along the bottom half of the room had broken pieces. There was an expansive curving staircase that led down into the foyer from the second floor. She took in the exquisitely carved banister and could almost feel the smooth wood under her hand. Mercy waited for a wave of familiarity to sweep over her, but as she looked around the room, the only impression she had was that the house needed some tender loving care.

An older, elegantly put-together woman appeared at the top of the staircase. She looked down on them.

"Oh, good afternoon," she said. "I didn't realize we had visitors."

As she started down the stairs, Beau reappeared in the foyer. "There you are. I've been calling for you."

"I heard," she said. "*Everyone* heard."

"We have guests," Beau said.

"So I see," she said.

He grinned at her. "Do you?"

"Don't be impertinent, Beauregard," she said, continuing to descend the stairs. "My vision is perfectly fine …"

"So you say." His grin widened. "And yet, no reaction …"

Beau swept his hand toward Mercy.

Elijah relaxed the arm Mercy's was tucked into, and took a step back. All eyes were on her.

The woman had only three steps left to reach the floor. "Good afternoon," she said. "I'm Suzanne Chapman …"

And then Mercy saw that moment of recognition she had seen on Beau's face. Suzanne's hand fluttered to the lace collar of her pale yellow day dress, and she nearly stumbled on the last step of the staircase. She reached out to grab the banister.

"Charlotte?"

At this, Mercy could only nod. She felt rooted to the spot and wondered if this was going to happen to her anytime she came face-to-face with someone from her past. Suzanne exchanged a wide-eyed look with Beau, then descended the last few steps.

"You've come home!" It was easy to hear the emotion in Suzanne's voice. The catch in her throat. She hurried toward Mercy, arms outstretched, tears in her eyes.

"Darling girl," Suzanne said, drawing Mercy into the circle of her arms. For the second time in less than an hour, someone from her family was hugging her. When Suzanne stepped back, she pulled a hankie from her sleeve and daintily wiped at the corner of her eyes.

"I can't believe it. To think after all this time you would turn up like this. I knew it was possible, of course, but as time went by and years passed, I assumed … well, I assumed the worst. Welcome home, Charlotte," she said.

Tears filled Mercy's eyes. *I'm home. My name is Charlotte Chapman, and I have a brother and a mother.*

A young woman entered the foyer. She appeared to be about the same age as Beau, had the same fair skin and blonde hair. "I heard shouting. What's going on?"

Suzanne stepped back away from Mercy. Beau swept a hand in her direction and grinned. "See for yourself."

The young woman looked at Elijah first, and then Mercy. Her eyes widened with recognition. "Charlotte?"

Suzanne nodded. "Yes, Victoria. Your sister has come home to us."

I have a sister, too!

Victoria squealed with delight and rushed forward, all but shoving Suzanne aside, and wrapped her arms around Mercy.

"Charlotte!" she said. Her Southern drawl was the most pronounced of all. "Oh my Lord, I can't believe it's really you. Where on earth have you been?"

"I … I, umm …"

"There will be plenty of time to talk about that," Suzanne said. "Let's not overwhelm the dear girl the first five minutes she's home."

Suzanne turned to Elijah and smiled. "I'm afraid the emotion of seeing Charlotte again has made me forget all my manners." She looked pointedly at Mercy. "We haven't been introduced."

"I'm sorry," Mercy said. "This is my … friend, Elijah Hale."

"For safety sake, he has been her escort while traveling," Beau said.

Suzanne's brows lifted. "Really? How chivalrous."

Victoria was the first to hold out her hand to Elijah. "Pleased to make your acquaintance, Mr. Hale. I'm Charlotte's younger sister, Victoria."

"It's a pleasure, Miss Chapman," Elijah said, taking her offered hand.

Suzanne offered her hand next. "Suzanne Chapman, Mr. Hale. Welcome to our home."

Elijah tipped his head in acknowledgement and took her hand. "Thank you, Mrs. Chapman."

A young Negro woman entered the foyer. In Mercy's estimation she couldn't have been more than eighteen. She stood uncertainly for a moment.

"You be needin' me, missus?" she asked.

Suzanne turned. "As you can see, Rose, we have guests."

Rose came toward them, her hands twisting in front of her apron. "I know I'm s'posed to take da hats and da coats," she said. "But dey don't seem to have none."

"We'll be going into the parlor, Rose. Perhaps you might see about refreshments."

"Yassum," Rose said. "You meanin' like sumpin' to drink, missus?"

"Yes, Rose. That's what I mean."

Rose made her way back out of the foyer, and Suzanne forced a condescending smile. "It's a pity freedom didn't come with the brains to make it count, isn't it?" Her voice was syrupy sweet—a stark contrast to the barbed words.

The comment shocked Mercy.

"Rose joined us after you left, dear," Suzanne said. "I'm afraid you'll find the quality of available help has deteriorated faster than the landscape of the South."

She turned and raised a hand to cup Mercy's cheek. "Dear one. You've been so missed."

Before Mercy could reply, Suzanne turned to go into the parlor with Beau and Victoria on her heels. Mercy glanced at Elijah, who smiled his encouragement, and the two of them entered the parlor.

She started across a threadbare carpet that was as faded as the furnishings and drapes and immediately recognized Colonel John Chapman in the portrait hanging over the fireplace. Beau and Victoria took seats like bookends around Suzanne on a flowered divan just wide enough for the three of them. Suzanne gestured to two wingback chairs across from them.

"Please sit," Suzanne said. "I admit I feel as if I'm dreaming right now. I've thought of the moment when I might see you again so many times, I wonder now if it's real."

Mercy felt exactly the same way. The house, the room, the people. The only thing of any familiarity to her was John Chapman's face. They were staring at her expectantly. Mercy cleared her throat.

"It's real, but I still can't believe I'm sitting here with you," she said.

Victoria shook her head. "Me, either. Where have you been, Charlotte?" Her voice held a hint of reproach, but her slow Southern drawl softened her words. "Beau and I were positively bereft when you left with no word at all as to where you'd gone. Completely devastated."

"I'm sorry," Mercy said. "Very sorry to make you worry like that." She looked to Elijah for some kind of support. He nodded his encouragement, and she went on. "I do have a bit of an explanation," she said. "But I think it would be best if everyone heard it at the same time."

"Everyone?" Suzanne asked.

"Yes. Perhaps we should wait for my father before I explain?" Mercy said.

The three of them stared at her. Suzanne frowned. "I don't understand."

"I just thought it would be easier for me—all of us, really, if I could tell you my story when my father can hear it too," Mercy said.

"I feel perfectly certain that your father can hear you from his place in heaven," Suzanne said.

"I'm sorry?"

Suzanne looked crushed. "Please don't tell me you've stopped believing in an afterlife, darling."

"I like to think of Father watching over me," Victoria said. "Makes me feel safe."

"He's … dead," Mercy said.

Suzanne and Beau exchanged a puzzled glance. "For three years," Beau said. "You *were* at his funeral."

Mercy heard Elijah say he was sorry. Her gaze flew to the portrait. The only person she'd felt any kind of connection to was gone. She'd never know him. Never be able to see if she could look him in the eye and recapture her past. In her heart, she'd hoped he would be the one person who might be able to give everything back to her—all the memories that had so inexplicably disappeared from her life. She felt crushed by the news, heartsick that she would never get to know her father's love.

"Ah, here's Chessie with some beverages," Suzanne said.

Mercy pulled her eyes from the portrait and looked toward Chessie. The old Negro woman entered the room carrying a silver tray with a pitcher and some glasses. Her ebony skin was a stark contrast to the silver of her hair. Chessie's focus was on balancing the tray as she carefully put one foot in front of the other.

"Rose is doin' her chores in da kitchen, missus," Chessie said. "She ask me to serve."

"That's perfect, Chessie," Suzanne said. "As you can see … we have someone very special back in our midst."

Chessie continued forward, glancing around the room. But when her eyes connected with Mercy's, they widened with disbelief and she stumbled. The tray started to drop. Beau jumped to his feet and saved it from falling. "I've got it."

"Sakes alive," Chessie said.

"Yes, Chessie! Charlotte has come back to us!"

"Yassum. I see." Chessie looked right at Mercy. "Welcome home to you."

"Thank you," Mercy said. Chessie gazed at her for a few more seconds, then looked toward Suzanne as she shuffled toward the table where Beau had placed the tray.

"I 'pologize for nearly spillin' the lemonade, missus," she said.

"I completely understand, Chessie," Suzanne said. "It is a little … shocking to see her."

"Your arrival home has left us all quite breathless, Char," Beau said. "But then, you always knew how to stir things up."

Chessie lifted the pitcher and began to fill the glasses.

"I'm sorry to shock everyone," Mercy said.

"I misspoke, darling," Suzanne said. "Seeing you here is an answer to prayer."

"I can't tell you how much I've missed those late-night talks we used to have, Charlotte," Victoria said. "It just hasn't been the same here without you."

Mercy looked up at Chessie, who held out a glass of lemonade with a trembling hand. "Juba's special recipe."

Mercy smiled and took the glass. "Thank you."

The old woman stood for a second and stared at Mercy, but Mercy was getting used to it. She seemed to provoke long looks from the members of her own family and from the servants, too. Chessie moved back and forth from the tray, pouring the lemonade and delivering her drinks. She wasn't in the room more than five minutes before she took one more look at Mercy, then shuffled out of the parlor.

"How long has Chessie worked here?" Mercy asked.

Suzanne tipped her head to the side and frowned. "You seem a little—preoccupied somehow. Three years is a long time, but it's not a *lifetime*. You seemed surprised that your father has passed. You're wondering about your very own mammy, Chessie, and … are you all right, dear?"

Mercy looked at Elijah, who again nodded his encouragement, then finally sputtered out the truth. "I should know, but I don't. I can't remember any of it. That's what I wanted to tell you. I don't remember Chessie, or that my father passed away. I don't remember anything about this place or any of you. In fact—I don't even remember myself."

CHAPTER THIRTEEN

Mercy's blunt confession was met with stunned silence.

Suzanne's jaw dropped, and then she shook her head and tried to laugh. "You're joking. This is one of those silly things you like to do …"

"I'm sorry to have just blurted it out that way," Mercy said, "but it's not a joke. It's the truth. I have amnesia. Amnesia is a condition where the memory is either gone or impaired …"

"We're not uneducated darkies," Beau said. "We know what amnesia is."

Mercy paused, then said, "The point is that I wasn't even sure when I arrived on the property who I would find in this house."

"You've always had an overactive imagination, Char, but this is too much—even for you," Victoria said.

"If you can't remember us—then how did you know to come here?" Suzanne said.

"I was at a military post and I saw a portrait of a man I felt I recognized." Mercy looked at the portrait over the fireplace. "That man. John Chapman. I had no idea who he was—just that his was the first face since my memory loss that seemed remotely familiar to me. We did some research and found he owns this plantation." She paused. "I suppose I should say owned."

"You don't remember all the times we stayed up talking into the wee hours of the night?" Victoria asked. "You don't remember—me?"

Mercy could see she was genuinely upset. "I'm so sorry. I don't —"

"So you're saying we are virtual strangers to you." Suzanne searched Mercy's face intently.

Mercy hesitated. "That sounds so—cold. But in a manner of speaking, yes, I'm afraid that's true. I don't know anything about you."

"I married your father when you were two years old. Beau and Victoria are fraternal twins. They were born when you were four."

Mercy stared at her in confusion. "You married my father when I was two?"

"That's right," Suzanne said. "Your mother died giving birth to you."

Mercy let that sink in and felt a stab of grief. *Both parents dead. And I'll never get to know them.* "You're my stepmother."

"Yes, though we never really made that distinction," Suzanne said. "I've always just been mother to you."

Suzanne paused and shook her head. "I'm so … so … I don't understand. What happened to make you lose your memory?

People don't just go to sleep and wake up without a fundamental sense of who they are."

"That's what it felt like," Mercy said. "I was brought to a doctor's clinic with a head injury. I'm told I was unconscious for a few days. And when I woke up, I had no memories of anything personal. I couldn't say where I was from or what I was doing. I couldn't even tell the doctor my own name."

"Oh, my darling girl, how awful. How long ago was this?" Suzanne fiddled with the handkerchief in her lap.

"A little over a year ago," Mercy said. "My memories begin with the day I woke up."

"But you've been gone for three years. Are you saying you don't know where you were all that time?"

Mercy nodded. "That is exactly what I'm saying."

"So when you left here? No idea where you went? Or why you left?" Beau asked.

"Believe me, I have more questions than you could possibly think of," Mercy said. "I feel as if my life is a puzzle missing over half the pieces."

"Maybe it would help if you answered some of Mercy's questions," Elijah said.

"Who is Mercy?" Victoria asked.

"I am," Mercy said. "I didn't know my real name. Some nuns I stayed with began calling me Mercy—and it's what I've used ever since."

"This is all so—upsetting," Suzanne said. "You're gone and we don't know if you're dead or alive. Then by God's grace you come back to us, but you can't tell us where you've been."

"I know it's a lot to digest," Mercy said.

Suzanne took a deep, steadying breath, then smiled. "What can we do to help? What would you like to know?"

"When was the last time you saw me?" Mercy asked.

"It was about a week after your father's funeral."

"And that was?" Mercy asked.

"August eleventh, '63," Suzanne said. "We had supper together as a family—albeit a fractured family. You had been so sullen and morose, not that I'm criticizing, considering the circumstances, but that night it seemed as if you might get your grief under control. You talked about the thresher on the lower field and how we could improve it once the South won the war and our lives went on."

"I thought the South would win?" Mercy asked.

"Of course, dear. We all believed it to be a foregone conclusion," Suzanne said. "Anyway, my point in bringing that up is you seemed more like yourself that night. But by the end of the meal, you said you had a headache and were going to turn in early. I believe Chessie brought fresh water to your room."

"How long has Chessie been with the family?" Mercy asked.

"Your grandfather owned Chessie and gave her to your father when you were born."

"But now she's free …"

Suzanne waved a hand in the air. "Yes, yes, free. She may leave if she wants to, but in all actuality, Charlotte, where would an uneducated seventy-year-old colored woman go? Mr. Lincoln didn't think about *that* when he opened the floodgates with the blood of thousands of men, and then pushed illiterate coloreds into a world they can't possibly understand."

Now Mercy was sorry she asked. Of all the things she didn't want to get into at the moment, it was the moral issue of slavery.

"So … I went to my room with a headache that evening, and then?" Mercy asked.

"Chessie went to check on you the next morning, and you were gone," Beau said.

"At first we weren't worried," Suzanne said. "You had a habit of disappearing for hours at a time and not telling me your where-abouts. So the first few hours you were out of the house I assumed you needed time alone. But as the day wore on and you didn't return, Beau and a few of the house servants went out looking for you."

"And obviously didn't find me. I was actually … gone."

"From then, until now," Suzanne said. "We had no idea what had happened to you. As far as we could tell, you didn't take any-thing with you. There was some talk that you'd taken the gun your father gave you, but in all honesty, I don't know one weapon from the next and we had several. We asked everyone we could think to ask: friends, neighbors, anyone who you might have confided in about plans you may have had. But we could never uncover a trace of you. As the years went on, we just assumed … well, we assumed you would never leave us and not send word. It would be so rude, so mean. So … unlike you. We assumed the worst, I'm afraid."

"How old are you, Beau?" Mercy asked.

Surprised at the question, Beau raised his eyebrows. "Victoria and I are seventeen."

"That makes me twenty-one?"

"Twenty-two next month," Suzanne said.

Doc Abe was close when he said he thought I'd barely seen twenty summers. She felt a small thrill of satisfaction to know this fact. In the space of a couple of hours, she had a name, an age, a brother, a sister, and a stepmother. She had done it—she had found her home.

Chapter Fourteen

Mercy looked up at the portrait of her father. She thought she saw bits and pieces of herself in his features. The dark hair and eyes. She even recognized the line of her own nose on his face. How strange to see she resembled someone.

"He was a very handsome man," Mercy said.

Suzanne glanced up at the portrait of her late husband. "Yes. Very handsome." She turned and looked at Beau. "I always thought Beauregard favored him."

Mercy looked at her half brother and didn't see an ounce of resemblance to their father. Beau was fair skinned, blond, and blue-eyed, just like his mother and sister. But she smiled and said what she thought was expected of her.

"Yes. I see the likeness," Mercy said.

"You always looked more like Father than we did," Victoria said. "When I was little, I used some of his black boot polish on my hair to make it dark like yours, and his."

"That was a mess," Suzanne said. "Took me a full week to get it all out."

"I would like to know what happened to him," Mercy said. "How did he die?"

"It really *is* remarkable that you don't remember," Suzanne said.

"*Frustrating* would be the word I'd use to describe it," Mercy said.

Suzanne shook her head with a look of concern. "Are you sure you want to have this conversation on your first day home? It might prove to be too much for you."

"I assure you, I'm not all that fragile. I can certainly hear the truth about what happened." *Please, God, let me be right.* She looked to Elijah for his reassurance on the subject. He kept his eyes on her but addressed the others in the room.

"Charlotte ... is stronger than you might think," he said. "I don't know what she was like *before* she left, but trust me, you can tell her the truth."

Mercy shot Elijah a grateful look, but thought about how strange it seemed to hear him call her Charlotte.

Suzanne sighed. "I think it's safe to say that Charlotte has always possessed a certain ... I suppose we could call it strength."

Beau shook his head. "I can't get a grip on this. And I'm sorry, Char, but it's just too awful to think you don't remember anything. *Us.* What did the doctor tell you about your condition?"

"He made no promises to me about when or *if* my memory might return. Now, about my father ..."

"Unlike you, I remember all the details of your father's death nearly every day, even when I try hard not to," Suzanne said. "The subject is very painful for me and I try not to dwell on what happened but instead to go forward with my life. Now, the joy of having you return home to us is almost more than I can comprehend. Maybe you would indulge me in hearing about the part of your life you *do* remember, before we discuss John."

Before Mercy could respond, another colored woman entered the room. She looked about the same advanced age as the maid, Chessie, but she moved with a speed that defied that age. She stopped in the middle of the parlor and pressed gnarled hands over her mouth while she shook her head and hummed a few high notes.

Suzanne raised her brows. "I see Chessie shared the good news, Juba."

Juba bobbed her silver-haired head, then rushed toward Mercy. "Cain't believe it, cain't believe dese poor ol' eyes."

Mercy stood as the old woman stretched out her arms and smiled.

Juba, though barely five feet tall, felt like a bigger presence when she hugged Mercy. "You home, Miss Charlotte. You home! I be fixin' yo' favorite foods fo' sure. Gimme time and I make 'em all."

Mercy gave Juba a little pat on the back, then straightened from the embrace. She smiled at her. "Thank you."

Juba stepped back. Her face had wrinkles so deep it looked like someone had folded her skin like paper and then unfolded it again. There were white clouds of flour that drifted across her dark blue apron. "Thought I'd hafta meet mah Maker a'for I see you again."

"No. I'm … here now. Safe and sound," Mercy said. *Safe and basically sound.*

Juba shot a look at the portrait of Mercy's father. "Massah would shorely be a happy man you home. He shorely would be …"

"Yes, he would be happy, Juba," Suzanne said. "We're all happy."

Juba didn't acknowledge Suzanne's statement. Instead, she dipped her head at Mercy. "Sorry to interrupt, jes had ta see fo' myself you was here."

She hustled out of the room almost as quickly as she'd come into it.

"That was Juba, our cook," Victoria said.

"She's been with us since we were children," Beau added.

Suzanne cocked her head to the side and looked at Mercy. "You do well 'meeting' people without calling attention to your memory issue."

"I don't know about that," Mercy said. "It's hard to tell someone who seems to know and care about me that I don't remember them."

"I suppose you'll have to find a way, darling. You will see a lot of people who knew and cared about you," Suzanne said. "Now … I believe you were going to tell us what you know about these past three years?"

"I can't talk much about the first two years I was gone, because all I do remember about my life—my *entire* life—is this last year. What happened before the injury that caused the amnesia is a complete blank. It's as if my life began on an April day in 1865."

"So where you went and what you were doing when you left us will remain a mystery?"

Mercy hesitated. "I can't say for certain where I was—but I do think I know what I was doing."

They stared at her expectantly. "I have it on good authority that after I left here, I enlisted in the Confederate army," Mercy said, with a quick glance at Elijah.

They stared at her for a moment of stunned silence.

"That's the most ridiculous thing I've ever heard," Beau said. "Women can't be in the army."

"It seems I cut my hair, bound my chest, put on a wool shirt and a pair of trousers, and passed myself off as a man."

Suzanne looked at Elijah, who confirmed the story with a nod.

"You marched with the other soldiers?" Suzanne asked.

Mercy swallowed. "Not exactly. I believe I was a sharpshooter."

Suzanne studied her, then sat back and crossed her arms over her chest. "At last, something that makes sense. Your father taught you to shoot before you could read. He told me you could shoot out the eye of a pigeon from fifty yards away."

CHAPTER FIFTEEN

Her father had taught her to shoot a gun. So strange to use the word *father* in context with herself. *My father taught me.*

"Why teach a daughter to shoot?" Mercy asked, then immediately regretted the question when she saw the irritated look on Beau's face. "I'm sure he taught us all?"

"Absolutely not," Victoria said. "I wanted nothing to do with his horrible guns." Mercy looked at Beau, hoping to find some sibling link between them. "Did we practice together?"

She thought she saw a quick flash of annoyance cross Beau's face, but he covered it with a smile. "Once in a while we did. But honestly, Char, you were Father's star pupil."

"He was a marksman, then?" Elijah asked.

"Among other things," Suzanne said. "John was a career military man."

"He didn't run the plantation?" Mercy asked.

Suzanne raised her eyes to the portrait of her deceased husband. "Between wars he did. He was educated in the art of warfare. His degree in engineering was almost an afterthought for him."

"A West Point man?" Elijah asked.

Suzanne arched a brow. "Yes. You've heard of it, then."

Elijah nodded. "Some of the highest-ranking commanders came from the Point. Good men, all of them."

Suzanne's face clouded. "Yes, good men. But so many dead men. Former classmates pitted against one another in a war that never should have happened."

Elijah didn't comment, and it seemed to Mercy it was the lack of comment that caused Suzanne to study him a little more.

"You have the presence of a military man, Mr. Hale," she said. "Did you fight?"

"Yes. It's how I met Mer … Charlotte," he said.

She smiled. "A fellow patriot."

Elijah smiled but said nothing.

"Seems everybody got to fight the despicable Yankees but me," Beau said. The bitter tone of his voice spoke of a wound that had never healed.

"You were only a child, darling," Suzanne said. "You know your father wouldn't hear of it."

"And if you'd been away fighting in that nasty war, you wouldn't have been here to protect us from those vile Yankees that came into our home and acted like the barbarians we know them to be," Victoria said.

"The Northern army was here? In the house?" Mercy asked.

"Evidence of their unwelcomed presence is all around you." The icy tone of Suzanne's voice gave away her deep feelings. "The broken floorboards and torn wallpaper. The gouges in the wood and the splintered furniture. Yankees used our home for a staging place, if you will. Complete disregard for us, our property. Rode their horses through the foyer just for the fun and spectacle of it! Victoria calling them barbarians is accurate. It is precisely the way they acted and why I wish they all would burn in hell."

Mercy didn't dare look at Elijah for fear she'd give him away. He had been right. The wounds were still too fresh to sit in a parlor and have a conversation with someone who was still their sworn enemy.

"Maybe in time the country will look back on the war and see the passion people had for their own ways of life and not focus on all the lives that were lost," Mercy said. "The bitterness will eventually fade—won't it?"

Suzanne shook her head. "The bitterness will never fade for me. Your father is dead because of that war."

"Was he shot in battle?"

Suzanne shook her head and tried to clear her throat. Mercy could see how difficult the conversation was for her newfound family. "Really, darling, I beg of you to leave this dreariness until another day."

"Of course," Mercy said.

"I think you should count yourself lucky you don't remember what happened, Char," Beau said. "I wish I could forget it."

"In any event, it's in John's memory that we strive so hard to bring this plantation back to the level of success we enjoyed before the war. Back to the glory days of when your father was alive and well and impressing us all with his newfangled methods for growing and harvesting rice."

"That must be quite difficult without your former labor," Elijah said.

Suzanne nodded. "At one time we had nearly three hundred slaves working the property, but now, to say there are fifty families working as sharecroppers is probably generous. Each and every day is a struggle, but we're doing fine."

"Life goes on," Victoria said. "Even when your father dies and your sister flees."

"Again, please accept my apologies for leaving the way I did," Mercy said.

Suzanne smiled. "We are just so happy to have you home, darling. Now, I'm sure you're exhausted and would like to freshen up before supper?"

"Yes, thank you, Mother," Mercy said.

Suzanne turned to Elijah. "Mr. Hale? I don't know what your plans are, but surely it's too late in the day to leave us now. You'll spend the night?"

Elijah glanced at Mercy, who nodded. "I appreciate your kind invitation."

"Nonsense. It's the least we can do for the man who provided a safe journey home for our Charlotte. Now, if y'all will excuse me, I'll see about supper preparations."

"What about Isaac?" Mercy asked before Suzanne could leave the room.

"Who is Isaac?" Victoria asked.

"The young man we arrived with," Mercy said. "He was sent to take care of the horses."

"The *colored boy* you arrived with," Beau corrected.

For a moment, Suzanne looked confused. "Beau will make arrangements for him in the colored camp."

"I am indebted to Isaac as well as to Elijah," Mercy said. "Is there a room in the house for—"

Elijah stopped her short with a meaningful look and a barely perceptible shake of his head. She turned to Beau. "I'm sure Isaac will appreciate whatever accommodations you make for him."

"Splendid. All settled, then." Suzanne made her way to a velvet rope hanging from the ceiling and pulled it. Rose appeared moments later.

"Please make sure Miss Charlotte's room is freshened," Suzanne said.

"Chessie already seen to it, missus," Rose answered.

"Then see to the green room down the hall from Miss Charlotte's," she said, "and make sure Juba knows there will be two more for supper."

"Yassum," Rose said. She hurried from the room.

"Your friend Isaac can have his meal in the kitchen with Juba or in the colored camp with his own kind."

Mercy nodded. "All right."

"Now, I'm sure you would both like to clean up," Suzanne said. "Change into something suitable for supper."

"I'm afraid I don't have anything more suitable," Mercy said. "This is my only dress."

"Hardly, darling. Though they are outdated now, you have a wardrobe filled with dresses upstairs in your room."

Mercy was touched. "You've kept a room for me all these years? Kept my clothes?"

"We never stopped praying for your return," Suzanne said. She crossed the few steps to Mercy and put a hand on her cheek. "Tonight I will be thanking God that He answered those prayers. Even against all the odds that seem to have been stacked against you." She pressed her lips to Mercy's cheek. "Welcome home, my dear Charlotte."

Mercy felt the emotion bubble up in her own throat. "Thank you, Mother."

Her stepmother stepped back. "Your room is at the top of the stairs. Third door on the right. Mr. Hale—fourth door on the left from the staircase. I'll see you both in the dining room at half past the hour."

Suzanne swept out of the room. Beau looked at Mercy. "I couldn't enlist. Too young, Father said. It was all I wanted. To fight for the South." He issued a curt laugh. "So typical that you managed to do what I couldn't."

"I'm sorry," she said.

"Don't be." He shrugged. "It's old news, your capability against my ineptitude. But I am happy to see you looking so well, big sister. Welcome home."

He kissed her cheek and then left the room. Victoria also moved toward Mercy and placed a delicate hand on her arm. "It will be just like old times, Char. I can't tell you how happy I am you're home!"

"Thank you, Victoria," Mercy said.

"Now, if you'll excuse me, I need to change for supper," Victoria said. She left, leaving Mercy and Elijah alone in the parlor.

Elijah looked at her. "Well? How do you feel?"

"It's so strange to be in this house with those people and hear them calling me Charlotte. I keep wanting to turn around and look for her—for Charlotte." She frowned. "I'm sad about my parents. Sad I'll never get to know them now." Then she smiled. "But I'm happy too. Happy to finally have some answers to my questions."

"I'm happy for you," Elijah said. "And I don't want to be the damper on your first evening with your family. Are you positive you want me to stay tonight? It's not too late for me to leave …"

"In spite of my behavior or things I may have said in the past … I do appreciate all the help you've given me, Elijah, and strange as it may be, you and Isaac are the only things familiar to me right now. I'll admit it will be nice to have you at supper."

"Fine. Then I'll stay for tonight," he said. "I don't know what Isaac is going to do, but I will be on my way in the morning."

When they reached the top of the staircase, Mercy turned to Elijah. "I trust you can find your room?"

"I think as well as you can."

"Touché," she said. "I will see you at supper."

Chapter Sixteen

Mercy opened the double doors that led to her bedroom and paused at the threshold. Part of her wanted nothing more than to hide in the room and think about everything she'd learned in the past hour. But instead, she stepped onto the blue Persian rug that ran the length of the floor and took it all in. The room must have been truly lovely at one time, but it now bore the scars of the Yankee invasion in the form of ripped wallpaper and gouged furniture. The four-poster bed was missing the canopy, and the marble-topped dresser was cracked in several places. Twin floor-to-ceiling windows were framed with heavy blue velvet drapes. An armoire sat against one wall, with a large wardrobe on the other, and a claw-foot tub half-filled with water, occupied a platform in the corner.

She crossed to one window, which framed a view of the rice fields and, behind them, a wide, meandering river. The lush greens were so varied it resembled an artist's rendering against a backdrop of shimmering water. Even the muted bluish gray sky was beautiful.

The door opened and Mercy turned to see Chessie enter the room. The old woman glanced in her direction, then without a word crossed toward the tub, her body tilting to the side from the weight of a bucket in one hand. Chessie started to pour water from the bucket over the side of the porcelain tub.

There was a quick knock on the door, and Victoria came breezing in. "I thought I should choose what you'll wear, just like the old days," she said. "I mean, just because you don't remember the old days doesn't mean we can't do it, right?"

Mercy smiled. "Yes, that would be nice."

Victoria went to the large wardrobe and threw open the door. "Let's see now … I'm going to wear yellow so—"

"Tub's full," Chessie declared.

"Thank you for doing that, Chessie," Mercy said.

"Jes doin' my job." Chessie started back toward the door.

Victoria rifled through dozens of dresses, then pulled a lavender gown from the rack. "Now we don't have to worry that we'll match, Char. Two unique sisters." Victoria laid the dress across the end of the bed and addressed Chessie. "Isn't Charlotte's news the strangest thing you've ever heard, Chessie?"

Chessie stopped and turned. "Dunno what'choo mean, Miss Victoria."

"Charlotte can't remember any of us—any of this," Victoria said, sweeping her hand around the room.

"I was hurt," Mercy said. "A head injury gave me something called amnesia. It means I've lost all my memories of this place. Growing up. My family. You."

Chessie took the news stoically. "You sayin' you don't 'member me one whit?"

"I'm afraid I don't."

"She only knows you were her mammy because Mother told her," Victoria said.

"I don't remember anything of my life here," Mercy said. "I don't remember any*one* from my life here."

Chessie stared at her. "Huh."

"Don't feel bad, Chessie," Victoria said. "She didn't know me or Beau—and we're blood kin."

"I'm sorry," Mercy said.

"Kin you help it?" Chessie asked.

Mercy shook her head. "No."

"Den being sorry don't make no sense."

"Just think about it, Char … if you hadn't seen that portrait of Father and thought he looked familiar, you might never have found us," Victoria said. "Such a lucky twist of fate." Victoria made her way toward the door. "I've got to change for supper. See you downstairs." She slipped out of the room, leaving Chessie and Mercy alone.

Chessie nodded at the tub. "Bath's ready."

As Chessie busied herself at the armoire, Mercy took the opportunity to maintain a little modesty and quickly stepped out of her dress and stepped into the tub. She sighed from the sheer luxury of the warm water and the scent of lemon soap. Chessie carried lacy undergarments back to the bed and put them beside the dress. She moved slowly, methodically, eyes anywhere but on Mercy. Finally, she brought a thick towel and draped it over the edge of the tub.

Mercy looked up at her. "I have so many questions …"

"Imagine so."

"I'm hoping you can answer some of them for me."

"I jes be da help. Ask yo' family," Chessie said.

"But if you raised me, you'd know me as well as, or even better than they would," Mercy said.

Chessie looked at her. "You kin raise a chil' and end up not knowin' 'em at all." She nodded at the towel. "I'll hep you into yo' dress when you done."

Chessie turned away from the tub, shuffled toward the bed, and Mercy rose out of the water. She wrapped herself in the towel. "Did you ever meet my mother? I don't mean Suzanne. I mean my real mother?"

"Jes one or two times," Chessie said. "I come here wit yo' grand-daddy 'afore you was born."

Mercy made her way across the room. "Can you tell me anything about her?"

Chessie shook her head. "No, I cain't." She shrugged.

"What about her name?" Mercy persisted, while she donned the things on the bed. "Do you remember her name?"

"Marie." Chessie picked up the dress from the bed and held both arms out in front of her to keep the material off the floor.

"Marie. That's a beautiful name," Mercy said. "It's strange, but until just a little while ago I didn't even know my *own* name. When I went to stay with some nuns for a time, they started calling me Mercy."

Chessie snorted derisively and shook her head.

"What?" Mercy asked.

Another shake of her head. "Ain't nothin'. You ready for yo' dress?"

"Yes, I suppose I am," Mercy said. "You really don't have to do any of this. I'm perfectly capable of getting dressed alone."

"Dis what we do here," Chessie said. "Like it or not."

Chessie lifted the dress and settled it over her head. Mercy pushed her arms through the sleeves, which stopped just above her elbows, and yards of material flowed over her hips. Stays in her corset pushed her chest up, the neckline revealed a deep décolletage, and the tight lacing made her waist impossibly tiny. She made her way to a mirror on the inside of the armoire door and looked at her reflection.

For a brief moment, Chessie's image was beside her as she put things back into the armoire. She went briskly about her business, not giving Mercy a second look. Mercy tried again to draw her into conversation.

"How long did you work for my grandfather before you came to work for my father?" she asked.

"Yo' granddaddy *owned* me twenty-five years 'fore yo' daddy did," Chessie said.

Mercy flushed. "That's what I meant."

Chessie leveled a look at her. "Den dat's what you should say— 'cause dat's da way it was."

"I'm sorry," Mercy said.

Another long look from Chessie. "You kin save yo' sorry for somethin' dat matters. You need anything else from me right now?"

Mercy shook her head. "No. Thank you for your help."

While Mercy watched, Chessie shuffled across the room with the empty bucket in hand, went out the door, and closed it soundly behind her.

CHAPTER SEVENTEEN

Mercy descended the staircase and dropped a hand to her waist where one of the corset stays was pinching. *This thing would explain what drove me to dress as a man,* she thought. She stepped onto the foyer floor and made her way toward the sound of voices in what she assumed must be the dining room. When she stepped through the door, the faces of her family turned toward her. Mother, Victoria, and Beau all smiled, and she felt a thrill. She was home. She was where she belonged.

"Ah, here is the woman of the hour," her mother said. "Right on time. You look lovely, dear."

"Thank you," Mercy said. She took a moment to look around the room. It was spacious and beautiful. The heavy mahogany pedestal table would easily seat twelve, and the high-backed chairs were upholstered in wine-colored brocade. In here, as in other rooms of the house, there were floor-to-ceiling paned windows with heavy draperies drawn back and tied with braided gold rope. A crystal chandelier hung from an intricate plaster medallion etched into the ceiling over the table. Two huge sideboards sat against opposite walls, but were noticeably bare of any kind of decorative adornment. Looking closer, Mercy could see further evidence of the Yankee occupation of the house. Wainscoting along the bottom half of the walls was damaged with dents and black marks, and the floral wallpaper on three walls was faded and had actually been stripped off in some places. There seemed to be no rhyme or reason for the damage, other than to be simply—destructive. Beau must have seen her glancing about.

"Think of the countless meals we've had in this room," he said.

"I wish I could," Mercy said.

He reddened. "I'm sorry, Charlotte. That was thoughtless of me. I keep forgetting that you've …"

She smiled. "Forgotten?"

He returned her smile. "Yes."

Her mother weighed in. "I hope you'll forgive us when we say things—well, things like Beau just said."

"There's nothing to forgive," Mercy said. "It's taken me a long time to come to terms with my memory loss. I can't expect you to get used to it in one evening."

"What's it like?" Beau asked.

Mercy thought for a moment. "Think of a book you've never read. Though it's filled with pages, you open it halfway through. The story doesn't make sense, so of course you flip back to the beginning to see how it all started, but the pages are blank. There are no answers, nor descriptions. No settings or plot points. No clever phrases written down or even the names of the characters—not even the story's main character."

"Sounds … frustrating," Beau said.

"Frustrating. Frightening. Maddening," she said. "I feel as if it's a miracle I'm even here at all."

"It does seem miraculous you were able to find your way back with so little information," Beau said.

"Yes. Miraculous," Mother said.

Before Mercy could answer, Elijah entered the dining room, wearing a clean white shirt and a pair of black trousers.

"I hope I'm not late?" he said.

"Not at all," Suzanne said.

Beau moved to the sideboard and opened one of the doors to retrieve a glass decanter half filled with a dark liquid.

"Would you care for some brandy, Mr. Hale?" he asked.

"No, thank you," Elijah said. "I fear it would be put me straight to sleep."

Beau looked at Suzanne. "Brandy, Mother?"

"After all the excitement this afternoon, I think a brandy would be welcome," she said.

"I'll have one too," Victoria said.

"No you won't," her mother said. "You're too young."

"I'm the same exact age as Beau minus three minutes," Victoria said.

"You're a woman." Suzanne accepted her glass from Beau.

"So are you," Victoria said.

As Beau added his two cents to the banter, Mercy tried to cover a smile by turning toward Elijah. She spoke with quiet, but evident amusement. "So this is what it's like to be part of a family."

Elijah smiled. "At times. You'll get used to it." She felt his appraisal of her appearance, but it didn't feel the least bit intrusive.

"I must say you look very much at home in this room—that dress," he said.

"I'll take that as a compliment," she said.

"That's how it was intended."

"Sorry, apparently I'm an unrepentant eavesdropper," Beau said, "but I'd like to add my compliments as well, Char. I don't ever recall seeing you in lavender, but the color becomes you."

Mercy raised her brows at her sister. "Thank you. The dress was Victoria's choice."

Victoria smiled. "I have a little confession. You've always said you hated lavender."

"Oh. Then why did I have this dress?"

"I actually had that made for you on your seventeenth birthday, dear," her mother said. "I always thought the color would be beautiful on you. I'm happy to say I was right. Shall we sit?"

Beau made his way to pull out the chair for his mother, then did the same for Mercy. Elijah pulled out Victoria's chair before taking his own.

As if on cue, Rose, the housemaid, and a young Negro girl entered with trays and began to serve.

"I hope you enjoy venison, Mr. Hale. It's just about all we eat these days," Suzanne said.

"I do," Elijah said. He looked at Beau. "You must be the hunter."

Beau nodded. "Luckily, the deer are plentiful around here. I've got a blind at the edge of one of the rice fields, and they wander right past me."

"I think, had Sherman's army figured out a way to do it, they would have wiped out the entire deer population," Suzanne said.

"We lost nearly all our pigs to a half-disciplined regiment of Yankees wielding knives and whooping it up." Beau shook his head. "Our new piglets aren't up to the proper weight to butcher yet."

"Aren't y'all going to mention the disaster with the chickens?" Victoria asked with a trace of sarcasm. "It seems to fit right into this conversation."

"Chickens?" Mercy said.

"Something got inside the chicken coop about two weeks ago," Beau said. "Nothing left there but feathers and cracked eggs …"

"Complete negligence on the part of the darkies," Suzanne said. "Time and time again we've told them to latch the door to the coop, but did they listen? No. So the loss is coming from their wages. It's the only way to make an impression …"

"All right, my appetite is officially ruined now," Victoria said. "Not that it matters, because personally, I'm sick to death of venison."

The young Negro girl put a basket of bread down on the table in front of Mercy who looked up at her and smiled. "Thank you."

The girl ducked her head. She shot a look toward Suzanne, then said quickly, "Welcome home, Mizz Charlotte."

"This is Biddy, Charlotte," her mother said. "She was born on the plantation. Her mother and father work the fields now and Biddy is old enough to help Rose here in the house."

"Dey calls me Biddy on account of I's an iddy biddy babe when I be born," Biddy said. "You knowed dat once but Rose tell me you's got a broken memory."

"I do, so I appreciate you telling me," Mercy said. "Have you met my friend Isaac, Biddy?"

"Yassum. He be havin' a meal in the colored camp."

"I would really appreciate it if you would make him feel welcome."

"Yassum, Miss Charlotte," Biddy said. "I surely will."

"Thank you, Biddy. That will be all now." Suzanne waved her hand dismissively. The young girl made her way out of the dining room and Suzanne directed her attention to Elijah.

"I'm wondering, Mr. Hale, if you and Charlotte were in the same regiment?" She shook her head at her own question. "It still sounds so odd to say …"

Elijah fleetingly looked at Mercy before he answered. "No. We weren't."

"How long have you known each other?"

"I'd have to say we really weren't formally introduced until about six months ago," he said.

Shifting her gaze to Mercy, Suzanne lifted her brows expectantly. "And where did you two meet?"

"St. Louis. We were both at a social function and saw each other again," Mercy said.

"I had a pal who was imprisoned at Gratiot Street Prison in St. Louis," Beau said. "Thankfully, he escaped and the town was so filled with Southern sympathizers, he found sanctuary in a home a block away from that horrible place."

Just hearing the name *Gratiot Prison* made Mercy shudder involuntarily. She drew in a breath, reached for her water glass, and found Suzanne staring at her with a quizzical expression.

"Are you all right, Charlotte?"

Mercy forced a smile. "Yes, I just had a chill is all."

"Someone just walked over your grave," Victoria said.

"Excuse me?"

"You remember that old saying, whenever you get a chill, it means someone walked over your future grave."

Oh, how close I've come to that, Mercy thought. She smiled at her younger sister. "I don't remember hearing that."

"I'm sorry, Charlotte," Victoria said. "I keep forgetting you have—forgotten everything."

"Please don't apologize anytime you say something that I don't remember."

"Forgive me for asking, Char," Beau said, "but I'm wondering if you remember basic things? Reading, writing, how to figure numbers?"

"It seems strange," she answered, "but I do remember all of that. I even kept a journal for a while to help me get things straight."

"At least you didn't have to relearn simple skills," Victoria said. "That must have been a relief."

"Yes, it was."

"Where are you from, Mr. Hale?" Suzanne asked. "You don't sound as if you're from the South."

"I grew up in Philadelphia," he said. "In fact, I tried to get into West Point, but the appointment went to a senator's son from our state."

"Money talks," Beau said with an air of satisfaction.

Elijah nodded. "Something like that."

"You came from a Yankee state and fought for the South?"

"He just said he met Charlotte in St. Louis, Mother," Beau said. "A city of split loyalties. Think about General John Pemberton. He was a Unionist rebel if there ever was one. Am I right, Hale?"

Elijah nodded. "Yes, you are. General Pemberton grew up in the North but fought for the South."

Mercy wasn't ready for the direction their conversation was headed, nor, she could see, was Elijah. So far he hadn't said anything that wasn't true, but surely he couldn't keep it up. Then Victoria saved them all from what could prove to be a heated discussion.

"I'm sick to death of war talk," Victoria said. "Surely there is another topic we can discuss without the words *rebel* or *Yankee* coming up in conversation."

"I would love to hear about the plantation," Mercy said. "The way you are all managing to cope day to day."

Victoria sighed. "Oh pooh. Another boring topic."

"That *boring topic* is what puts food on this table and pretty dresses on your back, darling," her mother said. "Without this place we'd all be homeless. You would do well to remember that."

"How could I *not* remember that?" Victoria said. "You won't let me forget it." She turned her gaze to Mercy. "I think you have the best of both worlds now, Char. You get to live in the present but can't remember the awfulness of the past. I envy you."

Mercy caught an unvarnished look between Beau and their mother at Victoria's comment.

"Anyway," Victoria continued, "I think we should talk about the homecoming party we're giving in Charlotte's honor!"

"Homecoming party?" Mercy asked.

"Yes, darling. We want all our friends and neighbors to know you've come home at last. We haven't had a party in ages. Not since … well, not since your father and the war and all the unpleasantness."

"I wish you wouldn't go to all that trouble," Mercy said.

"Oh, Charlotte … don't spoil it," Victoria said. "We're finally going to have some fun around here. I wish we could get Uncle Thomas and Aunt Sarah here for the party."

"I have an aunt and uncle?" Mercy asked.

Her mother nodded. "My brother and his wife. They live in Atlanta, but I'm afraid he's not well enough to travel."

"I'm sorry to hear that," Mercy said.

Suzanne sighed. "I used to go visit, but they live in the tiniest little house you've ever seen …" Her voice trailed off, and then she turned to Elijah. "Mr. Hale, we'd love to have you stay for the party. You brought our darling Charlotte home and we're so grateful."

"Yes, Mr. Hale. You must stay," Victoria said.

"Maybe Hale has a job to get back to," Beau said.

"As a matter of fact, I *had* planned to leave in the morning. I have responsibilities to attend to …," Elijah said.

"We're planning the party for Saturday," Suzanne said. "It's only a few days from now."

"Surely a few more days won't matter," Victoria said.

"I really shouldn't …"

Mercy had been watching him and listening to his polite refusals to her newfound family. How could one man evoke so many different emotions from her? She should speak up and let him off the hook. It was the kind thing to do. She saw him look across the table at her, so she did.

"I wish you *would* stay for the party, Elijah," she said.

His eyebrows rose and his mouth opened in surprise. "What?"

"Please stay. You helped me get home. I would like you to stay and help celebrate with me."

For a moment, it seemed as if it were just the two of them in the room. He held her gaze for a heartbeat longer.

"Thank you. I'd be happy to stay for the party."

"Splendid!" Victoria clapped her hands. "I can hardly stand it, I'm so excited. Now, if we could only find a few eligible bachelors to come to the house, I'll be the happiest girl in McIntosh County."

"Really, Victoria, is that all you think about?" Beau asked.

Victoria smiled unapologetically. "Yes."

"Charlotte, you and I and Victoria will go to Darien tomorrow," her mother said. "We'll issue invitations and pick up some of the things we'll need for Saturday. And, Beau, maybe you might give Mr. Hale a tour of the plantation?"

Beau looked at Elijah. "If you're interested, that is?"

"Very interested," Elijah replied.

"You never did say what you do for a living, Hale? Obviously not still soldiering?" He narrowed his eyes. "Or did you take that insulting oath of allegiance to stay on?"

"No, I didn't take the oath," Elijah said truthfully. "You might say I work on behalf of the railway companies out west. Making sure the workers and the trains go through without interference with the Indians in that region."

Victoria squealed her delight. "My, Mr. Hale, that sounds very exciting."

"Some days are more challenging than others," Elijah said. He glanced around the table. "And, please, call me Elijah."

Rose made an appearance with a pitcher of water and began to refill glasses around the table.

"Juba ask me to see if everything be the way you like it, missus?" Rose asked.

"Tell her it's fine, Rose," Suzanne said.

As Rose left the dining room, Suzanne shook her head. "I find it absolutely ridiculous that anytime one of our Negroes does the job they are supposed to do, they are fishing for compliments. For the love of God, we are *employing* them now. They receive compensation we can ill afford—but they need constant acknowledgment when a weed is pulled, a field is plowed, or a meal is cooked!"

"Biddy turned down my bed last night and you'd think she performed a miracle," Victoria said.

Mercy kept her head down and her fork full as the conversation between her rediscovered family members continued. She had a sobering thought. *Is that what I used to sound like?*

CHAPTER EIGHTEEN

Mercy was tired as she and Elijah climbed the stairs to their respective rooms later that evening. They reached the top of the stairs and Elijah looked at her.

"You're sure you want me to stay for your big evening?"

"Yes. Positive."

"I could just as easily leave as I planned in the morning and you wouldn't have to worry about anyone finding out about my ... occupation."

"You told them what you do," she said. Then she frowned. "*Is* that what you do? Do you really keep the railways safe from attacking Indians?"

He smiled. "It's one of my jobs, yes."

"It sounds dangerous."

"Less dangerous than the war the two of us fought." His chuckle was soft and wry.

She shook her head. "I always forget that."

"Has this been anything like you imagined?" he asked. "The house, your family—your homecoming?"

She hesitated for a moment. "I think I imagined—no, I *hoped* that I'd set foot in the door and everything would come flooding back." She barely lifted her shoulders in a shrug and offered a wan smile. "Silly, I know."

"Not silly."

"It's strange, though," she said.

"What?"

She sighed. "I find it ironic it was the portrait of my father that brought me back—and now he's the one who is gone."

"Sounds like he was quite a man."

She nodded. "Yes, it does." A smile. "I *am* happy to be here. Happy to know that I have a place in the world."

"And a lovely place it is, Charlotte," he said.

"We're alone, Elijah. You can call me Mercy."

He shook his head. "You're Charlotte now. If you want to reclaim your home, your past—your family. From here on out, even when alone, you've got to reclaim your name as well."

Thoughtful, she nodded. "You're right." She cocked her head to one side. "Are you always right?"

"If I have you believing that now, maybe I should leave in the morning before I prove it wrong."

Charlotte smiled. "Good night, Elijah."

Charlotte stepped into her room and closed the door. She was blessedly alone and could go back over the events of the day at her leisure. A fire burned cheerily in the fireplace—Chessie evidently had been there. The evening had grown quite cool once the sun set. The warmth of the fire felt good, and so did Charlotte.

She'd been truthful when she told Elijah she was happy to be there. Maybe things would finally settle down and life would fall into a predictable rhythm. She'd had enough surprises and adventures to last a lifetime.

She was humming when she went to the closet to hang up her dress. For once, she actually looked forward to the next day, what new things she'd learn. Who she would meet. She stepped closer to the bar to hang her dress, then looked down when her foot connected with something. Her saddlebags. More importantly—her journal. She pulled the leather book from the pouch and sat down on the bed. She thumbed through the many pages where her innermost thoughts were penned. Her hopes, dreams, fears—even bad decisions—were all written there for anyone to see. And the last people she wanted to see it were living in this house. Where to put it? The armoire or the desk? Maybe under the mattress. She knew what happened when the wrong people read it—knew it was as if she were baring her soul. She couldn't risk it. There was no place safe enough to hide it. She made her way to the fireplace. It felt good to decide; felt right that she was going to erase any record of the past year of her life.

Charlotte turned to the very first page of the journal and skimmed a few lines. It was as if a different person had written those things. A terrified young woman who wasn't even sure she could get along in the world. She closed the book. Thought about how much had changed since the day she'd first dipped the nib of a pen into a jar of ink and written in that very book—*I have woken up thirteen different times without a name.*

The search was over—and so was the need for the journal. Charlotte stepped closer to the fireplace. *It's the only answer. The only choice.* Quickly, before she lost her nerve and changed her mind, she tossed the brown leather book into the flames. The flames danced around the cover of the journal, licking up the sides and devouring the pages. She watched as the pages turned to tiny bits of ash—then floated up and out of sight in the chimney.

CHAPTER NINETEEN

The train rumbled down the tracks with clouds of smoke billowing back past the open windows. A good-sized piece of black ash from the smokestack landed on the back of a passenger's hand that rested on the window ledge. Luther, a tall man who could appreciate the luxury of stretching out his long legs, flicked the ash from his hand and continued to stare at the ever-changing view of the countryside. He looked placid, calm, but his thoughts moved faster than the train he rode. He couldn't make his mind still enough to match his outward countenance. Couldn't stop his brain from going over the recent events that had led him to that very train.

His traveling companions, Newt and Harland, had quickly found a high-stakes card game shortly after embarking at the Dover station, and had been holed up in the club car for most of the twenty-four hours they'd been traveling. The way Luther figured it, one or both would be so deep in debt from his losses, he would have to kiss the bounty money good-bye almost as soon as it hit his palm. Luther knew they were both marginal card players at best— but neither could resist the lure of a good game. Luther had never been a gambling man—couldn't see risking his hard-earned money on the chance that luck would be with him. The biggest gamble he'd ever made was joining up with the army when Lincoln called for volunteers. He had gambled with his life that he'd live to see the end of the war—and he had. It seemed to Luther he'd used up all the luck allotted to any one man during those battles when he came away with both arms, legs, and even his sanity intact. Now he was in charge of his own providence. A man who made his luck based on his own wits and decisions.

His thoughts went to poor, dead Shane. The kid had launched himself out the window of that boardinghouse, fueled by pure enthusiasm, which had led to his early demise. That kind of spontaneous action nearly always spelled disaster. Gus should have had a firmer hand with the kid. He wondered how Gus had fared with Pauline when he took the boy home. He'd always been a little jealous of Gus's marriage. In Luther's eyes, Pauline was the perfect woman. Looked good, but not so good you had to worry constantly about other men trying to steal her away. Amiable in most situations—even when Gus went off to war she hadn't sniffled and blubbered like a lot of other women he'd seen. Yes, as far as luck went with women, Gus had been blessed with it while Luther had not. Still, he knew Pauline's Achilles' heel had been Shane. Even as the boy was growing into a man, Pauline couldn't see it. To her, he would always be an eight-year-old with a crush on his mama. For once, Luther hadn't envied Gus one bit when he went home to his wife to tell her their son was dead.

The train rumbled around a curve in the tracks, and he had to flick another ash from his hand. His lips turned up in a slight smile when he thought about the days ahead. Gus had always been the leader in their little missions, the one who had the connections that brought them the work. So even though it had never been stated categorically, Gus was the boss. But with Gus out of commission, Luther had been more than happy to step into the role. At first, Newt and Harland had balked when he'd started to lay out his plan to find Mercy. A small skirmish had erupted between them over who was really in charge, but Luther prevailed. He'd pulled a map from his saddlebag and traced the route that made the most sense.

Now that she was positive someone was after her, he figured Mercy would take the quickest route south. It made sense—and Luther liked things to make sense. Newt and Harland had followed his plan grudgingly, and by the time they rode into Dover, Tennessee, they were convinced Luther was leading them the wrong way. *She would'a crossed back over the state to throw us off, Luther. This is even more of a wild-goose chase than what Gus had us doing.* But in a moment of loyalty, Luther reminded them that Gus had been right. And now they just needed to trust that Luther, too, would prove himself to be just as adept at finding her as Gus had been.

The idea to stop for the night had been Harland's. He'd refused to go any farther and, rather than incite mutiny, Luther agreed. But Luther already knew that depending on their successful outcome of finding Mercy, when he told this story in years to come, the detail of who wanted to stop at the hotel would change. It would be all his idea. As would the little history lesson he'd provide to whomever was listening. "Yes, sir," he would say. "We rode into Dover and found the hotel in the heart of town. Little did we know at the time we were entering the headquarters of General Buckner, who used it as a staging place when he fought the Union for the rights to the Mississippi River Valley. Poor Buckner had to swallow his pride when he was forced to surrender to Union General Grant in that very same building. We walked in the door and stood where the first major Union victory of the War of the Rebellion had taken place."

Of course, upon entering, none of this mattered much. But when a travel-weary Luther decided to pull his photograph of Mercy from his pocket, things began to matter very much.

The clerk behind the counter pushed the registration book toward them. "How many rooms, gentlemen?"

"One," Newt said.

"*One?*" Luther echoed. "I ain't sleeping in the same room with the two of you, if I don't have to."

"We can split the cost three ways if we share a room," Harland said. "Makes sense."

Luther shook his head. "I want my own room." He scrawled his name across the register. "You two do what you want."

While Newt and Harland made their decision, Luther pulled his photograph from his pocket. He was starting to believe that lightning wouldn't strike twice. They'd had their lucky break when someone recognized her in Salem. What were the odds of that happening again?

"Wondering if you've ever seen this woman?" Luther asked, pointing to the photo.

The clerk picked it up and studied it for less than a minute. "Sure have."

The words were so unexpected, all three men just stared at him. The clerk smiled and pushed the photograph back to Luther. "So have you two gentlemen decided how—"

"You've seen her?" Luther interrupted.

The clerk nodded. "Yes. Now—"

"When?"

"Two—three days ago, maybe," the clerk said. He took the registration book back and ran a finger down the list of names. He tapped one. "This is it."

All three men leaned in for a closer look. "That ain't her name," Newt said.

"No. The gentleman she was traveling with registered for her," the clerk told them.

Harland straightened up. "Then it ain't her. Our gal travels alone."

The clerk looked miffed. "I assure you I don't forget a face, and I especially wouldn't forget *that* woman's face."

"How long did she stay?"

"Just the one night. She looked a little peaked—but by the next morning I swear she had color back in her cheeks. That's what a good night's rest can do, which is why I recommend three rooms …"

"Where did they go from here?" Luther asked.

"I have no idea," he said.

"Did they say anything, do anything unusual?"

The clerk thought for a moment, then shook his head. "No. Nothing."

Luther flipped the book back around and looked at it. "So this man, Elijah Hale, just handed you back the key and left without a word?"

"He asked me where the county courthouse was," the clerk said. "But that's hardly a state secret. It's only half a mile from here."

"And the woman? She say anything at all?"

"No. Wait, yes. She had the audacity to ask me if we rent to Negroes," the man said. "I assured her we do not."

The clerk at the county courthouse had been most helpful. Luther adjusted his legs, moved his right ankle over his left, and tipped his hat farther down on his face to keep the sun from hitting him. The swaying of the southbound train, the monotonous sound of the wheels against the tracks, and the pleasant warmth of the passenger car had finally wrought their magic, and he started to relax. Luther had a name and a place. He wasn't sure what he'd find when they reached the Chapman Plantation, but he was sure of one thing: he was finally going to come face-to-face with the ever-elusive Mercy.

Chapter Twenty

From a distance, the town of Darien seemed to be a patchwork of gray and black surrounded by the glorious green vegetation. Brick chimneys, blackened from fire, dotted the landscape like cornstalks growing toward the sun. Victoria, in the driver's seat of the four-place buggy, expertly steered the horse past the waterfront, where timber was being unloaded from a float next to the pier.

"The timber business is starting to come back," Mother said. She leaned forward, her gloved hand resting on the back of Charlotte's seat. "It's been slow like everything else, but Darien depends on the loggers to continue using the harbor."

As usual, the scents of the river evoked the sense of something familiar for Charlotte. As if she could read her mind, Victoria looked over at her. "I used to be so envious of you, Char. Father used to participate in the crew racing regattas when we were younger. I was too little, but he used to take you on his practice runs up and down the Altamaha."

"All the plantation owners had boats," Mother said. "Your father named his the SS *Chapman*."

"He didn't have the best imagination." Victoria grinned. "But, as I recall, he was very good."

"Yes, he was," her mother said. "He took home the prize for first place more than a few times. Those were good days." Charlotte could hear the wistfulness in Suzanne's voice.

"Do they still have the regattas?" Charlotte asked.

"No. Not since the war started," Suzanne said. "And after it ended, the wealth of the county disappeared. I'm almost happy your father didn't live to see what's happened to his beloved South."

When Victoria brought the buggy up the main street of town, the devastation and ruin was even more apparent up close. Chimneys were all that was left in the remains of burned-out buildings; the red Georgia clay still bore the hallmarks of fire. Charlotte could see where some places were being rebuilt, and farther down the road a row of new businesses had gone up.

"The entire town burned," Victoria said.

"And ironically, it wasn't even General Sherman and his ruthless soldiers who did it. In June of '63, a colored regiment of Federals came through here and set a torch to anything and everything that would burn. Three churches, a courthouse, and a market were lost, along with more homes than anyone took time to count. They were blue devils with black skin whose hate became a physical thing. I'm quite sure the citizens of Darien could say they saw the gates of Hades."

"Enough of this dour talk," Victoria said. "This is supposed to be a fun trip for Charlotte—and for us." She urged the horse on toward the new buildings. "Besides, look at all the new places," she said. "Victory from the ashes—see? The town is coming back and will be better than ever. Pretty soon Darien will be as big as Savannah."

"Bring the buggy over, dear," Mother said. "We'll start at Dooley's."

Victoria pulled the buggy along the side of the road in front of a white clapboard building with the name Dooley's Merchandise Market painted over the door. After tying the reins around the post out front, Victoria pushed her arm through Charlotte's and whispered in her ear. "Ready or not, here we go."

As soon as they entered the establishment, Charlotte became the focus of everyone's attention. She heard a few people say her name, and there were a couple gasps of disbelief.

"Good afternoon, everyone," her mother said.

Before they could move from the spot in front of the door, a young woman pushed her way to stand in front of Charlotte.

"Good gracious, it *is* you! I thought I saw you riding along the outskirts of town the other day and I even said to Betty Lou Hibbitts, I believe that's Charlotte Chapman, but then we both agreed it couldn't possibly be you passing through Darien as if you didn't know a soul. I'm positive you saw me with Betty Lou, yet you didn't so much as offer me a greeting!"

Charlotte opened her mouth to reply, but Victoria gave her arm a little squeeze and beat her to it.

"Since when did she *ever* greet you, Penelope?"

Mother issued a quiet warning. "Victoria … don't …"

"You and Betty Lou … y'all were the meanest things in the world to her when she wanted to sing in the church choir. We all know you bullied the choir director into leaving her out."

Penelope lifted her chin a fraction of an inch, looked past Charlotte, and addressed Victoria. "Well, I'm not sorry. She couldn't sing. Not a note. It was church, Victoria. God shouldn't have cater-wauling voices lifted to Him in praise." Penelope turned her attention back to Charlotte. "I don't know where you've been or why you left in the first place, Char, but welcome home."

"Thank you."

As Penelope walked away, Victoria leaned closer to Charlotte. "She's a vicious little thing, but she's right. You can't sing a note that's not sour."

"That's good to know," Charlotte said. "I think."

"Oh, for heaven's sake, Victoria. Do try and keep a civil tongue in your head while we're here," Mother said. "It's counterproductive to rile up Penelope Sawyer and anyone else like her. You know her father is considering us for his rice season this year."

Charlotte heard the forced contriteness in her sister's voice. "I'm sorry, Mother. I'll be good."

"See that you are," Mother said. Then she turned toward a man who stood behind a counter. "Dooley! Look who's come home to us!"

Dooley, the proprietor, had a wide smile on his face. "I saw her the second you entered," he said. "Welcome home, Miss Charlotte!"

Mother and Victoria ushered her forward, and Dooley held out his hands over the counter. Charlotte smiled and put her hands in his.

"I can't tell you how happy I am to see you," he said. Charlotte thought she saw actual tears shining in his eyes.

"Thank you. It's good to be home."

"There must have been quite a celebration when you walked in the door!" Dooley said.

"That is precisely the reason we're here," her mother said to Dooley and the room at large. "To celebrate Charlotte's return. We're having a party at the house at five o'clock on Saturday and y'all are invited. And, please, pass the word for us. We'd love to have everyone who knows Charlotte there."

Her mother passed a piece of paper across the counter to Dooley. "I've brought a list for you to fill."

Dooley perused it while people started to crowd around Charlotte, one by one, welcoming her back. She was grateful to have Victoria behind her whispering names of those who approached in her ear. And then one young man, head and shoulders taller than anyone in the place, pushed through the group.

"Hello, Charlotte."

"Umm, hello."

"Hello, Shorty," Victoria said.

Shorty nodded at Victoria, then looked at Charlotte. "I'm glad to see you're back."

"Thank you."

"I hope you're not still holding against me that little incident that happened before you left."

Charlotte smiled. "Consider it forgotten."

She heard Victoria giggle behind her. The young man frowned. "Really? Just like that. Not a word about something I've been worrying on for years now."

"I'm … sorry. I thought you wanted me to forget it," Charlotte said.

"Guess it was a bigger deal to me than you," Shorty said.

Victoria stepped around her sister. "Charlotte, this is Shorty Smithson. And, Shorty, when Char says she doesn't remember … she isn't joking. Her memory's scrambled. She's got something called amnesia."

Mother turned from the counter. "Victoria, maybe Charlotte didn't want to say anything just yet …"

"Well, that's just ridiculous," Victoria said. "Everyone is going to find out sooner or later. Tell them, Char."

Charlotte looked at the strangers surrounding her—including Shorty. "It's true. I have a condition known as amnesia. It means my memory is impaired and I don't remember anything about my earlier life. So please, I'll ask your forgiveness in advance if you know me but I don't remember you."

A ripple of conversation ran through the place. Shorty leaned down toward Charlotte. "So you really don't remember when I tried to steal that kiss from you?"

Charlotte shook her head. "No, I don't."

Shorty's face flushed with color. "Then could you forget I just said that?"

Charlotte tried to cover her smile. "I'll try."

"That's a cryin' shame about your memory," Dooley said. "I hate to think you can't remember your daddy. We were all so proud of John. The air just went out of the town the day he died."

Mother's eyes grew misty, and she dabbed at the corner of her eye with the fingertip of her white glove. "He's right, Charlotte. Everyone loved your father."

"He was a true war hero," Dooley said.

"Well, y'all, we have another war hero right here," Victoria said loudly enough for everyone in the place to hear. She put her arm around Charlotte's waist. "My sister didn't run away from home three years ago. She ran straight to the Confederate army and took up arms to fight for the South! That's right. Charlotte was a sharpshooter who probably killed dozens and dozens of Yankee scoundrels. And anyone who knows her well, knows she could do it."

At first, the people in the store were too stunned to say a word. They looked to her mother, who nodded. "She's telling the truth. We were just as surprised as y'all seem to be."

Dooley was the first to break the silence. "I just know your daddy is so proud of you, Miss Charlotte. Must be beaming his smile down from the heavens."

Charlotte, even more uncomfortable than she was before, smiled at Dooley. "Thank you. That is very nice to hear."

People congratulated her, reached to shake her hand, and patted her on the back. Victoria, who seemed to be enjoying the attention much more than her sister, looked at Shorty and grinned.

"You'd best not be trying to steal any more kisses from Charlotte, Shorty. She might just shoot you where you stand."

CHAPTER TWENTY-ONE

"It was my grandfather's vision," Beau told Elijah as they rode on horseback along the banks of the Altamaha, the river that bordered the plantation. "He knew this was the perfect climate and location to grow rice."

A flock of ospreys flew overhead. The huge birds had a wingspan of over five feet and made moving shadows across the rice fields.

"But before he came here and started the plantation, he was a Revolutionary War hero," Beau said. "Father was very proud of him."

"And apparently followed in his footsteps," Elijah said.

Beau nodded. "Yes. Makes the fact I didn't fight all the more painful."

"You can hardly be blamed for being the wrong age when war broke out," Elijah said.

"I know of boys who lied and joined at fifteen. I wish I'd had the foresight to do just that. I could have made a good soldier."

"Seems to me you've been invaluable here. Look at this place." Elijah twisted in the saddle and let his gaze roam over hundreds of acres of rice crops. "It's really something."

"It's kind of you to say," Beau said. "It's not an easy job. This place is really like a small village. Our goal is to be self-sustaining, just as we were before the war—and we're nearly there."

They started past a vegetable garden that spanned an acre of land. There were Negroes kneeling in the dirt, weeding. "That's the house garden," Beau said. "We've hired several darkies to work it. Some are former slaves of ours, some are former slaves from plantations or farms that folded during the war."

"Being employed must give them a sense of pride," Elijah said. But Beau shook his head. "You would think so, but that's not the case. We've appealed to them to be productive, even promised them some of the food for their own families if they produce more. But quite honestly, they don't like to work. And they especially don't like to work on Saturdays—even though they agreed to it in their contracts."

"You do that through the Freedmen's Bureau?"

Beau nodded. "They require it. Want to make sure each darky has a contract and makes his mark on it. Seems kind of crazy to me since they can't even read what they're signing, but we do it. Then the contracts get sent to the bureau to keep on file. Part of the government's grand plan for reconstruction."

"I suppose they think that's fair to everyone involved," Elijah said.

Beau issued a curt laugh. "There is nothing fair about any of this, Elijah. They say the contract is as much for us as it is for them, but the agents at the bureau will believe the wildest complaints of the Negroes and call the whites to account for some imagined offense.

"Mother was out here last Saturday, checking on the workers, making sure they were putting in a full day as we require. She ran across Cato—one of our old slaves who decided to stay on for hire after he was freed. Cato used to be a good worker in the fields, but Mother found him sleeping behind the corn. When she demanded to know what he was doing, he looked at her and said, 'What's the use of being free when I have to work harder than I did as a slave?'"

"It sounds like it's been a tough transition for everyone," Elijah said.

"They need a firm hand and an uncompromising example made of anyone who doesn't toe the line," Beau said. "We have an overseer who worked here when my father was still alive. Jonas is tough but fair. And under him is Bram, the driver of the colored gangs that work the fields."

"I suppose everyone needs a boss," Elijah said.

"Bram knows how to get the most work out his people," Beau said. "It's easier to take orders from someone who knows what it's like to do the job. He keeps them in line."

"Of course," Elijah said.

"What's it like working out west?"

"A lot dustier and drier than it is here. The landscape isn't nearly as green as all this, and any water I happen across is usually a meandering stream or a lake—certainly different from this. I think a man could get used to seeing the ocean every day."

"I don't suppose I ever thought about *not* seeing it," Beau said. "Besides, I've been raised to think of it more as a means to an end than something to gaze on."

"How is it used?"

"For our irrigation system—not the salt water itself, of course, but we manipulate our dikes and canals in the fields by using the tides. The river can be affected by rise and fall of the ocean as much as thirty miles inland."

They came upon a large building with a brick chimney that rose nearly eighty feet in the air. "What's that?" Elijah asked.

"Steam-powered rice mill," Beau answered. "Father's idea. We produce twice the rice as other mills in the county. There are dozens of small farms and plantations a third of the size of this one. They harvest their crop and bring it to us. We charge a fair price for them to use the mill, and we all end up happy."

Beau made a turn and they rode parallel to a quadrant of rice fields. Elijah could see dozens of workers in constant motion.

"You plant in the spring, I assume?"

"Usually the first of April if the weather cooperates," Beau said. "A good, solid crop can be harvested in September.

"We flood the fields three times during the growing season. The field hands are getting things ready for the lay-by flow. Once we do that, the crop will be underwater for about two months."

"The water doesn't grow stagnant?" Elijah asked.

"It can. Fresh water is periodically introduced to replace it— but the point is to keep everything wet and growing during that time. If we have a good season, we produce about a quarter of a million pounds of rice."

Elijah whistled. "Impressive."

"Not as impressive as the million pounds a year we produced before Mr. Lincoln's destruction of our way of life. We've got a dozen empty houses in the colored camp now," Beau said. "There was a time we didn't have room for one more slave, but now …" He shook his head. "There aren't enough hands for the work."

Elijah watched the field hands make their way up and down the rows of green shooting into the air. There were men, women, and even children in the fields. The work looked monotonous and backbreaking.

"Some of them seem to be wearing Confederate uniforms," Elijah said.

"There were quite a few Negroes who signed on to fight for the cause. When the war ended, they were free, but when they got home, they didn't get clothes from their masters anymore, so they wear the uniforms they had in the war. 'Course, now it's getting too hot for the jackets, but they'll wear them right on through summer."

They rode on toward the stables. Elijah could see Isaac in the corral currying a large black stallion.

"As you can see, we put Isaac to work with the horses. Seems like he's got an easy way with them," Beau said.

"He does," Elijah agreed.

"And I'll admit I thought it would please Charlotte. She seemed to be … unusually attached to the boy."

"I'm sure it does please her. She just wants him to have opportunities that will improve his life."

They got closer and Elijah called out to him. Isaac turned and lifted a hand in greeting.

Beau and Elijah rode to the fence and Isaac came running up. "Hello, Ca … Mr. Elijah," Isaac said.

"Isaac … you doing all right?"

"I sure am. Dey say I kin stay and work and get paid real money," Isaac said.

"Is that what you want to do?"

"Yassuh, I do. I like it here jes fine," Isaac said. "And dis way I kin be where Miss Mercy is."

"Just remember she's Miss Charlotte now," Elijah reminded him.

"It be strange to say it out loud like dat," Isaac said, "after thinkin' a' her as Miss Mercy all dis time."

Elijah smiled down at him. "I know what you mean, Isaac. Guess you'd better be getting back to the horse now. I'm staying here a few more days. I'll see you again before I leave."

"You gonna be here for da party?"

"You know about that, do you?"

"Yassuh. Ever'body here know 'bout dat." Isaac grinned. "But I know Miss Charlotte gonna be da purdiest girl dere."

"Isaac? You done with your work, boy?"

Elijah looked across the corral to see a white man in his thirties, hand on his hip, staring at Isaac. Beau acknowledged the man with a touch to the brim of his hat.

"That's Jonas," Beau said. "The overseer I told you about. He lives right here on the property."

"You probably should get back to work, Isaac. You don't want to make a bad impression on Mr. Jonas," Elijah said.

Isaac looked over his shoulder. "S'pose not," he said. "But he seen me be a hard worker. Besides, Miss Charlotte won't be lettin' anyone treat me in a poor way. I know she won't."

Elijah smiled. "Just keep up your good work, and I'm sure you'll get along fine."

"I keeping up with yo' horse and Lucky," he said. "Not to worry 'bout dem."

"Isaac!" Jonas yelled.

Isaac grinned. "I be seeing you, Mr. Elijah." He turned and ran back to the horse.

Beau and Elijah continued on their way. "Seems to me that boy speaks in a mighty familiar way about Charlotte."

Elijah heard the disapproval in his voice.

"He's just got a small case of puppy love." Elijah smiled. "It's completely harmless. Mercy—I mean *Charlotte*—was very kind to Isaac in St. Louis. She helped him out of a bad situation, and the boy is grateful."

"You give an inch with those people and they'll take a mile," Beau said.

"I'm not sure she sees it that way," Elijah said.

"She will. Now that she's home again, she'll get back into the way things are done."

Elijah turned in the saddle and looked at Beau. "What was she like before the war?"

"Hmm. Charlotte before the war. We've got over seven hundred acres on this plantation and to cover the subject of my sister, we'd need ten thousand more."

"That complicated?"

"Yes. And no." He laughed. "You've seen her shoot?"

Elijah nodded. "Stunning accuracy."

"I don't think there is anyone in the surrounding five counties who can touch her acumen with a rifle. For a while, I tortured myself over her abilities and my ... inadequacies. But then I realized I was the normal one. She was the anomaly. For some reason, that helped."

"I'm sure you were all very worried when she left," Elijah said.

"My father had just died. We were all still reeling from the shock of his death, and then Charlotte disappeared. Yes, you might say we were worried."

"It must have been quite a shock when she turned up yesterday."

"I had a moment when I couldn't even believe my own eyes," Beau said. He gazed into the distance, then shook his head. "Last night I looked at her across the table and felt as if she'd never even left."

"She's lucky she had such a good family to come home to," Elijah said.

Beau smiled. "Your turn. What can you tell me about my sister? You've spent time with her. You can probably describe the woman she is better than I can."

Elijah contemplated the question. "I wouldn't know where to start. I think trying to describe the woman I know as Mercy would be like trying to tell a blind man about the colors in a sunrise. It's impossible to get it right."

Beau raised a brow. "I think you just described how you see her quite well, Elijah. I've seen the way you look at her. If I didn't know better, I'd say Isaac isn't the only one who has a case of puppy love."

Elijah thought for a second and then smiled. "Maybe ... but if I did, it would be harmless as well."

Beau looked over at him with a shake of his head. "Whatever you say."

Anxious to get off the topic, Elijah broached a new one. "How do you suppose they're getting on in town?"

"I imagine they've caused quite a stir," Beau said. "It's just like Charlotte to be in the middle and both ends of a mystery."

Chapter Twenty-Two

The three women strolled down the street, with Victoria and Mother pointing out various shops and people as they passed. Whenever someone new greeted Charlotte, he or she was invited to the plantation for the party.

"Have you any idea how many might turn up?" Charlotte asked.

"No idea at all, dear," Mother said, "but it doesn't matter. It's high time the people of Darien came back to the plantation to see we are thriving and still quite important to this town's survival."

"And to welcome you home, Char," Victoria chimed in.

"Of course," Mother said. "That goes without saying. We want all our friends to help us celebrate."

"I'll admit it seems a little … overwhelming," Charlotte said. "So much fuss."

"We used to have the most delicious house parties when Father was still alive. Before the dreadful war. People would come from all across Georgia and stay for weekends filled with music and food and dancing," Victoria said.

"Your father loved to entertain," Mother said. "Now, to entertain on *that* scale would be impossible without the slaves. We just wouldn't be able to manage so many guests. The stables, the kitchen, the cleaning. No. Those days are over, I'm afraid."

"I think we should have tea and sweets at the bakery before we go back," Victoria said.

"Fine. But I have a few more errands to see to," Mother said. She gestured to the door of the feed and livestock store as they passed. "I planned to order more chickens today from Mr. Jackson, but perhaps I can put you girls on the task while I go to Myrtle's to see about flowers?"

"You want *us* to order the chickens?" Victoria said.

"Didn't I hear you complaining about venison during supper last night?" their mother pointed out.

"Yes, but …"

"Mr. Jackson can help you with the particulars—I trust his judgment," Mother said. "We'll meet at the bakery when we're through."

The inside of the feed store resembled a barn. The pungent odor in the store had Victoria covering her nose when they entered.

"Did you notice Mother gets the sweet-smelling florist, while we are here?" Victoria said.

Charlotte smiled. "It's not so bad."

Seth Jackson was restocking bags of seed when Victoria and Charlotte entered. He was a middle-aged man whose dark-brown hair had just started to gray. He saw them and smiled.

"Miss Chapman? Ma'am. What can I do for you today?"

"Hello, Mr. Jackson. My sister and I are here to order some chickens for the plantation," Victoria said.

He raised his brows. "Your sister?"

"Yes," Victoria said. "This is my older sister, Charlotte. She's just returned home from a long … absence."

"Welcome back," Mr. Jackson said.

"Thank you."

Victoria turned to Charlotte. "Mr. Jackson is relatively new to Darien. He only set up shop a couple of years ago."

Jackson made his way to a long counter and ducked underneath.

"I thought y'all had a good stock of chickens," Jackson said while he dug around under his counter.

"I'm afraid some kind of wild animals got into the coop," Victoria said. "Wiped us out."

Jackson straightened and shook his head. "That's terrible."

Victoria smiled. "But good for business."

Jackson shrugged. "Can't argue there. Can you excuse me for just a minute? I've got the catalogs for poultry in the back room."

"Certainly," Victoria said.

As Jackson started toward a door behind the counter, another, younger man came through it. He carried a silver bucket that seemed to weigh him down.

"Get the rest of that grain in the barrel, Sam," Jackson said, brushing past him.

"Get it in the barrel," Sam repeated. "In the barrel, barrel, barrel, barrel …"

He made his way around the counter toward a big whiskey barrel in the corner of the store. The women watched his slow progress.

"Victoria," Charlotte said, her eyes still on Sam. "How close was I with Chessie?"

"What do you mean?"

"I just wondered what kind of relationship we had."

"She just thought the sun rose and set on you, is all," Victoria said. "Beau and I used to call her an ol' black mama bear protecting her cub." She laughed. "I declare, you could do no wrong in that old woman's eyes. She just doted on you."

"But she didn't take care of you and Beau?"

"No," Victoria said. "Father was adamant that Chessie was *your* mammy—not ours. Besides, we had Mother."

Sam dumped his bucket into the barrel, then started back across the room as Jackson hustled back to the counter with a catalog in hand. "Ladies, if you'll come over here, we can write up an order for those chickens."

Sam went behind the counter and found a broom. He set to work sweeping while Charlotte and Victoria watched Mr. Jackson start to make some notes on a piece of paper in front of him.

"What kind of chickens you looking for? You want hens for laying? Bantams for eating? What are you thinking?"

Victoria looked perplexed. "I suppose we want both. I'm not sure about the number, though."

She looked at Charlotte, who just widened her eyes and shook her head. "I'm sorry, but I have no idea. Mother said to trust your judgment."

"Well, I'd say fifty bantams, and maybe twenty-four laying hens."

Behind him, Sam started to mumble. "Fifty, twenty-four. Fifty, twenty-four."

"Let's say we start with the hens—the ones who lay the eggs. Remind me how much feed we would need?" Victoria asked.

"A typical layer eats about four ounces of scratch a day," Jackson said. He started to make notes on the catalog as he spoke. "Twenty- four hens would require …"

"Ninety-six," Sam said, still sweeping, eyes on the floor. "Ninety-six, nine—six, ninety-six."

Jackson cleared his throat. "That would be ninety-six ounces a day. Or to put it more simply it would be …" He started to figure again on the page.

"Six pounds, six pounds, six—"

Jackson looked over his shoulder. "Sam, what have I said about this? Hush now, you're causing me to lose track." Jackson went back to his figures. "It would be about six pounds a day—so if you ordered for the whole year it would be …"

"Two thousand, one hundred ninety pounds," Sam said quietly. "Two thousand, one hundred ninety … two thousand—"

Jackson turned, his tone terse. *"Sam!"* He turned back to the ladies. "Sorry. Once he gets going I can't shut him up. Cousin on my mother's side. No one will hire him ..."

"It's fine," Charlotte said. "He's not bothering us."

Jackson sighed, went back to his calculations. "So I figure you'll need ... twenty one—almost twenty-two hundred pounds of feed a year just for the layers."

"That sounds like a lot," Victoria said.

"It does. It does sound like a lot," Jackson said, "but don't forget the return you'll get on the investment. The eggs."

"Oh, that's right. We can eat or sell the eggs," Victoria said. She frowned. "How many eggs exactly?"

Sam swept closer to the counter, but his eyes never left the ground. "Eight thousand, seven hundred sixty eggs. Eight thousand seven ..."

Sam's voice faded away as he moved around the floor with the broom.

Jackson offered a strained smile. "Let's just say you'd make a pretty good profit. Now do you want me to calculate the feed for the bantams?"

"You know, I think we'll just leave it to you," Victoria said. "Don't you think so, Char?"

Charlotte nodded. "Yes, Mr. Jackson. We'll just trust your calculations."

Victoria smiled. "Will you send us the bill?"

"Of course," Mr. Jackson said. "You can probably expect the chickens in about a month."

Charlotte and Victoria started toward the door. They could hear Sam mumbling to himself. "Seven hundred thirty, seven hundred thirty, seven three zero. Twelve in a dozen, seven hundred thirty dozen in three hundred sixty-five days …"

Charlotte found the bakery to be as charming and inviting as its owner, Virginia, who squealed with delight when they walked in the door. She appeared to be very settled into middle age: bony hips, sensible shoes, touches of gray colored her tightly braided hair.

"Welcome home, darlin'," she said. "I'm so happy to see you back safe and sound." She enveloped Charlotte in a bone-crushing embrace.

"Thank you," Charlotte said. She wondered at the small woman's strength as Virginia tightened her grip like a vise.

"Now don't squeeze her to death, Miss Ginny," Victoria said. "There's something we have to tell you …"

Virginia loosened her grip on Charlotte and stepped back. "No need. The gossip got here long before you did, honey," she said. "I sold some scones to Penelope, and she told me all about Charlotte's lost memory."

"She's fast, I'll give her that," Victoria said.

"I knew your mama, Charlotte. Has anyone told you that you have her eyes?" Virginia asked.

The comment touched Charlotte more than she could say. "No."

"Marie was a beauty—inside and out," Virginia said.

"Thank you for telling me," Charlotte said.

Mother came breezing into the bakery. "Good day, Ginny," she said. "Have the girls filled you in?"

Charlotte wasn't sure, but she thought the warmth left Virginia's eyes when she answered their mother. "Yes, they have. We were just discussing Marie."

Mother's smile froze. "Really?" She pulled off her gloves. "Shall we take the table by the window, girls?"

"Tea, Ginny? And maybe some of your lemon bars? As I recall, Charlotte loved those," Mother said.

Virginia smiled, but she shook her head. "She loved my raspberry tarts … not the lemon bars."

Mother pulled out a chair and sat. "I think I should know what my own stepdaughter liked."

"I agree. I think you should know—but you're mistaken," Virginia said.

So there *was* tension between the two women. "I may not remember what I used to like, but I do know I love anything with chocolate now," Charlotte said.

Virginia put a finger in the air. "Chocolate cake for everyone. "

They'd barely pulled their chairs around the table when a knock on the window startled the three of them. Charlotte looked to see the face of a little boy smashed up against the window, his nose flattened, his lips pressed on the glass. Holding fast to his hand was a young woman, who smiled broadly and waved frantically.

"Oh no," Victoria said. "This should be something."

"I assume I know her?" Charlotte asked as the woman yanked the boy's hand and they both disappeared from view.

But before either Victoria or Mother could get the answer out, the woman burst through the door, dragging the little boy behind her.

"Oh my gosh! Oh my gosh! It's true! It's you! I was in Dooley's, and someone said why, Betty Ann, I'll bet you're excited as a little girl on Christmas morning, and I didn't have the slightest idea what they were talking about, and then they told me Charlotte Chapman was back in town, and I just couldn't believe my ears! But here you are."

"Hello, uh, Betty Ann?" Charlotte said.

"Did you also happen to hear that Charlotte has amnesia, Betty Ann?" Mother asked.

Betty Ann frowned. "Someone did mention that, but I told them it's one thing to forget a few of the hometown folks, but you don't forget your very best friend in the world!"

Charlotte was so tired of repeating the same apology over and over again, yet she started once more. "I'm sorry, but I'm afraid I don't remember anyone or anything about my life here."

Betty Ann pressed a hand over her mouth and her eyes filled with tears. She shook her head, then finally cleared her throat. "You mean you don't remember me at all?"

Charlotte hated how sad she looked, but she shook her head. "I'm sorry."

"But we were practically joined at the hip growing up," Betty Ann said. "We shared secrets, Charlotte. Lots and lots of secrets. You knew more about me than my own husband."

"How *is* Bobby?" Mother asked.

"He's getting on okay," Betty Ann said. "You should come and say hello, Char. It would lift his spirits to see you again. And I'll admit I would love to sit down and have a nice long talk with you."

Charlotte nodded. "I will. Your son is adorable."

Betty Ann brightened when she looked down at the quiet little boy still holding her hand. "Thank you. I certainly think so, but I'm his mama, and mamas are always partial. I'm sure you're like everyone else and think he looks just like his daddy."

It took a moment for Betty Ann to realize what she'd said. "'Course you wouldn't know that now. But if you were yourself, you'd be saying, 'Betty Ann, I declare, that young'un looks exactly like his daddy. He is Bobby to a tittle.'"

"I'm sure I would," Charlotte said.

"Anyway, remember what I said about a visit," Betty Ann said. "If the past is gone, then we'll get to work building our new friendship."

Charlotte smiled. "I'd like that."

"We're having a welcome-home party for Char," Victoria said. "You have to come and bring Bobby."

A strained smile from Betty Ann. "I'll try. He's not feeling very social these days." She looked at Charlotte. "We really were best friends. I worried myself sick when you disappeared. I'm glad you're back—even if you don't remember me."

She offered up one more sad smile, then turned to leave, pulling her little boy out with her.

"I feel terrible that she's so upset," Charlotte said.

"She'll be all right," Victoria said. "After all, she learned to cope with things much worse than your memory loss."

"Oh?"

"Her husband Bobby came home from the war, but sadly left one of his legs on a field in Kentucky," Victoria said. "It's just too sad to think about."

Ginny came toward them carrying a serving tray. "Thank goodness for cake," Victoria said. "It always lifts my mood."

CHAPTER TWENTY-THREE

The house fairly hummed with activity in preparation for Charlotte's homecoming party. Field hands were brought in to help rearrange the furniture in the parlor and roll up the huge rug so the floor would be suitable for dancing. Two women, on hands and knees, spent hours bringing the luster of the herringbone wood of the floor back to life.

Mother barked out orders to the servants. "I want the furniture so highly polished I can see my reflection in the wood." She had them wiping down the walls, beating the dust from the smaller rugs, washing the crystals of the chandeliers. Copper pots in the kitchen gleamed, and the banister of the staircase was rubbed to a high sheen.

They were crossing the foyer when Charlotte asked her mother about the one major thing that seemed to be overlooked.

"What about the damage done by the Yankees?" she asked. "There are holes to fill and wallpaper to repair. I could paint or do something ..."

Her mother shook her head. "I want those battle scars to stay. They are a badge of our strength. Not something to hide."

"But wouldn't it be easier for you to forget what happened if you weren't reminded of it every day?"

"I don't ever want to forget—or forgive—what happened here."

Charlotte heard someone behind her and turned to see Elijah standing there. She could see by the look on his face, he'd heard every word of their exchange. As grateful and happy as she was he was staying for the party, a part of her would be relieved when he left. She wouldn't be able to stand what her family would say or do if they found out about him.

Mother looked at Elijah. "Have you had tea or coffee yet, Elijah? I could have Rose bring it to you on the veranda. It's a lovely morning."

"Thank you, but I've already made a visit to the kitchen. I'm just inquiring if there is anything I can do to help?"

"You're a guest in our home. We don't normally put our guests to work," she said. Then she smiled and Charlotte thought it was something that she should do more often. "But, if you are sincerely offering ..."

"I am."

"Then I imagine Beauregard could use some help out front. I've asked him to make some more space for the buggies and provide a few more hitching posts for those who make an appearance but don't stay long enough to warrant their horses in the corral."

Charlotte thought Elijah actually looked relieved at the prospect of having been given a physical task.

"I'll see to it," he said. They watched as he made his way out the front door. When it closed, Mother looked at Charlotte with a quizzical expression.

"I don't know what your relationship is to that young man, but I think if you let him get away, you'll regret it," she said.

"We're friends," Charlotte said.

"Hmm. I suspected something more." Mother continued through the foyer, down the hall toward the dining room. Charlotte kept pace.

"I didn't mean to give anyone that impression," Charlotte said.

"Call it mother's intuition."

"I have entirely too much on my mind these days," Charlotte said. "And I don't want to make that mistake twice."

They entered the dining room, where Chessie and another colored woman had the silver laid out on the side table and were polishing each piece.

"Ah!" Mother said. "So there *has* been romance in your life since you left us?"

Charlotte glanced at Chessie, but the old woman was focused on her task. The other woman, Georgia, had a bent posture that revealed years of working in the fields. She was polishing with the same vigor as Chessie and studiously avoided a glance at the mistress of the house.

"I didn't mean to say that," Charlotte said quietly.

Mother was not to be put off. "Nevertheless … you did say it. Was the romance with Elijah?"

Charlotte sighed. "No. I was engaged to be married to another man, but I called off the wedding."

"How can this be the first I'm hearing of this?" Mother asked. "You obviously haven't told your sister?"

"I haven't, and I really don't like to talk about it," Charlotte said.

"I imagine a broken engagement would be a painful subject," Mother said. "But still, darling, these are the kinds of things mothers and daughters talk about. There should be no secrets between us."

Mother looked at the display of polished silver and frowned. "Make sure to find the coffee urn and polish that too, Chessie."

"Yassum. I will."

The thought gave Charlotte a warm feeling. She had someone to confide in—a mother who wanted to know her secrets. But just as quickly, the feeling disappeared. There were secrets she prayed would never come out. The subject of her broken engagement—and the reason for it—chief among them.

Mother turned her attention back to Charlotte. "I think I might find time for a cup of tea on the veranda. That would be the perfect spot for a chat—don't you agree?"

"Well, I—"

Rose entered the dining room with a lace tablecloth over her arm. "S'cuze me, missus."

"What is it, Rose?"

"Juba need you in the kitchen. She gots questions 'bout the party food."

Mother sighed with exasperation. "I've been over and over this with her. I may as well do everything myself."

Mother smiled distractedly at Charlotte. "I suppose we'll have to postpone our tea until after the party."

Charlotte smiled. "All right."

Her mother hurried from the room. Charlotte walked closer to Chessie and watched the two women for a moment. Georgia was slower and more methodical in her approach. Her hands were calloused, but efficient. Chessie reached for another piece of silver, her palm briefly displayed, and Charlotte sucked in a breath. She hadn't noticed the heavy, roped web of pink scars that covered the old woman's palm. It was clear to see something very painful had happened.

"That silver is beautiful. Has it been in the family a long time, Chessie?" Charlotte asked.

"Mm-hmm." Chessie looked over her shoulder at Rose, who had just settled the tablecloth over the enormous piece of furniture.

"I gots things to tend to in the parlor, Rose. You finish this for me?"

Chessie shoved her hands into the deep pockets of her apron, walked past Charlotte and out of the room. Charlotte turned to follow.

"I'd be happy to find that coffee urn for you if you can tell me where it might be," Charlotte said.

"I was tol' to do it and I will," Chessie said. She made her way around a ladder that had been placed directly under an ornate candelabra hanging in the foyer. A young colored man perched precariously on top, straining to sweep a feather duster over the fixture. The ladder actually teetered below him as he moved.

"Don't be fallin', Roscoe," Chessie said. "Ain't no one got time to tend to broken bones today."

"I won't, Chessie," he replied.

Charlotte veered around the ladder to follow Chessie into the parlor. Their footsteps over the bare wood echoed in the room. Chessie made her way to a corner cabinet to retrieve tall white tapers to replace the candles already gracing the fireplace mantel.

"I'm feeling a tad useless," Charlotte said. "Isn't there something I can do to help you?"

Chessie didn't look at her. "You can't help me now."

Charlotte frowned. "I don't understand."

"You findin' fault wit' my work?" Chessie stopped to ask.

"What? No," Charlotte said.

"Den I need to keep at it and not spend my time talkin'," Chessie said.

She continued to remove the spent candles from the holders, replacing them with the new tapers.

It was easy to see the tension in Chessie's posture, the rigidity of her back, the way she yanked the candles out and shoved the new ones into the holders. Charlotte couldn't help but feel the sting of Chessie's attitude with every move, every word she spoke.

"What happened between us, Chessie?" she asked.

There was a brief moment when Charlotte could see the question had caught Chessie off guard, but then she shrugged. "Nothin'."

"I don't believe you," Charlotte said.

Chessie finally turned and looked straight at her, and Charlotte was taken aback by pure anger in the old woman's eyes. "What difference do it make now?"

"I want to know. I want to fix what happened."

Chessie shook her head. "Some things cain't be fixed."

"Please. It's not fair of you to hold something against me that I can't remember," Charlotte said.

The taper Chessie held in her hand snapped in the middle. The unvarnished anger of the gesture shocked Charlotte.

"I'm not speakin' on what is fair to you," Chessie finally said. "You gots the great luxury of not rememberin'—and I gots the great sorrow of never forgetting. Leave it be, Miss Charlotte. Jes leave it be."

They both heard Victoria calling for Charlotte. Chessie pushed the broken candle into her pocket and turned away. Charlotte didn't know what else she could say. She took one more look at the woman who'd raised her, and then went in search of her sister.

CHAPTER TWENTY-FOUR

Charlotte stood at the top of the stairs and listened as the hired musicians tuned up in the parlor. The house fairly glowed in the candlelight, and fresh flowers had been brought in to fill every empty side table and wall nook. The scent of magnolias and jasmine wafted through the house. Servants had been admonished to be on their best behavior, and the whole affair promised to be a wonderful time.

Charlotte knew most of the people coming were friends of the family—even old friends of hers, but she couldn't help thinking curiosity would be the driving factor in getting half the town to the plantation that evening. She thought about the last party held in her honor. Six months before on a cold December evening, she'd stood at the top of another staircase in another grand home and descended to a throng of people, curious to meet the future daughter-in-law of Charles and Ilene Prescott. The Prescotts were widely considered to be the most patriotic of St. Louis citizens, loyal to Mr. Lincoln's Union cause and the fight to abolish slavery. It was also the night a certain young Union captain had been introduced to her in the receiving line and uttered words that would come to haunt her and eventually change the direction of her life. *"I'm sorry, but have we met before?"* Elijah's face and his words that evening were something she'd always remember—along with the way her heart had stuttered in her chest when she thought someone had recognized her. But then, just as quickly, he'd withdrawn his observation and said he'd been mistaken. Now they both knew his instinct had been right.

"Oh my, Char! You look beautiful!"

Charlotte turned and saw Victoria coming toward her wearing a light blue organdy gown that made the most of every one of her attributes.

"Thank you. So do you," Charlotte said.

"Give me a turn," Victoria said.

"What?"

Victoria made a spinning motion with her finger. "Turn and let me see the whole picture."

Feeling foolish, but doing as her sister asked, Charlotte turned slowly in her light green silk gown. The deep-cut bodice was covered with delicate glass beads, the skirt full and edged in scalloped lace. Once she turned full circle, she smiled.

"Will I do?"

Victoria clapped her hands. "Absolutely. The dress is a little dated now. Hoops are smaller than they were when that dress was new, but no one will notice. Half the women here tonight will be in dresses they bought before the war. No one has money anymore for frivolities."

"It seems we do," Charlotte said.

Victoria smiled. "Yes. It seems we do. At least for tonight."

The door was opening and closing now as people filed into the grand foyer, talking, laughing, looking around but trying not to be obvious. When Charlotte moved back to the banister to watch, Victoria stood next to her and pointed out guests.

"There's Wendell and Margaret Washington. They say they're direct descendants of George Washington," Victoria said. "Very highbrow and snooty. Mother loves them."

A silver-haired man and his wife entered the house. She handed her wrap to a maid waiting dutifully to take it.

"That's Ed and Mamie Nielson," Victoria said quietly. "They're like bookends—you never see one without the other. They're old as dirt."

"*Victoria*," Charlotte whispered. "That's so rude."

Victoria shrugged. "But true."

Charlotte looked back down as another group of people came in the door. She recognized Penelope, Mr. Dooley, and even Shorty Smithson. And then there was a sea of faces she knew she should recognize—but didn't. The thought of descending the stairs into the crowd made her feel sick.

"I don't think I can do this," she said. "Please, Victoria, make my excuses. I'm going back to my room …"

But Victoria grabbed hold of her arm. "Don't be silly, Char. You fought the Yankees, for pity's sake. You can certainly attend a party in your honor."

Charlotte took one more sweeping glance at the people in the foyer, and then she saw him. Elijah stood slightly apart from everyone, his face tilted up, his eyes on her. For a moment she couldn't place what was different about him, but then it dawned on her that he had shaved off his scruffy beard. He looked like he did that first time they'd met. She'd thought him handsome then—and certainly thought he was handsome now. He smiled and she wondered how long he'd been watching. For the first time since standing on the landing, Charlotte felt a measure of calm return. She smiled, then turned to Victoria.

"All right. Let's get this over with."

Victoria laughed. "Not quite the spirit of things, but it will have to do for now."

The receiving line had been just as much of an ordeal as Charlotte had thought it would be. She stood between her mother and Beau shaking hands, smiling. One of the first guests in line reached out and covered her hand with both of his. He smiled warmly at her.

"Welcome home, Miss Charlotte."

"Thank you."

Mother started to introduce them. "This is—"

"Adam Harper," the man interrupted.

"Mr. Harper is the family attorney," her mother said.

He glanced at the portrait of John Chapman, then looked at

Charlotte. "Your father was one of my closest friends." He smiled. "I can't tell you how many hours I listened to him bragging about you."

Charlotte returned his smile. "Then I should thank you for listening to him."

"It was my pleasure," Adam said. He released her hand and moved on.

One person after another offered their names and nuggets of information to help place them in her memory. Mother seemed to know almost everyone there, but occasionally a guest of a guest would come through the line and introductions would be made. Such was the case with Dooley. He arrived with a tall man that neither Mother or Beau seemed to know.

"Mrs. Suzanne Chapman," Dooley said. "May I present Mr. Reynolds? He's new to town and is very interested in purchasing the old Crowley farm."

"Welcome to McIntosh County, Mr. Reynolds," Mother said, offering her hand. "It would be wonderful to see the Crowley farm producing again. If we can be of any service, please let me know."

"I appreciate that, Mrs. Chapman," he said. "You have a magnificent home."

She turned and gestured to Charlotte. "This is my stepdaughter, Charlotte. The party is in her honor tonight."

Mr. Reynolds nodded at Charlotte and took her proffered hand. "A pleasure, ma'am. Dooley told me a little of your very interesting story."

He held her hand just a little too firmly, which made her uncomfortable, but Charlotte smiled and said, "The pleasure is mine, Mr. Reynolds," she said. "Good luck with the property, should you decide to purchase it."

He smiled. "Thank you. I hope luck will be on my side and I'll have a successful outcome."

Charlotte gestured to Beau. "May I present my brother, Beauregard?"

He smiled at her, then stuck out his hand for Beau. Charlotte turned to the next person in line.

"Betty Ann," she said. "I'm so glad you came."

Betty Ann's eyes widened. "You remember me?"

"Yes, from the other day at the bakery," Charlotte said. Betty Ann's face dropped. "Oh." She gestured to a man on crutches beside her. He had one pant leg pinned up behind his thigh. "This is my husband, Bobby. You two used to swim in the river together when you were kids."

"Hello, Bobby," she said, then looked at Betty Ann. "You were right. Your son does look just like him."

Betty Ann smiled. "I knew you'd see it. Everyone does."

The boy *did* look like his father—except Bobby was one of the saddest-looking men Charlotte ever remembered seeing.

"Glad to see you made it home in one piece, Char," Bobby said.

"Thank you."

"Betty Ann tells me you're missing your memories."

"That's true."

"She says you joined up with us Rebs to fight the Yankees."

"That's what I'm told," she said.

A ghost of a smile crossed his face. "Can't say I'm surprised," he said. "Guess you can't remember the war either?"

She shook her head. "No. Not a single day of it."

"Then I'd say your lost memory ain't a curse but a blessing." He started to move away, his shoulders hunched over the crutches under his arms, with Betty Ann trailing after him.

When the last of the guests had filtered through the receiving line, Charlotte's mother gave the signal for the musicians to start playing. Their opening song was "Dixie." The partygoers clapped, and couples started to dance. Charlotte started to make a hasty retreat to a corner of the room where she could take in the scene without anyone talking in her ear. But she wasn't quick enough. Dooley's friend materialized in front of her.

"I know I'm being bold, Miss Chapman, but might I have this dance?"

Charlotte hesitated. "I was just going to check on something, Mr. Reynolds."

He cocked his head to the side and lifted his brows. "Oh, come now, Miss Chapman, where is that famous Southern hospitality I've heard so much about?"

She forced a smile, then put her hand in his. "Right here, Mr. Reynolds. But I must warn you. My dancing is almost as impaired as my memory."

Chapter Twenty-Five

After the first couple of turns around the dance floor, Charlotte thought they were actually well suited—it seemed neither of them could find the proper footing. She wasn't the only miserable dancer, something made perfectly clear the third time Mr. Reynolds stepped on her toe.

"Apologies," he mumbled.

"It's fine," she said, her foot throbbing with each awkward step they took.

He finally looked up from the floor. "I've never met anyone with a story quite as unique as yours, Miss Chapman," he said.

"No?"

"You're the first."

She forced a smile. "A first for me, too. But if you don't mind, I'd rather not discuss it."

He looked chagrined. "Oh sure, sure. I understand."

"Thank you."

"You must be happy to be home," he said.

"I am."

He smiled. "No plans to travel to faraway places anytime soon?"

She was a bit confused by the comment. "No. No trips for me. I'm content to stay right here."

"Traveling can take a toll on a person," he said. "I'll admit I miss my home."

"Where are you from, Mr. Reynolds?"

"The great state of Missouri."

She faltered the next step, but he tightened his arm around her. Her heart quickened. "Where in Missouri?"

"Southwest corner of the state. A little town called Newtonia. Probably never heard of it."

Miles and miles from St. Louis, she thought with relief. "No. I never have."

"Great little town," he said.

"May I ask why you left?"

"Just hunting a better future for myself," he said. He smiled again, a smile entirely too intimate in nature. She shivered and wished the song would end. And then Elijah was there. He tapped Mr. Reynolds on the shoulder.

"May I?" Elijah asked.

A flash of annoyance crept across Mr. Reynolds's face, but then he smiled. "Of course. Thank you for the dance, Miss Chapman. Hope to see you again soon."

Charlotte nodded at him, then felt Elijah's arm go around her just as a new waltz began.

She prepared to concentrate on her footwork again, but Elijah wouldn't hear of it.

"Eyes on me," he said.

She lifted her face to look at him. "I've got two left feet …"

"Just relax," he said. "It's supposed to be fun. Get ready to turn …"

He swept her away and then twirled her flawlessly, and she went back into his arms with a grace she didn't think she'd possessed.

Charlotte became aware of the others watching them. Nervously, she looked back down at her feet again.

"Not down there—up here at me." She lifted her gaze again and this time couldn't seem to look away from his eyes. She heard him murmur things as they danced: "Turning, good … Left … now right … turning again."

She was gliding over the floor, dancing as if she spent every Saturday night in the arms of a handsome man, lost in time to beautiful music. She realized he had stopped his quiet instruction and was gazing intently at her while guiding her expertly around the room. She felt a blush creep up her neck and tried to untangle her complicated feelings with small talk.

"You're a wonderful dancer," she said.

"Lessons when I was a boy."

"Time well spent."

"You're doing well yourself," he said.

"Am I?"

"Yes. With all of it," he said.

For a moment, her guard came down. "I'm not so sure. I'm so … different than they are."

"Being comfortable in a family can be hard even if you have all your memories. You need to give yourself time."

"You think it'll be all right?"

"I do. It doesn't matter if you call yourself Mercy or Charlotte—you're a strong, capable woman. You have good instincts … just remember to listen to them."

"Good instincts?" Her eyes widened, but she lowered her voice. "I nearly married a man who ended up turning me over to the authorities, I actually made a plan to shoot you—I ran away from you and Isaac when you were only trying to protect me—and then I ended up at a Yankee army post I thought belonged to the South."

Elijah twirled her out and away from him, then took her hand again in that way that sent a thrill through her. "All right, you win. Whatever your instincts tell you—do the opposite."

She smiled. "Now *that* is good advice."

"I'm almost sorry to be leaving in the morning," he said. "I'm going to miss these little chats of ours."

She grew serious. "I will too. In fact, strange as this may sound, I'm going to miss you."

He looked into her eyes for a long moment, then said, "Mercy … I mean Charlotte …"

The music suddenly stopped and Charlotte heard Beau's voice. "Might I have your attention, please?"

Charlotte tore her gaze from Elijah's and looked around. She saw servants were circulating throughout the room carrying trays filled with crystal flutes. As guest after guest took a glass from the tray, she saw Beau, her mother, and Victoria move to stand by the fireplace, under the portrait of her father.

Beau cleared his throat. "I wanted to take a moment to thank you all for coming this evening. Mother, Victoria, and I are overjoyed to have our dear Charlotte home with us once again—and we are so pleased you came to help us celebrate her return."

There was a smattering of applause and Charlotte was embarrassed right down to her toes to be the center of attention.

"I hope everyone has a glass of champagne so you can all join me in toasting my sister. She went out into the world and, against difficult odds, managed to find her way home again. Raise your glasses to Charlotte ... John Chapman's daughter through and through."

"To Charlotte!" said the group in unison.

"Thank you," she managed to say. "Y'all are too kind."

She looked around at the smiling faces—people from her childhood, her family, friends, and neighbors who knew and admired her father. Betty Ann caught her eye and she smiled. Dooley waved. Even Shorty nodded in her direction before downing his champagne. And then she saw Mr. Reynolds staring at her, his glass of champagne untouched—his mouth set in a grim line that gave her a chill. But then he turned and said something to the woman next to him and she laughed. Charlotte shook off the uneasy feeling he gave her—hadn't she just admitted to Elijah she had terrible instincts?

"Everything all right?" Elijah said.

Charlotte turned to him and smiled. "Everything is fine." Then her smile broadened as she saw Victoria coming at them like a woman on a mission.

"Elijah," Victoria said with a bit of a pretty pout. "Charlotte has been monopolizing you all evening."

"I was just about to ask you to dance, Miss Victoria," he said.

"I accept," she said. "You don't mind, do you, Char?"

"No, I don't mind."

"How about it, Miss Charlotte?" Dooley stopped in front of her and held out a hand. "Dance with an old friend of your pa's?"

She fell into step with Dooley and they joined the others who were already dancing to the new piece the musicians played. Dooley was certainly not as good of a dancer as Elijah, but he was a sight better than Mr. Reynolds. She could see Elijah guiding Victoria expertly across the floor. Dooley was saying something about the plantation and the weather, but she wasn't paying attention. Instead, she had her eyes on Elijah, who was looking at her over Victoria's shoulder. The moment seemed to stretch, his gaze held hers, and then Dooley gave her a spin. She lost sight of him and was surprised at her own disappointment. It was going to be hard to say good-bye to Elijah Hale in the morning—much harder than she would have ever believed.

CHAPTER TWENTY-SIX

Charlotte hummed softly as she got ready for bed. She stepped out of her dress and laid it across the end of her bed. After putting on her nightdress, she padded barefoot to her dressing table, found her brush, and began to brush her hair. She heard her door open and turned to see Chessie crossing the floor. The old woman didn't so much as glance in her direction but went straight to her tasks. She picked up the dress, hung it in the closet, then went to the bed and turned back the quilt.

Charlotte had the thought she'd never heard so much heavy silence in all her life. Chessie went to the fireplace, tossed a small log onto the fire, and turned to Charlotte.

"You be needin' anything else from me?"

"No," Charlotte said. "Good night."

Chessie grunted an unintelligible reply and walked out the door.

Charlotte slipped her robe over her nightgown and went to the French doors. The moon struck the water from above and made it shine. She tried to push thoughts of Chessie out of her head and thought again about dancing through the parlor with Elijah.

She turned at the sound of Victoria's voice behind her. "I saw your light."

Victoria stood uncertainly in the doorway. "Come in," Charlotte said.

"I need to talk to you," Victoria said. As she got closer, Charlotte could see a small wooden box in her hands.

Charlotte took the box, examined it. It was rectangular, about a foot wide, and made from beautiful, burled rosewood. There was a small mechanism on the side.

Victoria squirmed. "Father gave it to you for your sixteenth birthday. I've always admired it, but I shouldn't have taken it."

Charlotte ran her hand along the smooth top. "It's lovely."

"As far as I know, you never kept anything in it. You were never much for trinkets and jewelry," Victoria said.

"Wait. It's a music box, isn't it?"

Victoria's brow creased. "As a matter of fact, it is."

Charlotte started to hum a tune.

Victoria's eyes became wide with excitement. "Char …"

Charlotte lifted the lid and sweet strains of a waltz tinkled throughout the room.

"Char! Do you hear that melody?"

"I was humming it."

"*Before* you opened the box!"

"Victoria, I remembered!"

Victoria was bobbing her head, eyes shining, smiling from ear to ear. "You remembered!"

"I can't believe it! I remember it! I remember the song!" Charlotte threw her arms around Victoria. She started to sing with the tinkling music—never missing a beat.

"La, la, la … la, la, la …"

The two sisters started to waltz around the room, Victoria giggling, Charlotte joyful. "La, la, la …"

"We should tell Mother and Beau," Victoria said, laughing at Charlotte's enthusiasm.

"We should tell everyone!" Charlotte replied. She twirled Victoria around and then hurried to the bedroom door. She flung it open and rushed out into the hall lit by two lamps.

"I remembered something!" she called into the quiet house. "I remembered!"

Doors opened. Mother and Beau came from rooms down the hall.

"What in the world …?" Beau frowned in the direction of his sister.

Charlotte threw her arms wide just as Elijah opened his door. "I've had an actual memory!" She twirled in the hallway, then ran to Suzanne and embraced her.

"Isn't it wonderful?"

"What exactly did you remember, dear?"

"A song. A song from the jewelry box Father gave me. I can hum it. I *did* hum it before I even heard it!"

"She did," Victoria said, "I heard her!" The two sisters exchanged a pleased look.

"That's wonderful, Char," Beau said.

"That is wonderful," Elijah echoed. Charlotte turned to look at him, her face radiant with joy.

"I know it seems like a small thing … but to me it means the world. It means maybe things aren't locked away forever. Maybe I'll start to remember more."

"We can only hope," Mother said. "Thank you for sharing your news, dear. Now I'll say good night."

Charlotte smiled again. "Good night, Mother."

Beau came forward, kissed her cheek. "Wonderful news."

"Thank you, Beau."

"I love when evenings end on a happy note," Victoria said, then giggled. "Or on a music box note."

Charlotte grew serious. "Thank you for giving it back to me. What a wonderful gift it turned out to be."

Victoria nodded. Her glance took in both Elijah and Charlotte. "Good night."

Elijah and Charlotte were suddenly alone. He studied her in the soft light. She looked radiant; her long dark hair cascaded around her shoulders, a dark contrast to her ivory robe. He had the fleeting thought that women always tried so hard to be dressed and primped and frilly, and here was a woman in a robe and she probably had no idea how lovely she was.

"I'm so happy for you," he said.

She smiled. "I hope you weren't sleeping when I came out heralding my news."

"No," he said. "In fact, I'm glad we have this opportunity to say good-bye. I didn't get a chance earlier. There were so many people, you were busy … I couldn't get Victoria to stop dancing …"

She smiled. "She is smitten with you, I'm afraid."

"I hope I didn't do anything to encourage that …"

"You exist. Apparently that's enough," she said. She grew serious. "I planned to be up to see you off in the morning."

"I saw Isaac earlier today. He offered to get my horse ready for me. I'm hoping to be gone by dawn. It's late and there's no need for you to get up so early."

"Oh. All right, then."

"I enjoyed this evening very much," he said. "I'm happy I stayed. And I'm glad I got to hear the news of your first actual memory."

"I'm glad too." She studied him. "I think it's finally time for me to thank you for everything—and I do mean everything. I wouldn't be here if it weren't for you."

"I hope it all works out for you with your family," he said.

"Thank you. I hope so too." She stepped toward him. "I won't ever forget you, Elijah." She rose up on her bare toes and kissed his cheek.

He thought a lot more about memories now than he did before meeting the woman before him. Elijah prayed the picture she made, looking like a vision in that softly lit hallway, would be remembered for a very long time.

"You take good care of yourself, Charlotte Chapman."

CHAPTER TWENTY-SEVEN

Juba was busy in the kitchen at dawn when Isaac came through the door. She turned and put a hand on her hip.

"I don't care for strangers comin' in mah kitchen, boy," she said. "What's yo' bi'ness?"

"I'm Isaac," he said. "I come here with Miss Charlotte?"

Juba nodded slowly. "I know who you are."

"Then I guess I ain't no stranger."

"Hmmph. You got a mouth on ya."

Isaac sidled a little closer. "Mr. Elijah be leaving today, and he ask me to get his mount ready and let him know when I done it."

"Ever'body in dis house be sleepin'," Juba said. "I don't wanna hear no ruckus or nobody fussin' 'cause dey gots woke up by a colored boy who don't know he 'pose to be stayin' in the stable."

"I'll be quiet," Isaac said. "I promise." He inhaled deeply. "It smell a lil' bit like heaven in here."

Juba pursed her lips together. "Mm-hmm. You don't fool me, boy."

Isaac lifted his brows. "Not tryin' to fool nobody, ma'am. Jes sayin' how good it smells in here."

"You get on wit' yo'self now. Get yo' errand done and quit wasting time butterin' me up," she said. "I might have a biscuit or two fo' you when you come back dis way."

Isaac grinned. "Kin you tell me which room Mr. Elijah be in?"

She pointed to a set of stairs against the back wall of the kitchen that seemed to disappear into the ceiling. "Take 'em up and go till you get to the third door on da right."

"I'll be back to claim those three biscuits," he said, making his way across the floor.

"I say one or two biscuits, you sassy boy," she said, "and you be quiet like a mouse. I don't even wanna hear no footsteps!"

Isaac nodded, then started up the stairs.

The door to Elijah's room opened quietly and Isaac slipped inside. He had the captain's horse all ready, and now he planned to get his things together. Anything he could do to help the man who had come to mean so much to him. Isaac hated to see him go, but knew his decision to stay behind and work on the plantation was the right one. There were plenty of people just like him. He was doing something he loved, and he had a new friend in Moby. For the first time, he was earning his own keep and it felt good. Besides, the captain was going back to fight the Indians, so he couldn't go with him anyway.

Isaac saw the worn Bible lying on the table next to the bed. He picked it up and carried it to the bureau, placing it next to a pocket watch, revolver, and hat. Making mental notes, Isaac decided if he worked quietly, he could get out a clean shirt, polish his boots, and have everything set to go before the captain woke. He started to carry out his plan, but his eye was drawn back to the revolver he had long admired. He brushed his fingers over the gun, lingering there a little longer than he should. He knew picking it up was a bad idea, but once the captain left, it might be a long, long time before he'd ever get the opportunity to hold an actual pistol. Maybe he'd hold it and hate it. He needed to find out. If he was going to be a lawman someday, he should at least know how it felt to have the gun in his hand. He lifted it and felt the weight in his palm. He didn't hate it. He liked how it felt—powerful.

Morning light slanted in through the window, giving Isaac a view of his own reflection in a full-length cheval mirror in the corner of the room. He faced the mirror, drew the gun and tried to look menacing. He drew again. Faster this time. Once more—even faster. He was cut out to be a lawman. A train-riding lawman. He'd have a future his father and grandfather had never even dared dream about. He glanced at the captain, on his side, still fast asleep. He faced the mirror one more time, legs apart, shoulders squared. He would be Sheriff Isaac and keep law and order in towns across the land. He prepared to arc his arm up one more time—this time he did it with lightning speed. Satisfied he was quick enough, he inspected the gun a little more closely. He tested the chamber and felt it turn, then pulled back the hammer with his thumb—it was harder than he'd imagined. He was pleased he knew how to do it. A noise from the other side of the room startled him. He swung toward one sound and nearly died from fright with the other as the gun exploded. His shoulder jerked back and he dropped to the floor, but not before he saw the surprised eyes of the captain—just as the bullet slammed right into him.

At first, there was more shock than pain. Elijah reached for a burning spot in his gut and pulled away a hand covered in blood. He could see it in the early dawn light—just as he could see Isaac on the floor. The gun dropped out of Isaac's hand. The shock on the boy's face nearly equaled Elijah's own disbelief at what had just transpired.

Isaac started to scoot backward against the wood floor, his heels pushing him toward the opposite wall.

"Oh, no, no, no, no, Cap'n," Isaac said. The words were almost a low, keening moan from the boy.

Elijah saw the fear and deep regret on Isaac's face. *Boy with a gun. Colored boy with a gun.* Over the blood pounding in his ears, he could hear doors opening up and down the hallway and people spilling out of their rooms.

"What was that?"

"Was that a gun? It sounded like a gun!"

"Isaac." Elijah pushed out the words. "Hide."

"Where did it come from?"

Any minute now someone would come into his room. Isaac was lost in the misery of his own actions and couldn't seem to move.

"I didn't mean … was a bad accident …"

Elijah grabbed hold of the edge of the bed and felt the stickiness of blood on the sheets. "I know," he said. Gritting his teeth against the spreading pain in his torso, he pushed himself off the bed onto the floor. "Hide."

Elijah pushed himself along the floor toward his pistol.

"Beauregard! Is everyone all right? What is happening?"

"Charlotte? Victoria?"

"Cap'n!" Isaac sobbed out the word. "So sorry …"

"The wardrobe!"

Elijah, sweating profusely now, was next to his gun. The blood from his torso began to pool on the floor. He looked at Isaac, huddled against the wall, his face racked with guilt.

"Get in the wardrobe … *now!*"

The commotion in the hall grew closer. He finally saw Isaac scramble to his feet and disappear into the wardrobe just as the bedroom door burst open.

"What the devil?" Beau stood in the threshold of the room, a shotgun in his trembling hands. "Elijah! What happened? Who did this?"

Beau, shocked at the scene, stepped back. He stood half-shielded by the doorframe.

Servants congregated behind him. Beau scanned the room, took in the bloody sheets, the pistol—Elijah bleeding on the floor.

Mother and Victoria tried to see past him, but Beau yelled.

"Stay back!"

Ignoring his order, Victoria peered around his shoulder to see Elijah on the floor. She immediately jerked back, away from the scene. She pressed her hands over her ears. "Don't say he's dead. Don't say it!"

"Not again," his mother pleaded. "Please—this can't happen again."

Charlotte moved past everyone in the hall, tried to get by Beau, but he put out a hand to stop her.

"Don't, Char, we don't know if—"

But she ignored him and pushed into the room. She saw Elijah on the floor, a puddle of blood spreading from his middle.

"Elijah!"

She ran to Elijah's side and dropped to her knees.

"Charlotte—get out of there," Beau said tersely.

She put a hand on Elijah's chest. His eyes were open, but when he tried to speak, no sound came out.

Beau finally raised his gun a little higher and left the perceived safety of the door frame. He stood over Elijah, but his gaze never quit roaming the room. "Who did this, Elijah?"

Elijah couldn't make his lips form the words to tell them it was an accident. It was easier just to close his eyes and not try anymore.

"Someone get a doctor!" Charlotte yelled.

Suzanne kept shaking her head, her hand clutched her robe, her brow furrowed in disbelief. "Not again."

Victoria turned to the group of servants in the hall. "Rose, go tell Jonas to fetch Doc Hawkins! Hurry up, now!"

Beau, seemingly emboldened by his audience, made his way around the room with his gun. He dropped to one knee and peered under the bed, looked behind the heavy drapes that hadn't been pulled the night before, then finally went to the wardrobe.

"So much blood," Charlotte said. "Victoria, get me something to press over the wound."

"What if he dies, Char?" Victoria's voice held tears. "What if he dies?"

"He's not going to. He can't. Get me something!"

Victoria grabbed Elijah's shirt from the bureau at the same time Beau yanked open the wardrobe to reveal Isaac.

"You!" He grabbed Isaac's arm and hauled him out of the closet. "Here's your shooter."

Charlotte took the shirt from Victoria, pressed it over the wound, in Elijah's belly and looked with disbelief at Isaac. "No. Isaac?"

"You do this, boy?" Beau asked.

Isaac nodded, tears running down his face.

"You're coming with me." Beau grabbed Isaac's arm and hauled him out of the room.

Elijah groaned. Charlotte focused on stopping the bleeding. "It's all right. A doctor's coming."

Elijah could smell lemons. He opened his eyes and looked at her. She was in her nightdress, hair in disarray from sleep. Her eyes looked so dark and concerned. He wanted to tell her not to worry. It didn't hurt. He wondered if this was how his brother felt when he lay dying from a bullet wound. He wished someone would say a prayer over him, send him home as he'd done for Jed. His eyes closed again. It was so much easier that way. He felt her hand on his chest, something soft brushed his cheek. A quiet voice filled with angst and regret whispered next to his ear.

"Please, God, don't take this man."

He felt such relief. There was the prayer. Now he could go.

CHAPTER TWENTY-EIGHT

Doc Hawkins was washing up at a basin when Charlotte entered Elijah's room.

"How is he?" she asked, glancing toward the bed. Elijah's eyes were closed. He was so still, so pale.

"I managed to locate and remove the bullet," Doc Hawkins said. "It was lodged between two ribs under the upper abdominal wall." He shook his head, rolled his shirt sleeves from his elbows back down to his wrists. "He'd lost a great deal of blood by the time I managed to get here. It's lucky he even made it through the surgery."

"But he'll be all right?" Charlotte asked.

"He'll sleep the rest of today, probably tomorrow too with the help of some of the laudanum I'm going to leave with you," he said.

"The threat now is infection. And in his weakened condition, it'll be harder for him to fight it off."

"What do I need to do?"

"Keep an eye on the sutures I used to close the wound. It needs to stay clean and dry. If you notice any kind of fever, that usually means infection."

Charlotte nodded at his instructions. "I'll stay by his side."

"Do you know who we might contact regarding his condition?"

Charlotte reached up and her fingers closed around the mercy medallion she wore. *My mother gave me this …*

"I think his mother is still alive," she said. "But I don't know where she is."

"I can go through his things if you like. Maybe there's something to give us an idea of where to write."

Her eyes flew to his saddlebags and things on the bureau. The sight made her nervous. What would happen if he stumbled across anything having to do with Elijah's military affiliation?

"No, you needn't do that. I can," she said.

"Charlotte?"

She looked at the doctor. "Yes?"

"I know how you take things on, shoulder responsibility. But you can only do what I just asked you to do," he said. "Nothing more. I've done my job, you'll watch for infection, but ultimately his fate rests with God now."

"I know."

He smiled, then took off his glasses and wiped them with a handkerchief from his pocket. "I know you don't remember, but we've had this conversation before, you and I."

"I was delivering a baby last night or I would have been here at your welcome-home party."

Doc started to pack up his surgical instruments. "I'm sure your father is rejoicing in heaven that you're home safe and sound. And I'm probably one of dozens or more who've told you this, but John adored you. Thought you hung the moon and stars. You were his life until the day he died and I don't think there's a person this side of the Mississippi who didn't know how proud he was of you."

Charlotte's eyes filled with tears, but she smiled. "Thank you for telling me."

"All right," he said. "I'm going to see myself out, but I will be back in a few days to check on him."

"Thank you so much," Charlotte said.

"You're welcome," he said. "And let me also say, welcome home."

Charlotte, going through Elijah's pack, pulled out a handful of papers stuffed into a side pocket. His orders granting him official leave from Fort Wallace were on the top of the pile, and she had a moment of gratitude that it was she who was seeing them and no one else from the family. There were maps of Tennessee and Kentucky, and a copy of a telegram he'd sent from Fort Donelson. *Thank God he stopped to send that telegram …*

And then she unfolded a piece of newspaper. She turned it over and stared in surprise at an engraving of her photograph that had appeared in the St. Louis *Gazette* with the announcement of her engagement to Rand. The edges of the paper were worn from handling, and she wondered how many times that picture had been pulled out and shown to strangers in different towns. She refolded the newspaper and put it back with his other papers on top of the bureau next to a Bible. The Bible was a surprise because she hadn't seen him reading it, but when she picked it up, she could tell it was well used. There were several pieces of paper stuck between the pages. She'd seen the nuns do the same thing with passages and verses particularly meaningful to them. Maybe Elijah had the same practice. Charlotte opened the Bible, intending to go to one of the marked passages to read, but as she flipped through the pages, a piece of paper fell out. It was folded in quarters, and when she opened it, she could see it was a letter. Though she didn't want to intrude on his private correspondence, she reminded herself she was going through his personal things for his own good. The letter might provide a clue to a family member or friend she should notify. Moving over to the window for better light, she started to read:

My dearest Elijah,

As always, I was overjoyed when the post came today and with it, your letter. I know I don't have to tell you the correspondence we exchange always lifts my heart and my spirit. Though today, dearest, I could read between the lines and sense the trouble of your own heart with the dilemma that has been presented to you. You are a good man, Elijah. I hope the guilt you feel will be assuaged with time and you will accept the grace we all receive when we believe as we do in the Lord. I pray you will come to realize the motives concerning your actions of late were prompted by your own conscience and the desire to do what is right and just according to God's law. I know the girl left you of her own accord, but you said yourself fear motivates us to do things in the moment that don't make sense. And she must be so afraid. I know your letter was to let me know of your plan to follow her, and yet I felt you also needed me to tell you my feelings on the matter and give your quest my blessing—which, my dear son, I most wholeheartedly do. Find Mercy and see her safely home, Elijah. Nothing less will quiet the need of your heart to do that. May God enable you to do this task, keep you safe in body and spirit—and bring you back home someday to me.

Forever your affectionate and loving mother

Charlotte was so engrossed in the letter she didn't hear the door open, or her mother step inside the room.

"I just came to check on him—and you too," she said.

Charlotte turned toward her, saw the pile of Elijah's incriminating papers in her peripheral vision, and made her way to the bureau.

"The doctor says he'll sleep now for several hours." Charlotte put the letter back between the pages of the Bible, then placed the book on top of the other papers. "I appreciate your concern, though, Mother."

Her mother took a few more steps into the room. "I'm so sorry this terrible thing has marred your homecoming."

"Bad things happen we can't help," Charlotte said.

After a light tap on the door, Beau entered the room and directed his comment to their mother. "Just letting you know I've taken care of things."

Mother nodded. "Good."

Beau glanced at Elijah. "How is he?"

"The same," Charlotte said. "How's Isaac? Were you able to get him to tell you what happened?"

Beau glanced at their mother. Charlotte thought she saw the slightest of nods from her mother.

"What is it?" Charlotte asked. "What did he say?"

"He told me it was an accident," Beau said. "He came into the room early this morning to tell Elijah his horse was ready, and to help him get his things together. According to the boy, he picked up the pistol and it accidentally fired. All a terrible accident, he said."

Every word he said dripped with skepticism, and Charlotte heard it immediately. "But you don't believe him?"

"Frankly, no."

"Well, I do. I know Isaac would never intentionally hurt anyone—least of all Elijah. He looks up to Elijah—respects and admires him. I know and trust this boy. Believe me when I say he would never do this on purpose."

Beau looked resolute. "You can *never* trust a colored man—even one that's still a boy. They harbor secrets and hate, and their desire for revenge can take over in an instant!"

"You can't believe that's true about all Negroes," Charlotte said. "And you're wrong about Isaac. I know him—spent weeks traveling with him. I've seen him with Elijah. There is absolutely no way he had any motivation to shoot him."

Charlotte caught another glance traded between her mother and brother. "You can't agree with him on this, Mother."

"I do agree with him," she said. "Beau and I have our reasons for being wary of Isaac. In fact, the reasons are intimately tied to the death of your father."

"I don't understand …," Charlotte said.

"Your father didn't die on a battlefield. He was murdered right here in this house."

"How?" Charlotte's voice sounded strained to her own ears. They were talking about a man she didn't remember, but she'd already begun to piece together the father she wanted to remember from the things people had told her about the man. Murder didn't fit in that picture at all.

"John was shot by a Negro man named Lewis," Mother said. "Lewis was born here on the plantation. He was raised here, played with you, Victoria, and Beau. We trusted him, fed, clothed, and provided shelter for him. We made sure Lewis and his family had medical care and even a gift at Christmas. To anyone watching—to all of us here—Lewis seemed to respect and admire your father." She paused. "So it seemed."

"Father's regiment was in the area, and he wanted to come home for a couple days to see us all," Beau said.

"We had the most wonderful, loving visit," her mother said. "When it was time for him to return to his men, we were saying our good-byes in the foyer." Charlotte heard the catch in her mother's voice, and Beau reached out to put a comforting hand on her arm. She smiled at him distractedly, then continued. "I remember John being near the front doors in his uniform. You were coming down the stairs, Charlotte, when …" Her mother frowned with the memory. "I saw Lewis from the corner of my eye, but that wasn't strange. He was often in the house for errands and things. But that day there was something different about him. His expression—his eyes. I remember turning to look at him and thinking he looked so angry. So filled with hate. And then everything happened fast. He lifted his hand and he had a gun, and my mind wouldn't comprehend it. Even after he shot your father in cold blood, I was so confused. The sergeant who'd been traveling with John heard the shot and came through the doors with his gun drawn just as Beau ran into the foyer. I remember being scared that the sergeant would get it wrong and I think I yelled, 'Don't shoot my boy' as I pointed toward the killer." She shivered. "He killed Lewis with a single bullet. And there were two dead men in my foyer."

Charlotte couldn't believe what she'd heard, and she realized she was crying. She swiped a hand across her cheeks. "That's why earlier you kept saying 'Not again.'"

Mother nodded. "Yes."

"But only *one* shooting was intentional …," Charlotte said.

"Even *if* Isaac is telling the truth and it was an accident, he had no business even touching that gun. The black codes in Georgia prohibit any person of color from using a firearm," Beau said.

Charlotte couldn't get the mental picture of her father's death out of her mind. She wondered if the picture she conjured up was worse than what her memory might have been.

"You're going to find out sooner or later, so I'd rather you hear it from me," Beau said. "But I had a public punishment carried out for Isaac's offense."

Her eyes flew to her brother. "What kind of punishment?"

"A few lashes across his back," Beau said. "And I'd say that was lenient."

Charlotte shook her head. "No! Please tell me you didn't use a whip on a child!"

"The only thing keeping the newly freed blacks in line is fear. Without that fear, what's to say we all won't be shot dead in our beds by our former slaves?"

"He's right, Charlotte. They hate us. They hated us for owning them as slaves and even now when they're free, they hate us because they aren't equipped to take care of themselves. Every weed they pull or dollar of debt they incur is somehow our fault and they've been very vocal about that," Mother said. "They want me to apologize for the life I was born into—as if their lot in life is my doing."

Charlotte shook her head, trying to hold her anger in check. "But to use a whip on a boy like Isaac ..."

"News runs rampant through the colored camps," Beau said. "Isaac's offense had to be dealt with swiftly and without remorse. Even if you can't remember how we did things here, and even if you don't approve of them, you need to stand with us when we make these kinds of decisions. You can't be a chink in our armor if you intend to live here as a Chapman."

"So I'm to say nothing, even when I think something is wrong?" she asked.

"Before the war, my sister Charlotte would have been the first to make sure a message was sent to the Negroes for an offense like this," Beau said. "It's what needed to happen, what Father would have done. You need to decide where your loyalties lie. With your family, or with some colored boy who picked up a gun and shot that man right there."

Beau offered a smile as if to soften his words. "I'm sorry. I really am. I wish we could have had a few more days of fun and parties and happy stories. But it seems real life has come calling much sooner than any of us wanted."

He looked at Elijah. "If and when he wakes, we'll ask Elijah for his side of the story. If Isaac told me the truth, then he's already received his punishment for handling and firing the gun."

"And if Elijah doesn't tell you the same story?" Charlotte's voice was cold with dread. She was afraid she already knew the answer.

"Then he'll hang for shooting a white man," Beau said. "Your mind might not remember what's true, but in your heart, you know that's what has to happen."

"Your father loved you very much, Charlotte. He was a fine man—held in great esteem in this county and around the state. I'm sure you've heard that time and time again," her mother said.

Mutely, Charlotte nodded.

"There was nothing in the world he wouldn't have done for you—it's probably why his portrait was so meaningful for you ... why you took a chance and came here to find out who he was. Now, the least you can do for his memory is to be loyal to it and never forget he died by the hand of a trusted servant."

Chapter Twenty-Nine

It was the end of the day when Charlotte sat dozing in the chair next to Elijah's bed. Her fingers were given a gentle squeeze.

"Mercy."

She opened her eyes to find Elijah's hand over her own. "You're awake!"

His voice was hoarse. "So it seems."

"How are you feeling?"

"Like I've been shot," he said.

"You've been out for the better part of two days," she said. "You've got to be thirsty."

She helped him drink. "Let me bring you something to eat."

He shook his head. "Not now. Maybe later."

"All right. But you *do* have to eat something …"

"How is Isaac?"

"Can you tell me what happened?" Charlotte asked, evading his question.

"*Where* is Isaac?" he asked again.

"He's in the colored camp," she said. "He was found hiding in the wardrobe the morning you were shot, Elijah. You need to tell me what happened."

"As best as I can figure, his curiosity about my gun got the better of him. It went off and I had the bad luck of being in the bullet's path. But it was an accident. I know that without a doubt."

She nodded. "He told Beau it was an accident."

"And Beau believed him?"

"Beau wants to hear it from you, but then it will all be over," she said.

His face was creased with worry. "And there won't be any repercussions for him?"

Charlotte weighed the truth against a lie that would lessen his concern. "No. I know Isaac's been very worried about you," she said. "I'll go and talk with him in a little while."

Elijah relaxed against his pillow. "So, what's the damage?"

"We had a doctor from town come, and he performed a surgery to remove the bullet. It could have been so much worse, Elijah. You're lucky to be alive at all."

"Another day or two and I can be on my way …"

"I don't think so," she said. "Doctor Hawkins will be back in a week to remove your sutures and then he recommends another three weeks before you can be on a horse."

Elijah sat up quickly, then sucked in a painful breath. "I can't possibly stay here another month. I've got a post to get back to."

Charlotte slipped a hand behind his back. "Judging by the way your face just paled, I'd say you might be rethinking that day or two." She helped ease him back against his pillow. Beads of sweat appeared across his forehead.

"Maybe three or four days," he conceded. "I'm a quick healer."

She cocked an eyebrow. "Is that right? How about bouncing up and down in the saddle for hours on end?" she said. "The very least you can do is give that bullet hole the respect it deserves."

Elijah chuckled, then immediately grimaced. "I'm respecting it now."

"Good."

He grew serious. "You know, the longer I'm here, the better the chances are of your family finding out what I did in the war. I don't want you to have to face the consequences of that."

"I'm doing all I can to make sure they don't find out." She wiped his brow with a cool cloth. "It's not something you need to worry about."

"I appreciate all the worrying you seem to have done on my behalf."

She could see he meant it by the look in his eyes. She held his gaze a little longer, then busied herself by folding the cloth in her hand.

"Mother, Beau, and Victoria have all been worried about you too," Charlotte said. "And this whole incident has brought back some very painful memories for them."

"Something you want to share?"

"It's about my father and how he died," she said, then shook her head. "You don't need to hear this right now. Later, when you're more rested …"

"You just told me I've slept for nearly two days," he said. "I'm sure I'm more rested than you are."

She hesitated, then nodded. "As you already know, my father died about three years ago. His regiment happened to be in the area, and according to my mother, he wanted to come home and spend a few days with the family. After a wonderful visit, it was time for him to rejoin his men. Apparently we were all to meet in the foyer to see him off …" Her voice trailed off.

"If you don't want to continue …"

"No. I do," she said. "There was a slave named Lewis. He was born on the plantation, was a playmate of ours growing up. As he grew, he became a trusted servant, coming and going in the house when the need called for it. The general feeling was that Lewis greatly admired my father—and to hear it told, it sounded like my father had affection for Lewis. That morning, just as Father was to tell us all good-bye, Lewis entered the foyer, shot, and killed him."

For a moment, Elijah was speechless. "And you were all right there to witness it."

Charlotte nodded. "They remember the nightmare vividly. Finding you shot in this house … well … as you can imagine, it brought a lot back to them."

"And Lewis? What happened to him?"

"He was killed by the sergeant who'd been traveling with my father."

Elijah slowly shook his head. "Survived the battlefields only to die in his own home."

"Is it cowardly to say for once I'm glad I don't remember?"

"No. Not cowardly at all. It would be a hard memory to live with," he said. "But at least now you know what happened."

"Yes. Now I know," she said. "And I also know you need to eat something to help you gain back your strength."

"I don't think I can right now. But soon …"

"All right."

He relaxed completely back into the pillow, fought the heaviness of his eyes for a moment until he gave in and was back asleep. She fussed with the sheets and quilt that covered him, then sat back down in the chair next to the bed. All the while, she recited a litany over and over in her head. *Thank You, God. Thank You for hearing my prayer.*

CHAPTER THIRTY

The setting sun cast gold shadows across the red clay dirt beneath Charlotte's feet as she made her way across the property to the south end of the rice fields. The humidity felt heavy and slick across her skin, and though the sun was slipping toward the horizon, the evening was warm. A slight breeze stirred the air and on it, the familiar scent of the ocean. She added that to the things in her recent memory that were comfortable, like slipping into the only dress she'd worn for ages, the smell of lemon verbena and the taste of tea laced with sugar. Every memory she could add to those she could call up at will made her happy.

Charlotte turned down the path to the colored camp. The closer she got, the more dismayed she became at the condition of the houses. Made of thin wooden boards stacked one upon the other, they looked like a strong wind would flatten them back against the earth. She could see space between the boards and wondered how the inhabitants stayed dry in the rain or warm in the winter. A few of the houses had rickety porches that appeared to have been tacked on as an afterthought. Several people were outside having an evening meal, sitting on squares of burlap in the grass. Children looked up as she approached. Somewhere she heard a baby crying. The men and women seemed to avoid her glances, eyes averted and faces turned down. It seemed they would look anywhere but at her. The thought crossed her mind that many of these people may have known her before she left. It seemed strange that no one was welcoming her back—or was it? She had been as much a slave owner as the rest of the family. As her father had been. She desperately wanted to believe she'd been fair-minded and kind, but she knew the answer because Beau had given it to her. *"Before the war, my sister Charlotte would have been the first to make sure a message was sent to the Negroes for an offense like this."*

"Good evening," she said to no one in particular.

People going about their evening rituals stopped and stared at her, but no one said a word.

"I'm … Charlotte Chapman," she said. It was the first time she'd spoken it aloud like that. The first time she'd introduced herself instead of someone in her family making the introduction. She approached a young Negro woman with a baby riding her hip. "I'm looking for a boy called Isaac," she said. "Do you know him?"

The young mother quickly shook her head. "No, miss."

She moved slowly through the row of houses, asking one person after another about Isaac but kept hearing the same answer. "No, miss."

A white man on horseback rode up and dismounted, and the Negroes seemed to physically shrink from his appearance. She remembered meeting the stocky, barrel-chested man at her party. The plantation overseer doffed his hat as he approached.

"Miss Charlotte," he said.

"Mr. Jonas."

"Can I help you with something?"

"No, thank you," she said. "I'm here on a personal errand."

"I don't know if anyone's told you, ma'am, but we don't got no call to be traipsing through the colored camp no more. These folks are sharecroppers, paying rent on their homes and working for their coins, just like regular people."

"I'm not going to bother anyone, Mr. Jonas," she said. "I'm looking for someone."

"Excuse me for sayin' so, Miss Chapman, but you shouldn't be here come dark," he said. "Wouldn't be safe."

The people around them were listening, but doing all they could to avoid looking like they were listening.

"I appreciate the warning," she said.

"Ma'am …"

"Please, Mr. Jonas, I have some business I'd like to attend to and then I'll be on my way."

Jonas touched the brim of his hat. "Evening, Miss Charlotte."

Charlotte spotted a familiar face sitting on the dilapidated porch on the house next door. His chin rested on the knees he had drawn to his chest. She walked toward him.

"Moby, isn't it?"

Moby eyed her but didn't say a word. She tried again. "Please, Moby. I'm looking for my friend Isaac. Do you know him?"

Moby nodded. "Yassum."

"Good. Can you tell me where to find him?"

Moby glanced over his shoulder at the shack, but then shook his head. "He don't come out now."

Charlotte started to go up the steps, and Moby suddenly stood. "It ain't fit in dere for you, missus." He ran up the steps, disappeared inside, and moments later, a very scared-looking Isaac stood in the doorway.

"Isaac," she said. "Please. Come and talk to me."

"Not sure I wanna hear what you gots to say to me, Miss Mer—Charlotte."

She held out her hand. "It's all right, Isaac. Please …"

He slowly descended the rickety steps. Before she could even say a word, he shook his head. "I be the mos' sorrowful person in dis place. I didn't mean to do it … would take it back even if I had to die to do it."

"I know, Isaac. I know it was an accident. Elijah is going to be all right. He told me what happened, and I told Mr. Beau," she said.

Isaac's chin fell against his chest. He stood there until his shaking shoulders told Charlotte he was sobbing. She reached out to put a hand on his shoulder and he flinched, then stepped up, back onto a step.

"I don't want no comfort," he said. "Mr. Elijah be the best man I know in the world and if he'd a' died on account a' my foolishness, I'd be throwing myself in da bottomless ocean."

"He didn't die, and there will be no more talk about throwing yourself in the ocean."

"I be so, so sorry," he said.

"I know, Isaac. And in a few days, you can come to the house and see Mr. Elijah for yourself," she said.

"And ask him to forgive me."

"If that's what you want, then yes," she said.

He nodded, wiped his face with the back of his sleeve. "Thanks to you for tellin' me 'bout him."

"Of course," she said. "And, Isaac … I know about the—the punishment you received. Are *you* all right?"

He backed up another step but nodded. "Yassum, I be fine."

She hesitated. "Who was it that whipped you?"

He shook his head. "Don't wanna say."

"Was it Bram? The man I saw chasing Moby?"

Isaac looked around. "He didn't start it, but he done what he could for me by sayin' he finish it. Don't blame him, Miss Charlotte. He look scary for da white men but he ain't scary to me."

"I've just been so worried about you," she said.

He shook his head. "Don't fret on me," he said. "I ain't makin' no more mistakes, and I make you a promise right now, front of God, that I ain't never, ever in my life, gonna touch another gun."

She nodded her understanding.

"You'll tell me if anyone isn't treating you right?"

"You best get back to the big house now. Sun's sinking and it get mighty dark out here."

"I'll send for you when Elijah is up to visitors," she said.

He nodded, then went back up the steps, past Moby and into the shack. She turned and pretended not to see everyone's eyes on her as she made her way past the shacks and the families having a meager supper.

Lights from the house began to flicker through the windows. It looked comforting, safe, inviting, and a world apart from the one she'd just walked away from.

Chapter Thirty-One

Elijah couldn't seem to get comfortable. There was little he could do for himself, and it made him moody and irritable. He fidgeted against the pillows behind his back and thought about how predictable life used to be, before he met Charlotte. He knew his own heart and mind then—he could count on certain things happening when he woke in the morning and went to sleep with the expectation that the next morning would probably be the same. A small voice in his head told him he was behaving badly because of his pride. *When pride cometh, then cometh shame: but with the lowly is wisdom.* Sometimes, that small voice could be very irritating. He shouldn't be sitting in bed on a Georgia plantation. He should be out West, riding the range, doing the job he'd signed on to do.

Charlotte entered with a bright smile and a tray in hand. "Good afternoon," she said. "I've come with something new to tempt you."

"I'm sorry for the trouble you've gone to ... up and down those stairs. But I'm still not hungry."

"It's no trouble. There's a wonderful contraption in the pantry called a dumbwaiter," she said. "You put the tray inside the wall and pull a rope and it comes right upstairs." She put the tray on the bureau, then pulled a chair closer to the bed.

"What are you doing?"

After retrieving the tray, she sat next to him. "You're going to eat—even if I have to feed you myself."

"No, I'm not. And I'm not a child." He pressed his lips together.

She raised her brows. "Then quit acting like one." She slid the tray onto his lap, being careful of the site of his wound. "It's biscuits and gravy. I'm told it was one of my favorites growing up, and after tasting it, I believe it."

"It looks like a gray mess," he said skeptically.

"Trust me."

"Why aren't you eating too?" he asked.

"I had a late breakfast with Victoria before she left to spend the day in Darien." Charlotte pointed at the food. "Try it."

He forked a tentative bite into his mouth and his eyes widened in appreciation.

She nodded. "See? Delicious, right?"

"It is. My brother and I would have fought over the last bite of a dish like this."

"You and your brother fought over *food*?"

The food was quickly disappearing. He had been starving and didn't realize it. "We fought over everything, but my mother's cottage pie was always good for a brawl or two." He grinned with the memory. "Beef, gravy, and a crust of creamed potatoes. We almost always came to blows over the last serving. Mother would defuse the situation, of course. Sometimes with dessert—but most often with a look that would make us both freeze in our tracks."

"That makes sense, then," she said.

"What does?"

"You talked about Jed in your sleep," she said. "Something about pie and telling your pa."

Elijah chuckled. "Brothers are always scrapping about something."

"I wonder if I did that with my brother and sister," she said.

He finished the last bite of food on his plate, and she took the tray from him with a smile. "Thank you for being so accommodating and eating all that without an appetite."

"You're welcome." He studied her. "How are you faring with your family?"

She put the tray back down on the bureau and returned to the chair, and he found himself relieved she was staying.

"My family." She grew thoughtful for a moment. "Sometimes, when they're telling me a story about the past—as in what happened to my father—I can accept it without question. But when they're talking about *me*—something personal I've said or done—they're telling me about a stranger I've never met, and it's harder for me to accept. I don't know if that makes any sense."

"And what do you think of this stranger Charlotte they talk of? If you were introduced somewhere, do you think you might be friends?"

"I honestly don't know," she said. "But I'd like to think so." She smiled. "I'm so tired of always talking about me. Tell me about you—your family."

"There isn't much to tell," he said. "My father died when I was sixteen. My brother, Jed, died the day you and I met."

"I'm sorry the day we met was one of the saddest of your life," she said quietly.

He cocked his head to the side and studied her. "I know it's strange, but when I think of that day, the part I remember about you was your compassion—not that we were on different sides of the conflict."

She gave a little nod, then asked, "What about your mother?"

"A wonderful woman." He shifted his weight. "I need to be up more. How am I supposed to get my strength back when I'm lying in this bed all day long?"

"I'll bet your mother would tell you to be patient," she said.

He smiled. "That's what she said when I was twelve and broke my leg trying to get Jed out of a tree. It turned out he was a much better climber than I was. He climbed down and I took the shortcut and fell from one of the highest branches."

She winced. "Ouch."

"I snapped my leg in two."

"I'll bet that took a while to recover from," she said.

Elijah nodded. "I thought I'd go crazy that summer, sitting on the grass while Jed could run and play. I was so mad at him." He smiled. "My mother has no tolerance for self-pity or grudge holding. She told me I should forgive him. It was an accident, but I refused. I think I liked the idea of being able to blame my sour mood on someone."

He shook his head. "You'd think I would have outgrown that."

She smiled. "I don't know what you're talking about."

"The thing is, what I remember most about that day is how disappointed she looked when I said I wouldn't forgive him. Of course I knew she still loved me, but that look of hers nearly undid me. I was sitting under the eave of our house in the shade, watching Jed and some boys play stickball. Mother leaned down and kissed my cheek and said, 'Remember, son, those who are furthest from giving mercy are furthest from receiving it.' She went back into the house, and I forgave my brother for an accident that was probably my own fault. Even though I'm a grown man, I still seek her counsel."

Charlotte looked guilty. "I have a confession to make."

"All right."

"When you were in bad shape, the doctor wanted to go through your things to see who your next of kin was to notify in the event things didn't … go well. I volunteered. I had no idea if you had papers identifying you as a member of the military."

"Good thinking on your part," he said.

"I found a letter from your mother in your Bible. It touched me very much. Her words made me wish my own mother had been like her."

"Maybe she was."

She smiled. "Maybe."

"I'm all my mother has left," he said. "She worries, but has the strongest faith of anyone I know."

"If you want to write about what's happened, I'll post it in town," she said.

"I need to write to Fort Wallace too. I don't want to be reported as a deserter."

So as not to arouse the suspicion of anyone in Darien, it was decided that the letter to Fort Wallace would be sent with the letter to Elijah's mother and she could send it on from Pennsylvania to the fort.

Through the window that faced the front of the house, they heard the sound of a buggy arriving. A minute or two later and heavy footsteps had Elijah looking in that general direction.

"Sounds like company," he said.

"Yes, Mother and Beau are meeting with some men over lunch today," she said.

"I shouldn't be monopolizing all your time," he apologized. "If you'd like to go down …"

She frowned. "No, I'm fine right here. Besides, from what I understand they're coming to talk plantation business. It's not as if I'm well versed in the art of rice production."

There was a short rap on the door and Biddy stuck her head inside the room. "Miss Charlotte, I sorry to disturb you but Miss Suzanne say it's 'portant you join dem on dah veranda for lunch."

Elijah thought momentarily that Charlotte looked disappointed at the interruption of their conversation.

She stood and smoothed out her skirt. "Seems I've been summoned, but you haven't seen the last of me. I plan to bully you into eating every meal."

He leaned back against the pillow after the door closed, and smiled. The food had been good but the company even better.

Charlotte came through the doors onto the veranda, puzzled as to what her presence could possibly lend to this meeting.

"Here she is," Mother said. "Thank you for joining us, darling."

As Charlotte approached the table, the men stood.

"Charlotte, you remember Mr. Reynolds from your welcome-home party?"

"Yes, of course," Charlotte said. "How are you, Mr. Reynolds?"

"Happy to see you aren't still limping from our dance," he said. "I'm afraid I stepped all over your toes."

She smiled. "No permanent damage."

"This is my attorney, Mr. Newton, and this is Mr. Harland. He'll be my overseer if I buy the property," Mr. Reynolds said. "Gentlemen—Miss Chapman."

Once they were all seated again, Charlotte's mother smiled at Mr. Reynolds. "Would you like to discuss business first, Mr. Reynolds, or shall I have Rose serve lunch?"

"We're at your mercy, ma'am."

Charlotte's mother caught Rose's eye. "You and Biddy may serve now, Rose."

"Yassum," Rose said.

"I had Juba make chicken and dumplings," Mother said. "Some have called her the finest cook in the county."

"You've gone to entirely too much trouble, ma'am," Mr. Reynolds said.

"Don't be silly, Mr. Reynolds. We may very well end up neighbors—and friends, too, I hope. Now, what can we do for you?"

Mr. Reynolds leaned his elbows on the table, and Charlotte tried not to smile at the look of disdain her mother was trying to tamp down at his social faux pas. "Well, Mrs. Chapman, we hear you run the most successful rice plantation in the state."

Suzanne corrected him. "In *three* states."

"I need to know that, if I buy the Crowley place, I'll have a fair place to trade when I harvest my crop."

"You're referring to our threshing mill?"

Reynolds nodded. "Yes. Your threshing mill."

"Just to clarify, we take our fee in cash, Mr. Reynolds. There is no trade."

"No wiggle room there, eh?"

She smiled. "None."

"It's a little late in the season to be planting rice," Beau said. "We're just about set for our lay-by flow."

Mr. Harland slapped at his neck. "Darn mosquitoes. Think they've had about a gallon of my blood since I got here."

Suzanne forced a smile. "We *are* in the lowlands here."

"Nuisance," Mr. Harland said. "Anyway, we aren't dead set on rice. Maybe we'll do corn."

Beau's brows shot up. "Corn?"

Newton exchanged a quick look with Reynolds. "He meant cotton."

"How many acres do you plan to harrow?" Beau asked.

Charlotte thought Mr. Reynolds looked confused at the question. Then he deferred to his overseer.

"What do you think, Harland? This is your area of expertise."

Mr. Harland stroked his chin. "I haven't really had time to plan it all out yet, but I'm thinking on about five."

"And you intend to make your living that way?" Charlotte's

mother seemed puzzled. "On just five acres? I believe Mr. Crowley utilized all fifty acres when he was producing."

"I'm not sure how much help I can afford," Mr. Reynolds said. "And once I hire 'em, how do you keep 'em? The work looks miserable."

Mother and Beau traded a look. "Don't worry about that, Mr. Reynolds. We can help you keep your workers. There are ways to … guarantee their return year after year."

"Is that right?" Mr. Reynolds pursed his lips in thought and nodded.

"I would suggest utilizing more than just five acres for cotton, though," Beau said.

"Well, we might have other … plants go in," Mr. Harland said.

"Oh. You're considering mixed-crop production?" Beau asked.

"Right," Mr. Reynolds said. "Mixed crops."

"How many acres do you have here, Mrs. Chapman?" Mr. Newton asked.

"A little over seven hundred," she said. "We're hoping to get back to our prewar production of a half million pounds of rice a year."

Mr. Reynolds issued a low whistle and Charlotte saw Suzanne flinch again. Charlotte had the thought that his table manners were on par with his dancing. *Dancing*. Her thoughts drifted to Elijah; it surprised her how much she enjoyed his company.

"Charlotte?" She heard a slight annoyance in her mother's voice.

"I'm sorry, yes?"

"Mr. Harland asked you a question."

"I'm afraid my thoughts were elsewhere," Charlotte said. "I'm sorry, Mr. Harland. What was your question?"

"Hell's bells, we all let our mind drift. No need to apologize."

Charlotte felt icy-cold fear run up her spine. *Hell's bells, he's down!* That expression—that voice. She tried not to let the fear show on her face but when her eyes darted to Mr. Reynolds, she saw the cold glare in his eyes. The same glare she'd seen the night of the party. Weeks of running from the men who hated her and now here she was at the same table. Having lunch.

Chapter Thirty-Two

Charlotte was immobile with fear, but her mind raced in a million different directions as Rose and Biddy arrived with lunch. While Biddy held the serving tray, Rose settled plates in front of the guests. Charlotte felt as if her mouth was too dry to even speak.

"Anyway, Miss Chapman, to repeat my earlier question, I wondered if you could show us around the plantation," Mr. Harland said as he turned to Beau. "No disrespect, but I'd like a woman's perspective. Not to mention she's more pleasing to the eyes."

"None taken."

Charlotte tried to swallow down the panic rising in her throat and forced a smile. "I must decline, Mr. Harland. I would be an inferior guide to my brother …"

"Inferior like your servants?" Mr. Newton said. "Or do you still refer to them as slaves?"

Mother frowned at his comment, then looked at Rose. "You may bring out the tea now, Rose."

Rose nodded. "Yassum." Rose and Biddy made their way back into the house. Charlotte didn't want anyone hurt, but she knew she needed to do something to protect her family. She glanced around the table, then locked eyes with Mr. Reynolds. His expression was one of satisfaction; hers, she thought, must reveal naked fear.

She pushed her chair back and stood. "If y'all will excuse me for just a moment …"

"Sit. Down," Mr. Reynolds said.

Her mother looked from one to the other. "I beg your pardon?"

Charlotte slowly took her seat. "It's all right, Mother."

Reynolds shook his head. "I don't think it is. And just so we all have the same information, *y'all* should know we ain't just got napkins in our laps. When the help comes back, act natural—you don't want your slaves in danger, do you? I wouldn't want a pistol to accidentally fire …"

"Who *are* you?" Charlotte's mother's voice quivered with fear.

"Do you want to tell them … Mercy? Or should I?" Reynolds asked.

"What's he talking about? Why is he calling you Mercy?" Beau asked.

"If you'd just let them go inside …," Charlotte said.

Reynolds offered a slow smile and picked up his fork with his free hand. "We aren't going to hurt your family, Mercy. But I am going to eat this very fine meal." He forked a dumpling into his mouth and rolled his eyes with pleasure. "I have to say I despise the climate here—the blood-sucking mosquitoes, the wet air, and the clammy way my clothes feel. Can't imagine anyone wantin' to work out in those fields—but I imagine that's what the slaves were for."

Newton and Harland chuckled. Reynolds swept his gaze over the trio they held at gunpoint, who just stared at him. He shrugged, dug his fork into another dumpling. "Anyway, to my way of thinking there is only one thing of merit here in the lowlands of Georgia— and that's the food. I will freely admit I *do* love Southern cooking."

"What do you want with Charlotte?" Beau asked.

"We want justice," Harland said. "Justice for the crime she committed, but never paid for. A few weeks in Gratiot ain't enough."

"Gratiot Prison?" Beau asked. "I don't understand …"

Charlotte looked at Reynolds. "Please, I implore you to leave them alone. They've done nothing to you."

"They're part of the reason this country nearly tore in two. Planter elite is what they are. Confederate scum who called human beings property and even after all the blood of the war still have the nerve to have blacks waiting on them." Reynolds spit on the wooden floor. "Rebel scum begets rebel scum!"

Rose came from inside the house with a pitcher of tea in hand. Reynolds raised a warning brow at his captive audience. Harland held his empty glass in the air and smiled. "Got a thirst like I been in the desert," he said. "Looks mighty refreshing."

Charlotte looked up at the window above—Elijah's *open* window. She prayed he hadn't fallen back asleep. Rose made her way slowly around the table, taking infinite care not to spill a drop of tea as she poured.

Reynolds started to talk again, in a pleasing, quiet tone that sounded more like a bedtime story than an indictment. "Guess you're mighty proud of this little girl, huh? Dressed herself up as a man, killed who knows how many God-fearing Union soldiers during the war, gets herself engaged to one of the biggest Union supporters in the country so she can wrangle an introduction to a congressman and then sets out to kill him." Reynolds smiled pleasantly. The other men were eating their food as if nothing was happening.

Mother shook her head. "What are you talking about? What is he saying, Charlotte?"

"Go ahead and tell her, Mercy. Tell her how a jury found you guilty and sentenced you to hang. Tell 'em how you sat in that prison until they took you to the gallows and then, by some inconceivable twist of fate, had a stay of execution just minutes before that hemp rope went around your neck."

"I'd had last rites and the hemp *did* go around my neck, but I was innocent of treason and the judge let me go!"

"If a judge set her free, then you can't take her back to prison," Beau said. Charlotte knew he was terrified; she could hear it in his voice. She had to do something—anything. She needed to get inside to find a weapon. And then Rose was there, over her shoulder, the pitcher of tea in hand. As she started to pour, Charlotte bumped back against her and the tea splashed down the front of her dress.

"Now look what you've done, you clumsy idiot!" Charlotte shouted. She jumped to her feet. "I'll need to change my dress now. I'm completely soaked!"

"I'm sorry, Miss Charlotte!" Rose said, her voice cracking with emotion. "I'll go fetch you a towel ..."

"No!" she shouted again. "Just leave us! Now!"

Rose hurried back into the house. Reynolds turned steely eyes on Charlotte.

"You got about two seconds to sit back down in that chair ..."

Charlotte dropped back into her seat. "You can see they know nothing about any of this," she said. "It's just me you want."

Elijah had been on the verge of napping since Charlotte left. He could hear bits and pieces of the conversation on the veranda below his window. Just fragments, really, nothing that concerned him. He mentally calculated the number of hours until he thought she'd be back with his supper. It was definitely something he looked forward to. But then he heard Charlotte shout, and he was jolted out of his daydream. Her words clearly carried through his open window. She would never use that word, never shout at Rose like that. He threw back the quilt and made his way to the window. He caught a glimpse of Charlotte dropping into a seat at the table. He saw two men and Suzanne but from his angle couldn't see anything else. He recognized Reynolds from the dance. What was happening? And then he heard Charlotte again. *"It's just me you want."*

Gritting his teeth against his pain, Elijah made his way to the bureau, pulled open the drawer and found his revolver. He opened the chamber, filled it with six rounds and made his way into the hall. He went to the stairs, yanking his shirt open as he started down the steps. Steeling himself against the pain from his belly wound, Elijah clawed at his own sutures, ripping the stitches out one by one. He nearly pitched forward from the pain, but kept descending the stairs. He pressed his hand over the wound, felt the blood under his hand and prayed he'd have the strength to see his plan through.

On the veranda, Newton put his fork down and pushed his empty plate away. "We been chasing this little woman since she left St. Louis," he said. "Kinda nice we're ending our quest with a good meal." He grinned. "Feels right."

"What do you intend to do with her?" Beau asked.

"We got our orders," Harland said. "But we ain't sharing 'em with you."

"Orders from whom?" Mother asked.

"There are some very important people who want to make sure that Mercy pays the price for her crimes—and consequently want to pay us to make sure that happens. Since the justice system is corrupt and blind, we'll use our own justice."

"This can't be happening," Charlotte's mother said. "This just can't be …"

A gunshot from inside the house echoed out on the veranda. The men got to their feet just as Elijah came staggering through the door—his belly a bloody mess.

Reynolds scowled. "What the …?"

"They're coming!" Elijah doubled over, stumbled toward them. He held up his blood-stained hand. "Someone help me!"

"Who's coming?" Reynolds jumped up from the table.

"Behind me! They're coming," Elijah said. He staggered forward. Chairs pushed back from the table. Reynolds and Harland raised their guns, arcing them back and forth. Newton took an immediate defensive position and jumped over the rail of the porch. Elijah straightened, aimed at Harland, hit him, and he dropped. Elijah took aim at Reynolds next, who made a fatal mistake by turning to watch Harland fall. Reynolds joined him on the ground a second later.

"He's getting away!" Beau yelled, pointing at Newton, who was only steps from his buggy. Newt turned and aimed at Elijah, but before he could get a shot off, Elijah hit him in the belly. Newt looked surprised and dropped his gun to grab his belly with both hands, then surprisingly turned and heaved himself into the buggy. He slapped the reins on the horse and headed out the drive. Elijah knew they'd never be able to get a horse saddled to give chase.

"Elijah!" Charlotte said. "He's still alive."

She was standing over Reynolds, who struggled to pull in each breath.

Elijah knelt by his side. "Who hired you?" he demanded.

Reynolds squinted at him. "Thought you … were … gone."

Elijah grabbed Reynolds by his shirt collar, practically lifting him off the ground. "Who put the price on Mercy's head?"

"It isn't over for … her. Never be over till she's dead," Reynolds said.

Charlotte stood, transfixed at the words Reynolds said. She could hear her mother weeping behind her. Beau was offering trite words of comfort, but he, too, sounded shaken to his very core.

Reynolds's eyes fluttered closed, a slight smile on his mouth. "More will come." His mouth went slack and his head lolled to the side. Elijah released his grip on the man, and looked up at Charlotte. "Are you all right?"

She swallowed hard and nodded. There were two dead men on the porch. She looked toward the door and saw Chessie and some of the other servants staring at the scene in stunned silence.

"Beau, go through his pockets," Elijah ordered. "Pile whatever you find on the table."

Elijah was doing the very thing he asked of Beau. He went through Reynolds's pockets, pulled out some paper money, a pocket-knife, and a compass. He also found the same image he'd carried of Mercy when he was looking for her.

"Elijah, you're bleeding again—badly. We need to send for the doctor."

Elijah pulled a faded yellow piece of paper from Reynolds's shirt pocket. He had to unfold it to read it.

"Elijah …"

He slowly got to his feet and turned to Beau. "Get my horse saddled. I must leave at once."

Charlotte shook her head. "You can't go anywhere! You're bleeding—you need stitches …"

"Then get me a needle and some heavy thread," he said.

"What? You can't be serious," Charlotte said.

"I am."

Charlotte looked at Chessie, still standing in the doorway. "Chessie, I need a needle and some sturdy thread right away." With a nod, Chessie was off.

"I want some answers, Charlotte. Right now," Mother said tersely.

"Not now," Elijah said as he turned to Charlotte. "I need my things from my room. Everything."

"I won't get them. You can't leave like this," she said.

"Beau, would you get my things, please?" Elijah said. "I'd rather not climb the stairs and bleed all over the floors …"

"Get his things," Mother said.

Elijah went to the table and rifled through the things Beau had pulled from Harland's pockets. There were some hard candies, a cigar, a piece of card stock with a list of farmer's terms written on it.

"What about the man who got away?" Charlotte asked.

"The bullet hit him in the gut," Elijah said. "I have to hope he won't get far."

Chessie brought the needle and thread to Charlotte. "Sturdiest thread we got."

Elijah folded the card stock and put it in his pocket. Charlotte handed him the needle and thread. "Do you need some help?"

He shook his head. "But I would like a few minutes alone, if you don't mind," he said. He lowered himself to a chair. Charlotte winced just looking at the open wound. "You aren't thinking clearly. The blood loss, the pain. You can't seriously propose you can …"

"I've done it before," he said. "Who knows, maybe you have too. Please—a few minutes alone."

Charlotte took her mother inside. Before they could make their way to the parlor, Beau was back downstairs with Elijah's things in hand. He glared at Charlotte. "You brought a *Yankee* into our house? We've had the enemy under our roof all this time and you never said a word?"

"How …?"

"I saw papers, Char! Orders and statements of leave …"

"It's true he's in the army," Charlotte said.

"He was in the *Union* army, wasn't he? A Yankee?"

"That Yankee just saved our lives!"

"Is there no end to the deception?" Mother said. "I don't even know what to think now—what to do!"

"We get the sheriff out here and tell him what's happened," Beau said. "And Elijah stays until he gets here."

"I'm not staying for that," Elijah said.

They all turned to see him standing at the door. He looked pale but resolute. "There could be more men coming for Charlotte. More men looking to do her harm. You need to protect your sister, Beau."

"You're leaving?" Beau said. "That's noble. Cut and run."

"I'm going to try and stop whoever has put a price on her head," Elijah said. "Charlotte, a word?"

Charlotte gathered the things from Beau and followed Elijah back out onto the veranda. As they made their way down the wide stairs, they could see someone leading his horse toward the house.

"I wish you wouldn't leave like this," she said.

"I have to go and find whoever is doing this. Convince them to call off the bounty."

"Maybe it's over now," she said.

He pulled the yellow piece of paper from his pocket and handed it to her. "A telegram." She opened it and read: *"Received location. Stop. Good work finding her. Stop. Send proof we require. Stop. Payment when proof received. Stop."*

"What does that mean?"

"It means when they don't receive proof you're dead, more men may be sent to do the job."

"You said you don't know who put out the bounty," she said.

"That's true, but I have some theories. I'm headed back to St. Louis," he told her. "In the meantime, stay close to the house. Don't go anywhere alone."

"I still don't understand the hurry," she said. "You could stay a few more days and give yourself a chance to heal."

"I need to get there and stop this madness before the people behind this realize their bounty hunters have failed—and they send out replacements."

"I'm worried about you," she said quietly.

He looked at the house. "I'm worried about you, too. You have a lot of explaining to do, and I don't think they're in a very receptive mood right now."

A stable boy arrived with Elijah's horse. He frowned. "Seems strange to see someone besides Isaac with my mount."

"I'll find him, tell him what's happened," Charlotte said.

"Good. Say good-bye for me."

She nodded, looking at his worried expression. "I'll be all right."

"See that you are," he said gruffly. She reached up and laid her hand against his cheek. He covered it with his own, then captured it and held it between them.

"If things get hard, remember who you are," he said. "Not with your head, but with your heart. Heart memories are the true memories."

Elijah mounted his horse. She watched him gallop away, then turned back to the house.

Charlotte made her way up the steps, and purposely stopped to look down the veranda at the men who had come to take her life but lost their own. She had survived another nightmare. But would the nightmare eventually win?

CHAPTER THIRTY-THREE

Charlotte had been vaguely aware of the number of people milling about the front yard, workers from the house and other spots on the plantation who had presumably come when they heard the gunshots. She hadn't paid attention to anyone but Elijah and the moment he was telling her good-bye. When Charlotte entered the foyer, she saw Jonas there with her brother. Both men glanced at her.

"He left, then?" Beau asked.

Charlotte nodded. "Yes."

"I'm sending Jonas to town for the sheriff and undertaker," Beau said.

She nodded distractedly. "All right."

Beau nodded at Jonas, who hurried out the door.

"The sheriff is going to be upset Elijah didn't stay and talk to him. Makes him look guilty of something," Beau said.

"Those men intended to kill me and who knows what they would have done with you and Mother. Elijah saved our lives, and that's all the sheriff needs to hear."

Chessie entered the foyer. "You wanted me, Mr. Beau?"

"Could you find some sheets to cover those men outside, Chessie?"

Chessie glanced at Charlotte, then nodded. "Yassuh."

"I'm going up to my room," Charlotte said.

"No, you're coming into the parlor with me. We want to talk to you," he said.

Victoria burst through the door, eyes wild. She nearly careened into Charlotte, and then saw Beau. "You're all right? All of you? Where's Mother?"

"We're fine. Relatively fine," Beau amended. "Can't say the same for our luncheon guests. There have been some … developments since you left."

"I saw Elijah tearing down the road, could barely get him to stop and talk to me," Victoria said. "He wouldn't explain what he was doing. Why he's leaving when he's in such bad shape." She looked at Charlotte. "He said you'd explain. And then I ride up to the house and see …"—she pointed toward the veranda—"that!"

"We were just about to hear Charlotte's explanation," Beau said. "Weren't we?"

Charlotte nodded, then made her way into the parlor with Beau and Victoria close behind her. Her mother looked like a woman who'd been through a trauma; her face was ashen, eyes seemed unfocused and glazed. She held a glass of brandy in her hand, but it shook when she raised it to her lips and took a drink. As if the play had been rehearsed, Beau and Victoria sat down on either side of their mother. Charlotte sat opposite them, and her mind went immediately back to the day she arrived. Was it really less than two weeks before when she'd sat in this very chair and told them she couldn't remember them? She didn't know quite how to start what she knew would be a difficult conversation. Her mother took care of that for her.

"You knew you were being pursued by bounty hunters?"

Charlotte nodded. "Yes."

"*What?*" This came from Victoria.

"And you came here anyway—put us all in danger?"

"I don't understand what you're talking about," Victoria said.

"Those men lying dead on our porch were bounty hunters—after our sister for apparent crimes she committed …"

Victoria's jaw dropped. She looked at Charlotte. "Crimes?"

"Wait—there's more," Beau said. "It also seems Charlotte has a penchant for Yankees. She was engaged to one—and then brought one home with her. Elijah fought for the North."

Victoria put a hand on her chest. "Do be quiet, Beau."

Though Charlotte tried to act calm, her mind raced during Beau's jabs to try and find the right words to explain the last year to her family.

"When Elijah told you that we'd met on a battlefield," Charlotte said, "that was true. But we were on opposite sides. According to him, I chased after him, but when I found him praying over his dying brother, I let him live. I didn't take the shot, and he thanked me for it. As a token, he gave his mercy medallion to the sergeant that spared his life that day. He walked away and I apparently did too. I don't remember any of it."

"All Yankees are liars and manipulators … and murderers," Beau said. "We've got two on the veranda who prove my point!"

"You know that's not true, Beau," she said. "You can't make a claim like that about Northerners any more than they can claim Southerners are heartless in their treatment of Negroes."

"How *do* you know he didn't lie to you about that encounter?" her mother asked.

"Because when we met again about eight months later—at my engagement party—he thought he recognized me. I obviously looked different than the sergeant. My hair had grown considerably—and I was wearing a dress. A far sight different than the brown wool shirt and green pants I'd donned for the army. He heard rumors about me. That I'd been found on the outskirts of St. Louis and brought to a clinic dressed as a man, had cuts and bruises—and amnesia."

"He could have told you anything and you wouldn't know if he was lying or not," Beau said.

"He was staying with some old friends of his in St. Louis while he waited for his next post," she said. "He came to me with his suspicions one evening. I didn't believe him, of course. I didn't know why he would lie to me, but I was convinced he was."

Victoria was hanging on every word. "But then …? What did he do that convinced you he was telling the truth?"

Charlotte nodded. "He described the mercy medallion he'd given to that rebel soldier." She slipped a finger under the chain around her neck and drew out her necklace. "He described *this* mercy medallion. Right down to a missing letter that's been rubbed off with time. It was his—and I had it."

"He must have seen you wearing it!" Beau said.

She shook her head. "No. I didn't have it on the night of my engagement party, or any of the other times I'd subsequently seen him. I knew he was telling me the truth."

"None of this explains why men are trying to kill you," her mother said.

Charlotte took a breath. "The man I was going to marry came from a powerful family in St. Louis," she said. "His father was part owner of the railroad, very wealthy—and used everything within his means to help the North win the war."

"What was his name?" Beau asked.

"Charles Prescott. I was engaged to his son, Rand."

Beau frowned. "Prescott. I've heard of him. Didn't he help design the armor the North used in their train engines?"

She nodded. "There were also some rumblings about a political office sometime soon," she said. "To be honest, they weren't happy when Rand wanted to marry some obscure girl who had no history—but they gradually accepted it."

Her mother shook her head. "I don't understand how you could fall in love with a Yankee!"

"I had no memory, Mother. No political leanings one way or another," Charlotte said, "but when Elijah came to me with what he knew, he insisted I tell Rand about my past. That I was a former Confederate sharpshooter. He reasoned if my memory returned one day, so might my former loyalties to the South. I would literally be married to my enemy. Elijah insisted I tell Rand the truth before our wedding day—or he would."

"So you told him?" Victoria asked.

She shook her head. "No. I couldn't do it. I knew he would hate me. His feelings about the South and the war were still so bitter."

"So that's why you broke off your engagement?" Mother asked.

"Yes. But not before I attempted something very foolish," Charlotte admitted. "I was desperate my secret not come out. I thought if I could stop Elijah from saying anything …"

Beau's brows shot up. "You went to kill him? Finally something makes sense."

She dropped her chin. Couldn't even look at them. "I did. I went to the home of the congressman before dawn, started a small fire and waited for them to come out of the house. But when Elijah did appear, I couldn't do it. I couldn't believe I almost *had*. I tried to get out of there as fast as I could and accidentally fired my gun.

"When the authorities came to arrest me, they came to the conclusion I was trying to kill the congressman. They said I used Rand and his family connections to gain access to him. They said it was my plan all along. I was a traitor—a Confederate who couldn't let go of the war and planned to execute a government official. The jury found me guilty of treason and sentenced me to hang."

"So this is all Elijah's fault!" Beau said.

"No. In fact, once Elijah heard about my sentence, he moved heaven and earth to get back to St. Louis from his post in Kansas and convinced the judge to commute my sentence."

"How?"

"Elijah told them if I'd wanted anyone dead, they'd be dead. He arranged for me to prove myself with a gun. When they let me go, Elijah offered to escort me to the state line. There had been rumors someone was very unhappy I was set free—and that someone was willing to pay men to find and kill me."

"So you're saying he's the hero?" Beau's voice dripped with sarcasm.

"I'm saying he's an honorable man who does what he believes is right. If I had told the truth about my past to Rand, I might have spared myself the nightmare of these past weeks."

"Maybe, if Rand loved you enough, the truth wouldn't have mattered to him," Victoria said.

Charlotte shook her head. "It mattered. He was the one who told the authorities where to find me. He was the one who sounded the treason alarm."

"Yankee revenge and scorn," her mother said. "We're all too familiar with it."

"I'm sorry I didn't tell you all of this sooner," Charlotte said. "I didn't believe the bounty hunters would find me here. If I did, I wouldn't have come back at all."

"I choose to acknowledge you fought for the South—you went to war because you knew the North was going to destroy our way of life," Mother said. "You knew it was the North that influenced Lewis to kill your father. You may not remember the hate you had for the Yankees, but in your heart you have to know that's who you still are. *That's* what I'm going to count on moving forward from this terrible day. That's what I suggest we all do."

CHAPTER THIRTY-FOUR

Charlotte hoped a good night's rest had done wonders for everyone's temperament and entered the dining room hanging onto that hope. But one look at the tired faces around the table told her otherwise.

"Good morning." Charlotte took a seat next to Victoria.

"Morning," Victoria said. Her usual enthusiasm was noticeably missing. Beau didn't say anything, but Charlotte noticed he had added something new to the table setting—a pistol was placed conspicuously next to his plate.

Her mother shook her head, reached for a china cup. "You're late."

The comment took Charlotte by surprise. "I am? I'm sorry."

"Rose has already been in to pour coffee," her mother said.

Charlotte reached for her own cup, then stood. "I can get my own."

"Don't!" Mother glared. "It is *her* job. When you do the work of the servants, you're undermining their very reason for being here."

Feeling chastened, Charlotte sat back down. "I wasn't trying to undermine anything. I was going to get coffee."

"Don't be impertinent, Charlotte," Mother snapped. "It isn't becoming on you."

Charlotte was shocked at both her tone and her biting comments. She stared down at her plate as Rose entered the dining room.

"You may fill Miss Charlotte's cup now, Rose," Suzanne said.

"All right, missus," Rose said.

Rose made quick work of pouring coffee, carefully avoiding any eye contact with Charlotte.

"Thank you, Rose," Charlotte said. "I apologize for my words yesterday …"

Rose dipped her chin in a nod and hurried away. Beau shook his head. "Why are you apologizing to her?"

"I was … I called her …"

"With everything else that happened yesterday, you're stuck on that?" Beau said.

"I'm sorry about yesterday," Charlotte said. "I truly am."

Suzanne glared. "Sorry doesn't change things. Sorry is said to lessen the guilt of the one who did wrong."

"It's not to lessen my guilt …"

Rose and her constant shadow, Biddy, arrived with plates of grits and pancakes. Victoria wrinkled her nose at the food.

"In my wildest dreams, I never imagined I would miss eggs so much," Victoria said. "I will never take chickens for granted again."

"When did Mr. Jackson say to expect the order you placed?" Mother asked.

"He said it would be about a month," Charlotte said.

"A *month*?" Their mother shook her head. "That's not acceptable. I want them sooner. You should have checked in with Jackson when you were in town, Victoria."

"I had lunch with friends yesterday, Mother. I wasn't there to see about chickens. Besides, there's nothing we can do about it now."

Mother sighed. "It's like everything else. I should have done it myself."

"I'll go to town," Charlotte said. "I'll speak to Mr. Jackson and impress upon him the urgency of the order."

Her mother looked at her. "I suppose …"

"You can't ride to Darien alone," Victoria said. "Have you forgotten what happened here yesterday?"

"She's right," Mother said. "It's not safe."

"I've got to check on repairs that were made at the mill, so I can't do it," Beau said.

"I'm perfectly capable of going," Charlotte said. "I'll take one of Father's guns."

"And what about the man who was wounded yesterday?" Victoria asked. "What if he's still looking for you?"

"He doesn't have to look for me," Charlotte said. "He knows where I live."

Mother sipped at her coffee, then looked at Charlotte. "Please be careful, dear. And tell Mr. Jackson we want those chickens in two weeks' time."

Charlotte nodded and wondered how fast she could eat her grits.

The ride into Darien on Lucky lifted Charlotte's spirits. She'd tucked her pistol into the reticule around her wrist and gave herself over to the ride. The horse seemed as happy galloping along the road as she was, and they reached their destination much too soon. She slowed Lucky to a walk through town. This time in town, Charlotte saw a few people whose faces she recognized, and they greeted her. She noticed a few curious glances as she arrived at the feed store, dismounted, and tied Lucky to a hitching post.

Charlotte entered to find Mr. Jackson and a young Negro man standing on opposite sides of the counter—staring at a ledger. Jackson looked her direction and raised his brows.

"Miss Chapman. I'm happy to see you looking so well," he said.

"Thank you, Mr. Jackson," she said.

"I heard about all the commotion at your place yesterday," he said.

"You did?"

"Word gets around," he said. "Just glad to see you're fine."

"Yes, I am. Fine. We're all … fine," she said. "When you have a moment, I need to speak to you about our order."

"Sure thing. Just let me wrap things up with Parker here."

"I'm in no hurry," Charlotte said. She noticed that Jackson's cousin, Sam, was at some shelves on the side of the small store, straightening things so that they lined up precisely against the wall. He was mumbling to himself.

Charlotte made her way to a bookshelf near Sam. Jackson was rattling off numbers as his finger ran down a page in the ledger.

"All the figures are right here, Parker. You can read 'em for yourself."

The black man called Parker stared hard at the paper, but shook his head. "Seems like too much, Mr. Jackson.".

"Look," Jackson huffed out impatiently. "You got five acres you're trying to cover. Takes you about thirty thousand seeds to cover an acre ..."

Charlotte heard Sam murmur, "Thirty thousand, thirty thousand. One hundred fifty thousand ..."

"And you divide that by two thousand seeds per pound ... giving you fifteen pounds ..."

"Fifteen, fifteen, fifteen, fifteen."

Jackson seemed oblivious to Sam's nattering. "You got about fifty-six pounds a' seed in a bushel— I'm charging you two dollars a bushel. So you can see right here you're needin' three bushels to plant your fields. That's six dollars."

Sam shook his head slowly back and forth, then spoke more softly. "One and a half bushels, one and a half, fifteen into fifty-six is one and a half."

Parker looked at him. "And then you's charging me on top a' that?"

Jackson nodded. "Got to, Parker. I'm basically lending you the money for your seed. The only collateral you got is your land. I take a quarter of the cash value of your crop when you harvest. Then there's the matter of the interest on that loan, but again thirty percent is standard practice."

Parker looked upset and undecided at the same time. Jackson sighed heavily. "It's up to you. But I don't see how you're going to get any planting done unless you accept the terms."

Parker finally nodded. "Fine."

Jackson smiled and tapped a finger on the bottom of the ledger. "I need your name right there to make it legal."

Parker scratched out something on the paper and shoved the book back at Jackson, who seemed to pretend not to notice the black man's irritation. "I'll get the seed as soon as I help Miss Chapman."

"No, Mr. Jackson, please help him first. I'm fine to wait," Charlotte said.

Jackson frowned. "No, he can wait …"

"Please. He was here first," Charlotte said.

Parker nodded at Charlotte. "Thank you, ma'am."

Sam finished his task and made his way back across the store and Charlotte followed him.

"Sam, isn't it?" she asked.

He didn't make eye contact with her, but bobbed his head. "Sam. That's right. Sam."

"I couldn't help but overhear your figures, Sam," she said. "It sounds as if you disagree with Mr. Jackson's numbers."

Sam went to the ledger on the counter and flipped it open. Charlotte glanced toward the direction Jackson and Parker had gone but then turned her attention to the columns of figures on the page. Sam started his litany of numbers.

"Two thousand per pound, fifteen pounds is thirty thousand seeds … fifty-six pounds in a bushel, fifty-six divided by fifteen is three point seven three. One-quarter bushel for an acre. One and a third bushels, not three. Not three … not three …"

Charlotte ran her finger down the numbers and could see not only was the total wrong, but the interest charges at the bottom of the page were more than fifty percent.

She could hear Jackson coming back into the store. Sam heard him too and turned away from the counter just as Jackson entered. He smiled at Charlotte.

"I apologize for the delay, but it's always the same thing with those people. They want something for nothing. Now what can I do for you?"

"My mother sent me to see if we might get a quicker delivery on the chickens, Mr. Jackson. She was rather put out with a month's wait."

Jackson slowly nodded his head. "I will certainly see what I can do to hurry it along, Miss Chapman. My supplier is in Savannah, but maybe there is transport coming sooner. I'll wire and check."

"Thank you," she said. "She also inquired as to the charges. I'm afraid neither my sister nor I asked you about that."

He frowned. "It will be the standard cost of doing business, Miss Chapman. If I need to carry the terms, the plantation will be charged two percent on the balance."

"Two percent?"

He nodded, then smiled. "Anything else I can help you with today?"

Charlotte stared at him for a moment. "No. Thank you."

Charlotte made her way to the door, but not before she heard Sam reciting in his monotone voice, "Two percent, two percent, two … two … two."

CHAPTER THIRTY-FIVE

Charlotte stepped outside the feed store at the same time a young couple came down the street in a small buggy. The man pulled the buggy over to the side of the road, jumped down, and offered his hand to his lady. As they strolled down the boardwalk, they seemed like two people who didn't have a care in the world. Charlotte's thoughts turned to Elijah. She wondered how far he'd made it on his journey back to St. Louis—if he was on the train out of Savannah by now. The thought that he might get some much-needed rest appeased her worry for the moment. Pensive, she didn't notice Dooley approaching.

"Miss Charlotte?"

"Hello, Mr. Dooley," she said.

He frowned. "You made it here awful quick."

"I'm sorry?"

"They only just brought the body into town less than an hour ago," he said.

"I don't know what you're talking about," Charlotte said, though her heart had stuttered at the mention of a body.

"Old Man Grice found a buggy in his field this morning with a dead man inside," he said. "Scuttlebutt is he's the missing man from the big dustup at your place yesterday."

Charlotte's jaw dropped, but when she didn't say anything, Dooley went on. "The sheriff made mention he'd have someone ride out to the plantation and bring back one of you to identify him."

"I just happened to be here to check on an order," she said. "Where did you say they brought the man?"

Dooley pointed down the road. "Undertaker's place is the last one on the right. Do you want me to come with you?"

She shook her head. "No, but thank you for offering. I'll be fine."

Sheriff Dan Klein stood silently by and watched as the undertaker, Horace Larson, led Charlotte to a table where the man she knew as Mr. Newton lay dead.

She stared down at his slack, pasty white face and shuddered. "That's him. Mr. Newton. He's the one who got away yesterday."

"We figured that was the case," Sheriff Klein said. He approached the body and peeled back his shirt to expose a tattoo inked right over his heart. The black star had the letters *GAR* inscribed in the middle. "Found the same thing on the other two."

Klein looked toward two other bodies, covered by gray tarps, lying on similar tables in the room. Charlotte followed his gaze, then turned back to Newton.

"What does that mean?"

"Grand Army of the Republic." Sheriff Klein sneered. "Union boys and their symbols to prove they fought. You won't catch us Southern men doing that. God knows we were on the right side of the war. Don't need to desecrate our bodies to say so."

Klein flipped Newton's shirt back into place. "He ran but he didn't get too far," he said with some satisfaction. "You and your family can rest easier knowing he's dead."

"How do you let *their* families know what's happened?" Charlotte asked.

Klein shrugged. "I don't have enough information on any of them to find out who their next of kin are."

"But people will start to worry about them—wonder where they are," she said.

"They should have thought of that when they set out to catch you!"

"I suppose that's true, but it's not their families' fault. Sometimes people make choices that cause others to suffer ..." She stopped. No one was more surprised than she was when her eyes welled. The sheriff and undertaker both looked away as she wiped at a single tear rolling down her cheek.

"What happens to them now?" Charlotte asked.

"There's a potter's field outside town. We'll bury 'em there," Sheriff Klein said. He nodded to Charlotte. "I appreciate you coming here, Miss Chapman. Saved us the trouble of bringing someone from the plantation to look at the body."

He left, but Charlotte remained behind, staring at Newton. Horace cleared his throat. "If it's worrying you, Miss Chapman, you should know I'm neither judge nor jury here. They'll be treated with dignity and respect until they're placed in their final resting place."

She looked at him. "It doesn't bother you they fought for the Union, Mr. Larson?"

"I had an uncle, two cousins, and a best friend who fought for the Union. They felt God was on their side just as we felt He was on ours. I'm not here to make judgments—just to ensure respect for the dead. Even for those who go into the potter's field."

She nodded but still didn't move. He smiled. "Surely you have someplace more cheerful to be, Miss Chapman. I'll let you get on home now."

He was prompting her to leave. *Someplace cheerful ... Cheerful?* Charlotte had the sudden realization she didn't want to go home. And the irony of that revelation wasn't lost on her. She should ride straight back to the plantation and let them know Newton was no longer a threat. She should—but she wasn't going to. At least not yet.

"Mr. Larson, you wouldn't happen to know Bobby and Betty Ann ... Betty Ann ... umm ..."

"Wilkes," he said.

"Do you know where they live?"

"Head about a mile east of town, then left at the biggest magnolia tree in the county. Gotta be ninety feet tall. Head about a quarter mile down the road. Theirs is the white house with green trim," he said. "You can't miss it."

CHAPTER THIRTY-SIX

There was a wine cellar under the kitchen of the house. The access door was nearly invisible in a kitchen wall; the entrance, cut along the lines of intricate wallpaper, would surely be missed by a casual observer. The room was long and narrow with a dirt floor. The ceiling was shored up by rough-hewn beams, and dozens of oak barrels, lying on their sides, lined the walls. Two small oil lamps brought warmth to the otherwise damp space and gave it an intimate air. Near the stairs from the kitchen were two rows of wooden shelves that held the other liquors of the house. Bottles of whiskey and rum, with glass decanters and empty pitchers standing ready to transport the wine from cellar to table whenever the need arose.

Suzanne stood with Beau between the golden-colored barrels.

"I wonder if Charlotte and her Yankee freebooter had a good laugh at our expense," Beau said. He leaned down to the closest spigot on a barrel and slipped a glass beneath it. With the twist of a lever on top, wine began to flow into his glass.

"Deceitful. Both of them. Keeping his identity a secret from us," Suzanne said.

"I should have known he was a Federal." Beau took a long drink of his wine. Then he said, "Word's going to get out she came home with a Yankee. Danced with a Yankee right in our own home. We look like fools."

"He's a Yankee, but he killed two Yankees on our porch," Suzanne said. "Somehow, she will end up being elevated in the town's eyes. She'll be the returning war hero who managed to turn a former Union soldier against men of his own political persuasions."

"I see what you're saying. To everyone she's still John Chapman's darling daughter, who can do no wrong," Beau said. "I think if we let it slip that she was convicted of trying to kill a Yankee congressman, the town would throw her a parade."

"I still can't believe she didn't tell us any of that," Suzanne said with a shake of her head. "She always was guarded about things—had secrets I suspect only Chessie knew, but I'll admit I'm surprised she could lie straight to our faces."

"Makes you wonder what else she's lying about," Beau said.

"If you're referring to her memory, I still don't think she lied about that," Suzanne said. "She seems too genuine."

Beau smiled. "And we don't? I think Charlotte would beg to differ."

Her response was a small smile. Then she frowned and shook her head. "But what if the music box was just the beginning of more memories? What if tomorrow, the day after, or next week, all her memories come crashing back? Then where are we?"

"You own the plantation. You decide who lives here and—who doesn't."

"I can't throw her out, Beau. Can you imagine the reaction we'd get in town if we turned John's daughter out of her childhood home? We'd be ostracized and probably have to pay the same for goods and services as the freedmen. The interest alone would sink us. No one would bring their rice here for processing, just on principle, because we pushed her away."

"Then we're stuck," Beau said. "Living on pins and needles that she'll remember it all."

"Never stuck, my boy. There are solutions to every problem."

"Does that mean you've come up with a solution?" Beau asked.

Suzanne sighed. "Not yet. But I need to. The incident with the music box has been her only real memory so far, but we can't live on the assumption she'll never remember anything else. We need to have a plan in place."

"Speaking of plans," Beau said, "I've managed to round up three more farmers to use the mill to cultivate their rice."

"Good. How many acres are you talking about?"

"Three darkies got a hundred acres each from the Standish place."

Suzanne shook her head in disgust. "Micah Standish loses his plantation because of the war fought over darkies, and the government gives away his land. Makes you wonder where the justice is, doesn't it?"

"It's not fair, but for us, it's profitable. We never got business from Standish before—he did all his own cultivating. At least this lines our coffers with more money, and we can hire more workers to put rice in those last fifty acres we haven't harrowed before now."

Suzanne's mind wandered as Beau continued. "Within a year— two at most, we should be back to where we were before the war," Beau was saying.

"Mother? Have you heard a word I've said?"

"I've been thinking about Charlotte," Suzanne said. "And I think we've been looking at our little problem the wrong way."

"How so?"

"As I said, we plan. We prepare for the day Charlotte's memory returns by protecting ourselves in the meantime," she said.

"How do we do that?"

"By changing the tide of public opinion. People don't generally want to stay where they aren't wanted."

The undertaker had been right. The Wilkes house was easy for Charlotte to find. Betty Ann opened the door with her son clinging to her leg. She squealed with delight when she saw Charlotte on her doorstep.

"You came to call?"

"I hope you don't mind," Charlotte said.

But Betty Ann was already pulling her into the modest house and closing the door. "Mind? Don't be ridiculous, Char. I'm so happy to see you. Come in and tell me all about being home. How has it been? Has anything jogged your memory? I've been completely cooped up here at home. Anything interesting happen?"

Anything interesting? Elijah was shot the morning after the dance. Three men who came to lunch are dead.

Charlotte, relieved Betty Ann didn't seem to know of the latest developments at the plantation, picked the easiest question to answer.

"I had a small memory," Charlotte said. "I remembered the tune my jewelry box played."

"Oh! The one your pa gave you for your birthday," Betty Ann said.

"Yes."

"That's so wonderful! It's a start, isn't it?"

"I hope so," Charlotte said, following Betty Ann farther into the house. She took in the main room. A chintz sofa and two worn chairs were grouped together on a huge braided rug. Some children's toys were scattered around the room, but the main thing that caught Charlotte's eye were the plants. They were near the windows, lined up against walls, even plants tall enough to be staked.

"I'm sorry about the mess," Betty Ann said. "We've just got one maid now and it's hard for her to keep up with everything."

"Your plants are—extraordinary, Betty Ann," Charlotte said.

Betty Ann smiled. "I love to grow things. Always have." Betty Ann led Charlotte farther into the room. "These are all seedling plants I sell for gardens. Practically everyone is growing food again now—and by keeping it all indoors like this, I get a jump start on the planting season."

"What a smart idea," Charlotte said as she sat down on the sofa.

"Bobby's the one who thought of it," Betty Ann said. She grinned. "I guess you could say he planted the seed. He's always telling me I don't just have green thumbs, I have eight green fingers too. I don't think he intended for me to start my own little business, but we can use the extra money these days."

"How is Bobby? I hope I'm not disturbing him …"

"Sometimes I think disturbing him might be good, you know? Get him out of that back room."

A woman entered the room. At first glance, Charlotte thought her to be older, but realized she was probably only in her midforties. It was her countenance that aged her—sad eyes, rounded shoulders, an air of defeat. "Good day to you, Charlotte."

Charlotte nodded. "Hello."

"This is my mother-in-law, Frances Wilkes," Betty Ann said. "You used to know that."

"My husband and I were friends of your family," Frances said.

"It's nice to see you," Charlotte said.

Frances frowned at her. "Robert is dead."

"I'm sorry?"

"You wouldn't know it since you were gone. Even if you had your memories, you wouldn't know my husband, Robert, died at Chancellorsville in May of '63."

"I'm sorry," Charlotte said.

Frances nodded. "I am too." She looked at the little boy, still clinging to Betty Ann's leg. "You come with Granny now, Bubba, and let your mama have some time to talk with Miss Charlotte."

The little boy shook his head.

"It's all right, Frances," Betty Ann said. "He can stay."

"Indulge a child, spoil a child," Frances said. She crossed the room and plucked little Bubba from the floor. The boy started to cry, but Frances settled him on her hip and left the room. Betty Ann forced a smile.

"I wish you could remember how nice she used to be," Betty Ann said. "Before the war took everything away from her."

"I'm sorry about your father-in-law," Charlotte said.

"And I'm sorry 'bout your daddy. I told you at his burial, but I felt like I should say it again anyway. You were so broken up about him—but then why wouldn't you be? There was nothing that man wouldn't do for you. My goodness, his face lit from the inside out whenever you walked into a room."

Betty Ann's forehead creased to a deep frown. "I still can't believe it was Lewis who shot him." She shook her head. "I don't think any of us could have imagined he had all that hate inside."

"I don't suppose you know anything about my real mother?"

Betty Ann sighed and shook her head. "Other than she died giving birth to you, no."

"The only thing I know is her name was Marie," Charlotte said, "and I practically had to drag that information out of Chessie."

Betty Ann smiled. "I would have loved to see your reunion with her. She must have been so happy to see you."

Charlotte shook her head. "I get the impression she isn't happy with me at all."

Betty Ann looked perplexed. "I can't believe that. She loved you like you were her own child. Chessie's the one who always fixed up our skinned knees and bruised shins. In fact, Chessie's the one who stitched your shoulder closed that time you ripped it on that tree branch."

Charlotte reached up to her shoulder, and she felt the scar under her fingers. "I wondered how I got that scar."

Betty Ann grinned. "You and I and Bobby were by the river. He was teasing me something fierce and said I was the slowest girl in McIntosh County and challenged me to a race. You were bound and determined for me to win, if for no other reason than to shut him up with all his pontificating about how fast he was … so when we started to run, you jumped on Bobby's back and he carried you like that till he ran under a tree and a low-hanging branch tore through your shoulder."

"Who won the race?"

Betty Ann giggled. "I did. He declared the prize to be a kiss from the loser and that was the first time he ever kissed me."

Charlotte laughed. "Sounds like the loser got what he wanted."

"He did. Got the kiss and the girl forever," she said. "Those were good days between us."

Betty Ann suddenly sobered. "I've been so angry at you, Char. So—angry and hurt. All we went through together and you didn't even tell me good-bye—never said you were leaving. You just—left."

"I'm sorry, Betty Ann. I wish I could explain it …"

"You and Bobby were all I had left here," she said, "and you *knew* that. Daddy lost his smithy shop halfway through the war and moved the whole family to Savannah. Then Bobby left to fight and a year later you said good-bye to me after your pa's funeral—but it wasn't the kind of good-bye that says I won't see you again for years, or even forever. It was a good-bye as if we'd see each other the next day or the next week. I didn't even know you were gone—I had to hear it from one of the slaves at Fox Burrows."

"Fox Burrows?"

"The Wilkes family plantation. Foxes everywhere when they built the place. Anyway, Bobby and his daddy had gone off to fight the Yankees, so Frances and I were left trying to keep things running at home, and one of our slaves told me they'd heard from one of your slaves that you'd run off.

"I didn't for one second believe it," Betty Ann said. "I high-tailed it over to see for myself, and Victoria told me it was true."

"I'm so sorry, Betty Ann. I can't tell you what I was thinking or why I did what I did … but I am sorry I hurt you."

Betty Ann studied her for a moment. "You know what? I don't care about that anymore. Here you are. Back in my life again."

Betty Ann got up and went to a curio cabinet against the wall. She opened the glass and pulled out a silver-framed daguerreo-type. She handed it to Charlotte. "Look. Our wedding day."

Charlotte studied the picture and was astonished to see herself standing next to the bride and groom. "I was in your wedding."

"Who else would have been my maid of honor? You were the reason I met Bobby in the first place. I never would have been in the same social hemisphere as he was, if it hadn't been for our friendship."

"It's so strange to see myself then," Charlotte said. "I've almost started to think of it as my other life."

"It kind of is that way now, isn't it?"

"Yes. I'm not sure what I expected when I finally figured out where I was from ..."

"At least it seems like your stepmother has buried the hatchet," Betty Ann said.

"What do you mean?"

Betty Ann shrugged. "The lovely party she had for you. They were so gracious about having you back. Made me believe they were actually happy you were home."

"I don't understand," Charlotte said.

Betty Ann made a face. "I'm sorry. I shouldn't have said that. Me and my big mouth."

"No, no. Tell me ...," Charlotte said.

"Let's just say that Miss Suzanne was always pleasant when your daddy was around," Betty Ann said, "but when he wasn't, she wasn't the sweetest thing in the world to you."

Charlotte frowned. "We didn't get along?"

Betty Ann shook her head. "Not even a little bit. And then when your daddy left for the war ... things got even uglier. They didn't have to put on a show for him anymore. Sometimes you'd ride over to Fox Burrows to see me, hide out until the dust would settle from your latest go-round with Beau or Suzanne."

"Was it always that way?"

"For as long as I can remember," Betty Ann said. "I tried to get you to talk to your daddy about it, but you wouldn't. I don't think you wanted him worrying about you.

"Here, I'll take that," Betty Ann said, holding out her hand for the daguerreotype Charlotte still held.

"You were a beautiful bride," Charlotte said. "And Bobby looked very handsome."

Betty Ann stared at the picture. "The girl in this photograph could not have imagined the life I'm living right now."

She looked up with a quick frown. "Don't get me wrong. I love Bobby as much today as I did the day we married," she said. "But all the changes since the war have made it hard for him to even want to get up in the morning. I grew up in a house half this size, but Bobby grew up privileged, like you. I think the day they lost the plantation was harder for Bobby than the day he lost his leg. Fox Burrows was his legacy—little Bubba's legacy. That's all gone now."

"It must be hard for all of you," Charlotte said.

"The world's a tough place right now. Not just for us, but for lots of folks," Betty Ann said. "Suzanne has kept your daddy's place alive and thriving. I don't know how she's doing it, but she is. That's something in these times."

"Knowing how they feel about me now, I'm not sure I can stay there," Charlotte said.

"I think your daddy was the problem. He loved you more and they knew it. Now that he's gone, I'd figure out how to get along with them, do things their way. It's too hard out there."

"That was my hope," Charlotte said.

"Unless of course you find a man that can give you the kind of life to which you've become accustomed. *Do* you have any husband prospects?"

Charlotte smiled. "No, I don't."

"What about that handsome Mr. Hale I saw you dancing with?"

"He's gone," Charlotte said, with a pang of regret she wouldn't admit to Betty Ann or anyone else. "He left just yesterday, as a matter of fact."

Betty Ann looked disappointed. "Oh. Too bad. I declare, unless I'm in town to hear the latest gossip, the whole world could be on the verge of collapse and I wouldn't know it."

Charlotte thought of the latest gossip that would be making its way around town and remembered she had a message to deliver to her family.

"I should be getting back home." Charlotte stood. "Thank you for the visit. I hope we can do it again soon."

Betty Ann got up and gave her a quick hug. "I know it's nothing as grand as Fox Burrows," Betty Ann said, "but if you ever need a place to run to till the dust settles, you're always welcome here."

CHAPTER THIRTY-SEVEN

When Charlotte entered the house, she heard voices coming from the parlor. She crossed the foyer, thinking she'd deliver the news about Newton to her mother, and then since she hadn't had a bite since breakfast, she would find something to eat. Maybe she could convince Juba to make her a middle-of-the-day snack.

Her mother was in the parlor with two women. Charlotte vaguely remembered their faces from the homecoming party, but for the life of her, couldn't remember if they'd been introduced or not. Mother turned at her entrance and smiled.

"Ah. Charlotte. I'm glad to see you're finally home," she said. "I was beginning to worry."

"I'm sorry, Mother," Charlotte said. "I didn't intend to stay gone so long."

One of the women, thick around the middle, with deep-set lines around her eyes, lifted her brows. "At least it wasn't three years this time."

Her mother laughed politely. "Very true, June, very true." Charlotte could see she was not amused. "Charlotte, this is June Clifton and Hattie Bedford. They came from town to let me know the third man who tried to attack us was found dead."

Charlotte nodded. "I was just coming in to tell you."

"So you already knew it."

"Yes, I went to ... identify him at the undertaker's earlier today. It was definitely him."

"And that was ... how long ago?"

Charlotte saw the two women trade knowing looks.

"A few hours ago, I suppose," Charlotte said. "I went to have a visit with Betty Ann after and ..."

"I know this entire thing has been very hard on you, dear, but I would think you'd have come straight home to tell us you were safe before you went on a social call. After all, we *have* been in fear for your life," her mother said. "And when you didn't turn up sooner, I was thinking the worst—until June and Hattie here arrived to dispel my fears with the news from town."

All three women looked at her expectantly, and she felt withered by their judgment.

"You're right, of course," Charlotte said. "I apologize. It was selfish of me."

Her mother's glare was cold, but her tone pleasant. "Apology accepted. It's all over now. And we'll sleep so much better tonight knowing there isn't another Yankee scoundrel lurking about the plantation waiting to do you harm." She smiled and it seemed frozen on her face.

"Are you going to join us, Charlotte?" June asked. "We'd love a chance to catch up with how you're doing. Other than this terrible ordeal you've just gone through, of course."

The look on her mother's face was anything but inviting and the very last thing Charlotte wanted to do was sit in the parlor with those women and be grilled about her recent past.

"I hope you won't think me rude if I decline, Mrs. Clifton," she said. "I have a bit of a headache and I think I'll go up to my room and lie down for a while."

"I'm sorry you aren't feeling well," June said. "Another time, then."

Charlotte nodded. "Yes. Another time."

"Go along, dear, and get some rest," Suzanne said. "I'll check on you later."

Hours later, Charlotte sat near the French doors in her room and stared out as the sun sank into the water. She heard the door to her room open, then close. She turned to see Chessie carrying a dinner tray toward her.

"I'm not hungry," she said.

"Den don't eat it," Chessie retorted.

Charlotte watched as she put the tray on the dressing table. "Did Mother ask you to bring that up to me?"

"No. Juba did," Chessie said. She turned to shuffle back across the room.

"I'm still not going to eat." Charlotte felt as irritable as she sounded to her own ears.

"Don't care one way or t'other," Chessie said.

Charlotte had had enough of the mystery, innuendos, and barely veiled hostility from Chessie.

"You raised me, took care of me." She could hear her voice rising in pitch and volume, the tone accusatory. "You probably held me when I was sick. You *should* care!"

Chessie turned, and for the second time, Charlotte saw raw emotion on the old woman's face—unveiled anger. Though Chessie didn't say a word, she trembled under the weight of her own silence.

Charlotte continued. "I want to know why people tell me we were close, while you barely look at me. Won't talk to me. I don't know what happened between us, because I can't remember!"

Chessie crossed a few steps back toward her. "How *nice* dat must be for you not to remember. Not to know all the ugly that happened."

"I want the truth! You owe me the truth!" Charlotte shouted.

Chessie's dark eyes flashed again with emotion, and her top lip curled back with contempt. "I had one livin' relative in dis world, and you took him from me!" Her next words seemed to tear straight out of her soul. "You took my grandson to auction!"

While Chessie seemed to heave out a pent-up breath with the statement, Charlotte felt as if all her air had been sucked out of the room.

"Dat's why I gots a problem with you and things ain't the same between us," Chessie said. "You think God take yo' daddy, and you gonna play God and take my Kitch 'cause he friends wit' da man who kilt da master! I owed you da truth?" Chessie gave her a curt nod. "Consider my debt paid." She turned and left the room.

Charlotte stared at the closed door, her mind refusing to accept what she'd just heard. *She's lying ... I could never do such a thing. Never.* But in her heart, she knew Chessie hadn't lied. What possible reason would she have to make up such a thing? She could have blamed the chasm between them on anything else. Maybe Charlotte had been a spoiled brat—disrespectful, ungrateful. Didn't say good-bye when she left home—anything. But not this. Not something so hateful and unforgiveable.

No wonder she looks at me the way she does. No wonder she can barely tolerate being in the same room with me.

Charlotte went to the dressing table and sat down. The food on the tray had cooled, the gravy congealed and unappealing. She had no appetite anyway. She picked up her brush and tugged it through her long hair. The face staring back at her was once more the face of a stranger. With this new knowledge of her past, she studied her reflection and wondered what she was really capable of doing. She'd proven she had a temper, proven when backed into a corner that she was capable of some truly terrible thoughts. She couldn't even blame her brokenness on the self she couldn't remember. The woman she was at this moment was also broken, also capable of making decisions pushed by fear and self-preservation. Her own reflection made her feel sick, and she pushed to her feet, crossed to the window, and looked outside. The moon glow made everything look so calm and peaceful—the opposite of how she felt. She thought about the heartache she'd caused Chessie—*"All the ugly that happened."* Charlotte knew nothing could ever make up for her past cruelty to the woman who'd raised her, knew that a violation of that magnitude could only be forgiven supernaturally. She hoped someday she'd be able to look Chessie in the eye again without seeing all the pain she'd put there. But in the meantime, she would give Chessie as much distance as she wanted between them. It seemed like the very least she could do.

CHAPTER THIRTY-EIGHT

Elijah tied his horse to a hitching post in midtown St. Louis. Every muscle in his body ached, every bone punished beyond repair. The wound in his belly made him feel as if he were on fire as he pushed through the revolving door of a Gothic-style four-story building. His bearded, ragged appearance garnered more than a few looks from people in the lobby. His shirt bore the hallmarks of heavy bleeding, and he hadn't slept properly in days. The constant pain had worn him down to a shadow of his former self. Suffice to say he was given a wide berth as he made his way across the marble floor. *At least this wound is coming in handy.* He stopped when he found what he was looking for. The specific office was well marked with a name etched into the glass of the interior door. He didn't bother to knock before he entered.

Rand Prescott, Mercy's former fiancé, sat behind a desk cluttered with files and paperwork. Only a few weeks before, Elijah had seen him standing in the dark outside Gratiot Street Prison the night Mercy was released. Elijah could see the shock on Rand's face at his presence.

"Hale?"

Elijah crossed to the desk and braced himself on the edge of the fine cherrywood. "We need to talk."

"What's *happened* to you?"

"Mercy."

Rand stood. "What about her?"

"You were right about her." Elijah put a hand on his belly wound. "All told, the woman's tried to kill me three times. I was lucky to get away when I did."

Rand frowned. "I don't understand. I thought you were trying to help her. Why—"

"She hates me. Sees me as the reason her life fell apart," Elijah said. His face broke out in a sweat and he glanced around. "I need to sit."

Rand went to grab a chair from the corner of the room. "Did you take her to the state line?" he asked. "That *was* the plan—right?"

"We went north, figured it would throw off anyone hunting her," Elijah said.

Rand put the chair behind Elijah, who promptly lowered himself into it. His relief wasn't an act, and nor was the grimace on his face from the pain.

"And are there people ... *hunting* her?"

Elijah slanted a look up at him. "You know the answer to that. You probably even know the price on her head."

Rand moved back around his desk, though he didn't sit. He faced Elijah but crossed his arms across his chest.

"I don't know anything about any of it," Rand said.

Elijah studied him. "I came here to tell you I was wrong about Mercy. I shouldn't have interfered with her hanging. I should have let the judge's sentence stand. But I felt too guilty about my part in exposing her as a Confederate."

"Her own words in her journal exposed her," Rand said.

"Words she'd never have written if I hadn't told her who she was. Must have been so confusing for her ... but it doesn't matter. I'm trying to tell you I'm on your side now. I can see she can't be trusted."

"I'm through with that chapter of my life, Hale. I don't even think about her much anymore."

Elijah indicated his bloody middle. "I'm afraid I still do—think about her, that is. Kind of hard not to right now. She's gotten under my skin."

"She's good at that." Rand eyed the wound. "Have you seen a doctor?"

"Not yet. I left her on the trail while she slept and came here to say my piece. I was going to give you whatever information I had on her location—but you say you're not involved in looking for her."

"I'm not."

"Do you know who is?"

Rand hesitated. "You want me to believe you're going to help the bounty hunters get her?"

"That *is* where we believe the justice to be—isn't it?"

"Does she know about your change of heart?"

Elijah heard the skepticism in Rand's voice and saw the confusion on his face.

"She forced my change of heart," Elijah said. "As I said, she blames me for her turn of fortune."

"Even after what you did to get her sentence commuted?"

Elijah nodded. "She says I forced her into the rash actions that got her arrested. I brought to light her Confederate past—insisted she tell you the truth …"

"Which she didn't do."

"No. She didn't," Elijah said. "She loved you. Wanted to be your wife. Anyone could see she was crazy about you. And to be blunt, anyone could see by looking at the two of you together you felt the same about her. She had a glorious future in front of her. I should have known she would have done anything to keep you from finding out about her past. She was desperate, and desperate people do and say all sorts of things in the name of love."

Rand took a moment to answer. "Yes," he said. "I think you're right."

The door to the office opened and a beautiful young woman stepped inside. She wore the latest fashion, from her dress to her hat, and was the very picture of wealth and privilege. She stopped when she saw the man in the chair.

"I'm in the middle of something right now, Cora."

Elijah struggled to his feet and turned toward her. "Hello, Cora."

It seemed to take her a moment to realize whom she was staring at. "As I live and breathe," she said. "Captain Elijah Hale."

Elijah was completely surprised at her appearance. The last time he remembered seeing Cora Vaughn was at a pheasant hunt hosted by the Prescott family, where she'd insisted he give her shooting lessons.

"I must say I thought we *might* meet again someday." She moved across the office toward Rand but kept her eyes on Elijah. "My goodness, Elijah, but you look simply dreadful."

Elijah forced a smile. "You look just as lovely as always, Cora."

"Thank you. If I'm glowing, it's all because of my fiancé here. I'm simply brimming with happiness."

"Fiancé?"

Was it Elijah's imagination, or did he see Rand flinch? Cora tucked her arm through Rand's. "Yes." She nestled closer to Rand. "You didn't share our good news with Elijah?"

"We've been discussing other things, Cora," Rand said. "Our engagement news wasn't the first thing that came to mind."

"Congratulations," Elijah said.

"Thank you," Cora practically purred. "It's an exciting time for me. Us. I'm marrying the man of my dreams." She looked up at Rand adoringly, but Elijah could see Rand's obvious discomfort at her display.

"Anyway, Elijah, I'm so sorry to have to spirit him away from you, but we have an appointment to keep with the officiant of our ceremony. Not that we're going to do anything on a grand scale, mind you. Just our families and close friends. After what that traitor Mercy put Rand through, we didn't want him to relive the planning and staging of a big wedding."

"He doesn't care about the details, Cora." Rand's tone was terse.

Cora smiled sweetly. "Of course not," she said. "We do have a full afternoon, darling. Don't forget, after the meeting we have the fund-raiser for your father." She looked at Elijah. "Did Rand tell you Charles is running for Senate?"

"No, he didn't," Elijah said.

She rolled her eyes but smiled. "He hates to brag." Then her smile dropped as she looked him over from head to toe. "Forgive me for saying so, Elijah, but you do look as though you could use a nice, long rest. Maybe a bath, a shave." She grimaced when she looked pointedly at his shirt. "A clean shirt wouldn't hurt either."

Rand put a hand on her arm. "I think you've made your point." He turned to Elijah. "But she is right, I think. It would do you good to see to some of those creature comforts. Maybe take a room somewhere. In fact, I'd recommend you go to the Lindell Hotel. It's not far—just over on East Sixth Street. I think you might find what you need there."

Cora brightened. "Oh, the Lindell is a beautiful hotel. In fact, my father has his lunch in the dining room five days a week. Noon on the dot … There he sits with his paper and cigar."

"Every day like clockwork," Rand reiterated.

"Tell them you're a friend of Howard Vaughn and I'm sure they'll treat you right, Elijah."

"Thanks for the tip," Elijah said. He looked at Rand and saw the slightest nod.

Cora smiled. "That kind of routine is comforting—don't you think?"

"I suppose so," Elijah said. "I'll get out of your way now. I appreciate your time, Rand. You've been most helpful."

He was making his way out of the office when Cora stopped him.

"How is Mercy, Captain Hale? Still walking the earth?"

"As far as I know."

Cora lifted her brows. "Hmm. More's the pity."

Elijah drew in a steadying breath and walked out the door.

CHAPTER THIRTY-NINE

The Lindell Hotel covered most of a city block. Elijah went to the Sixth Street entrance, bent his arm across the unsightly stain in his shirt, and nodded at the doorman who opened the door, but not before he looked at Elijah with a dubious expression.

"Are you a guest at this hotel, sir?"

"Meeting a guest," he answered.

"Enjoy the hotel, sir."

The interior of the place was a blur of activity—bellmen pushing luggage carts, people checking in and checking out. As he entered the massive lobby, he saw a concierge stand, a corner where books, newspapers, and magazines were sold, a gift shop, and finally, through an arched doorway across from him, the dining room. Two women made their way past him, and he felt their judging eyes as they took in his disheveled appearance. He ducked into the men's washroom and took a good, long look at himself in the mirror. He'd wondered if he looked as bad as he felt—and the reflection confirmed it. He was a mess inside and out. Thanking the good Lord for water, he splashed it from a basin onto his face, then slicked back his hair with the palm of his hand. Standing on shaking legs, he was surprised at the heat coming off his face. His dark beard covered much of it, but the ruddy red of his cheeks wasn't from the sun. He fought the urge to sit and wait for a wave of weakness to pass but summoned all the energy he had left and pressed through the door. He stopped at the counter where a hatcheck girl was handing out tickets for hats, handbags, anything patrons didn't want to take to their tables.

Elijah smiled at her. "I'm sorry, but I seem to have lost my ticket."

She smiled back. "If you describe the item you checked, sir, I'll be happy to look for it."

An older couple stepped up beside Elijah. "I'll be right with you," the hatcheck girl said.

"Please, go ahead and help them," Elijah told her. "If you don't mind, I'll go look myself."

"Thank you," she said. "That will be most helpful." As she turned her attention back to the older couple, Elijah slipped into the recesses of the coatroom. He made his way along the racks, found what he needed. Elijah entered the dining room wearing a navy-blue jacket that covered the stain on his shirt just fine.

It was easy to spot Howard Vaughn. He sat alone at a corner table with his cigar and paper, just as Cora has described. He was a man who looked right at home in the wealthy surroundings.

Elijah drew himself up, squared his shoulders, denied the groan that was aching to come out from the pain he was in, and quickly crossed to Vaughn's table.

"Mr. Vaughn?"

Vaughn lowered the paper to look at Elijah. "Yes?"

"We have some business to discuss."

Vaughn put the paper down and stared at him. "Do I know you?"

"Elijah Hale. We've never been introduced," Elijah said.

Vaughn waved the hand holding his cigar dismissively. "If you have something to discuss with me, make an appointment with my secretary."

Elijah pulled out a chair and sat. "I don't think so."

Vaughn was taken aback. "I'm having my lunch, young man, and I'm not discussing business with someone who is so ill-mannered ..."

"I'm here to talk about Mercy."

Vaughn's brows shot up. "Now there's a name you don't hear in polite circles."

"What circles *do* you hear her name in?"

"What is this about?"

"What do you know about the bounty on Mercy's head?"

Vaughn stuffed his cigar back into his mouth and shook his head. "Nothing."

"I think you're lying."

Vaughn blew out a cloud of smoke and leaned toward Elijah. "You have a lot of nerve, Captain, especially since you were the one who thwarted justice for that girl."

"I'm flattered you remember me."

"I heard about your theatrics—how you convinced the judge to let Mercy put on some cockamamie shooting show. The two of you had it all planned out, did you?"

Elijah just shook his head. "She was innocent of the treason charge, and you know it."

"But guilty of so much more."

"Just by virtue of being from the South?"

"Good enough reason for me," Vaughn said.

"I saw Cora at Rand's office a little while ago," Elijah said. "I assume both of your families are pleased with their engagement."

"Not that it's any of your business, but yes. Yes, we're very pleased. Cora and Rand are a fine match. Always have been."

"Must have made things a little sticky at your house when Rand planned to marry Mercy."

"Sticky?"

"Hell hath no fury like a woman scorned," Elijah said.

"Are you suggesting my daughter has something to do with this bounty nonsense?"

Elijah shrugged. "Why not? She's a young woman used to getting her way."

"It's a ridiculous notion, and it would be completely pointless. Rand had broken things off with Mercy, and she was in prison! Even when her sentence was commuted, she was ordered to leave the state. No, no, Rand came to his senses long before that trial. I guarantee my daughter hasn't wasted two seconds worrying about Mercy."

"Cora tells me that Charles Prescott is making a run for the Senate," Elijah said.

"That's right. I can't think of a better man to hold office than Charles," Vaughn said. "He's perfect candidate material."

"Unless someone from his past comes out of the woodwork," Elijah said.

Vaughn grinned, waving his cigar back and forth. "I see what you're trying to say here, Hale, and you're way off base. Everyone who matters knows about Mercy and how Charles had to suffer through that embarrassment with Rand. Mercy can crawl out of that woodwork and it won't matter one iota."

"I heard it wasn't Charles who was so angry about the whole thing—it was his wife, Ilene."

"I wouldn't know about that."

"Then again, I image your wife didn't care much for Mercy either."

"No. Not much."

"So really, if you think about it, both sides of the family would be more than happy if she disappeared and never surfaced again."

A waiter hustled up to the table with a tureen of vegetables and a plate heaped with pork. "Your succotash, Mr. Vaughn. Anything else I can get for you?"

"I'll have my usual custard in a bit, Tommy."

"Yes, sir," he said, then glanced at Elijah. "And anything for your guest?"

"No. He's leaving," Vaughn said with a pointed look.

When the waiter was out of earshot and Elijah hadn't budged, Vaughn settled his cigar in an ashtray. "I'd like to eat my lunch in peace, Captain, if you don't mind."

"I think Mercy would like to live her life in peace, Mr. Vaughn," Elijah countered. "I know you had something to do with the bounty."

"Oh, do you?"

"My theory is you're the one who put up the money to have her hunted like a dog."

Vaughn puffed out another cloud of smoke. "Think whatever you want, Captain. The world revolves around proof, not theory. I sleep with a clear conscience at night."

"And how do you think you'll sleep when I tell you the men you hired are dead?"

"Dead?"

"All of them."

Vaughn puffed away on his cigar. "Men like that know the risks. I'm sorry for their families. Now, I would appreciate it if you would leave me to my lunch. Any more of this talk and it might spoil my appetite."

"Then I'm afraid this won't help much," Elijah said, drawing the faded yellow telegram from his shirt pocket. It was blood stained, wrinkled, but still legible. "I found this in the pocket of one of the dead men."

Vaughn looked down at the telegram, then shrugged. "So?"

"Did you know it's possible to trace the origin of this, Mr. Vaughn?"

"No …"

Lord, I'm already asking forgiveness for the lies I'm about to tell.

"It is. Something I learned in the military. It takes some effort, but it's entirely possible … and I intend to do that. Track down the person who sent this. They say dead men tell no tales, but the men who came after Mercy did quite a bit of talking after their deaths."

Vaughn's lunch grew cold in front of him. The ash on the end of his cigar lengthened and the man himself looked ill.

"What do you want, Hale?"

"I want the bounty canceled, or I will let every newspaper this side of the Mississippi know that Charles Prescott is involved in underhanded tactics that resulted in the deaths of former Union soldiers."

"Charles has no knowledge of any of this!" Vaughn slapped the table with his free hand. "It was our wives who hated Mercy with a passion. Ilene hates her for the humiliation she's caused the family, and my Betsy—well, she'll do almost anything to ensure Cora's happiness. A man has to see to his wife's happiness and well-being. It's the duty of a good husband."

"And I'm sure it won't hurt that if Charles is elected to the Senate, you'll be his right-hand man. But not if Mercy comes back into the picture—riles everything up again."

Vaughn started to pick up the telegram, but Elijah snatched it off the table and stuffed it back into his pocket.

"No more men. No more threats against Mercy," Elijah said. "Or I will go public with this telegram and I'll see you prosecuted for your part in Mercy's attempted murder."

"I don't care for threats, Captain," Vaughn said.

"It's not a threat, Mr. Vaughn. It's a promise—one I'll make good on with my last breath if I have to. As you said, the world revolves around proof." He patted his pocket. "Are we clear? Do I have your word?"

Vaughn nodded. "Yes. I don't ever want to hear that woman's name again."

Elijah pushed back from the table, used every ounce of strength he had left to make his exit back through the dining room. He peeled off the jacket he wore, handed it to the surprised hatcheck girl, and using the wall for support, made his way back across the thick carpets on the floor.

Elijah could see the world beyond the hotel door—the carriages, wagons, and horses. People walking to destinations he couldn't see and didn't care about. With his mission behind him, his body rapidly started to betray him. It felt as if a wick of flame had started deep inside and was spreading its fire from limb to limb. The growing heat told him his wound was infected.

Elijah stopped to rest, leaning heavily against ornate plaster molding along the wall. He needed to find a place to stay, out of the way of maids and bellmen and anyone else's prying eyes. His thoughts started to drift. Light in the room started to dim. He shook his head and pushed on along the wall until, in his haze, he saw a door. *Basement. Staff Only.* Incredibly, it opened and he shoved through. The steps were wooden, noisy. Elijah wondered if the shaking he felt was his legs or the wood. All efforts were poured into getting down those stairs to the concrete floor below. Rectangular windows near the ceiling provided meager light. Cobwebs across the bottom stair wrapped around his skin and gave him reassurance the room wasn't often visited. He looked around for the perfect place, even as he swayed on his feet, felt the light in the room grow dim. He made it to a corner—behind the huge boiler that heated the place in the winter but stood quiet at the moment. The light dimmed in his head again, the room spun, and Elijah never knew exactly when he hit the floor.

CHAPTER FORTY

It was Sunday morning and Charlotte knew she should leave her room, face the day with her head held high and her shoulders back—but she didn't want to. There was no one in the house she wanted to see.

Mother, Beau, and Victoria were going to church. For the first time since Charlotte arrived home, they would make the trip to town and sit down together in the family pew. Except Charlotte had no intention of going. She knew if she timed it right, made the announcement of her severe headache just moments before Beau was ready to drive the buggy away from the house, they wouldn't be inclined to argue with her. After all, her mother had made it clear several times how much she valued punctuality.

In the hall outside her room, Charlotte could hear Victoria complaining that she had a spot on one of her white gloves. Beau told her to find a new pair, but Victoria was irritated that Rose hadn't put them in the proper place. Sundays without the help were always so inconvenient. There was a rap on her door and Beau called out, "Leaving in five minutes, Charlotte." She heard him walk away and waited.

They were already in their carriage when Charlotte came out the front door and stopped at the top of the steps. Beau held the reins, her mother sat beside him, and Victoria sat in the back.

"Hurry up, Char!" Victoria said. She moved over a little on the bench seat to make room.

Mother swept her eyes over Charlotte's simple day dress. "That's not suitable for church, Charlotte," she said. "And where are your gloves?"

"I'm sorry, Mother, but I don't feel up to church this morning. I have a headache and I didn't sleep well last night ..."

Her mother waved off the rest of her apology. "That's typical. The town expects to see us all together this morning, and you're going to dash those expectations by being absent."

"I didn't mean to upset you," Charlotte said. "I suppose if you'd just wait a few minutes ..."

Suzanne shook her head. "I'm not going to walk into church late." She turned away from Charlotte to stare straight ahead. "Go ahead, Beau."

Beau glanced at Charlotte, then gave the reins a shake, and the horse was off. Charlotte watched them go with a sigh of relief. She thought of Betty Ann's advice to try and get along with her family. There was something she needed to do, and now that they were gone, she could do it without upsetting them.

Charlotte walked toward the colored camp to have a conversation with Isaac. On the whole, the place seemed to be deserted. She knew it was their only day off for the week, so she was surprised there wasn't more activity. She saw a couple of old men squatting in the grass cleaning and scaling fish, and shuddered, remembering her experience by the river. A young mother hung clothes on a line stretched between two houses, with a baby tucked into a sling against her chest. Charlotte approached the house where she thought Isaac had been staying, walked across the brittle front porch, and knocked on the door. But no one answered. The morning was quiet, the wind still, and the air sweet with the scent of magnolia, in such contrast to the bleak homes around her.

And then Charlotte heard it. Clapping ... and singing. She walked between two of the houses until she came to the back. Although she couldn't see the water, she knew it was there, surrounded by tall reeds and overgrown vegetation. But what caught her eye, about forty yards away, was a magnificent oak tree whose branches spread out to comfortably shade dozens of Negroes standing in a circle, dressed in their Sunday best, clapping hands to the sound of the music they made with their own voices. Charlotte could see Chessie and Rose in the circle with men, women, and children who swayed and bounced with the energy of their fast-paced spiritual. She could just make out the chorus: *"Ev'ry time I feel the Spirit moving in my heart, I will pray! Ev'ry time I feel the Spirit moving in my heart, I will pray."* They sounded so joyful; the words rolled off their tongues and they raised their eyes to heaven. She started toward them when a familiar voice stopped her.

"Miss Charlotte?"

She turned to see Isaac standing there. "Isaac. I was looking for you."

He shrugged. "Found me."

The song continued and Isaac glanced that way. *"Up-on the mountain my Lord spoke, out of His mouth came fire and smoke! Looked all around me, it looked so fine, till I asked my Lord if all was mine!"*

Charlotte inclined her head toward the singers. "It's a beautiful hymn."

He nodded. "Yassum."

"You didn't want to join them?"

Another shrug. "Didn't feel like it, I s'pose."

She nodded. "My family went to church without me this morning. Didn't feel like it either."

"Why was you lookin' fo' me?"

"I wanted to check on you, see how you're doing," Charlotte said.

Isaac shook his head. "You shouldn't worry 'bout me."

She took a step toward him, and he took a step back, looking again toward the group still singing under the tree. The gesture stopped her cold. Isaac knew—he knew about her actions before she left for the war. Why hadn't she thought of it before? The former slaves of the plantation who stayed on as paid laborers would have talked, would have told Isaac what they knew about the white woman he'd traveled with from Missouri to Georgia. He knew she'd sold a black man as if he were a piece of furniture or a field cow. He was probably ashamed to be seen talking to her. The thought made her heart sink.

"I'm sure you've heard Elijah had to leave?"

He nodded. "Yassum, I heared it."

"He was sorry he couldn't tell you good-bye himself, but he was in a bit of a ... hurry."

"I'm glad he kilt those men," Isaac said. "I'm glad he be dere to protect you."

She nodded. "Me, too."

"Dat part over den? No more men comin' to find you?"

"I hope it's over. It's one of the reasons Elijah left in such a rush. He wanted to make sure there will be no more men."

"Dat's good."

"Are you doing all right, Isaac? I know they moved you out to work in the fields and I was worried …"

"I be fine. Never been 'fraid a' hard work. Long as it be fair work, I'm fine."

She shook her head. "I can't imagine life here is anything like you hoped it would be …"

"Didn't imagine anything, Miss Charlotte. Didn't even know dis be da place we be stayin'."

"Down in the valley, when I feel weak, it's when the devil use'ly speaks."

"I'm afraid you might have heard some things about me," she said. "Some … bad things."

"Because he's crafty and full of lies, I need the Spirit to keep me wise."

"I hear some things," he admitted. "Not all of 'em good. Don't know if dey real."

She looked into eyes that had held nothing but trust for her. "Some of them probably are."

"Dey's sayin' you did angry-type screamin' at Rose," Isaac said. "Dat one true?"

Charlotte hesitated. "That is true."

He studied her. "Den you must a' had a good reason for doin' it."

"I did."

"Ev'ry time I feel the Spirit moving in my heart, I will pray."

He nodded. "Da folks 'round here say you is showin' yo'self to be just like you was before you left fo' the war. Filled with hate, mad at the world, and takin' it out on the black folks."

"Ev'ry time I feel the Spirit moving in my heart, I will pray."

"You know I don't remember what I was like before I left for the war," Charlotte said. "But that could be true as well."

"Dey say it was a colored man who shot and kilt yo' daddy," Isaac said. "Said he used to be yo' friend."

"That's what I hear too," she said.

"Dey also say you sold off a slave that was kin to Chessie."

"Chessie told me that just last night," Charlotte said. She swallowed, tried to hold back the tears that threatened. "I don't know who I am, Isaac. I don't know which Charlotte is the real me. The one who said and did those terrible things or ..." She looked at him. "Who do you say I am?"

Isaac studied her. "You own Lucky's heart. God made that fierce horse, who probably got more good judgment than most people. And I think he's right about you."

Charlotte swallowed the lump in her throat. She looked toward the people under the tree, swaying together, singing with joy.

"Ev'ry time I feel the Spirit moving in my heart, I will pray."

She turned her eyes back to Isaac. "I suddenly feel like going to church."

Charlotte and Isaac entered the church in the middle of Pastor Daniel Brady's sermon. The sanctuary was packed with people—all of them white. Charlotte saw the pastor's eyes widen just a bit at their appearance, and he stumbled over a word or two, but to his credit, continued to preach without more than those brief hesitations.

It had been enough, however, to pique the curiosity of the congregants. In the quiet of the place, clothing rustled, pew benches creaked and groaned as they turned in their seats to see the new arrivals to the service. Midway up the aisle, Charlotte saw Betty Ann's face register disappointment with a small sad shake of her head. Beside her on the aisle sat Bobby, his crutches propped against the side of the pew. A man in the pew to their left turned and glared at her with one eye, his other covered by a black patch. Charlotte, trying to ignore the hostility in the air, scanned for empty seats, then locked eyes with Mother, sitting between Victoria and Beau in a front pew. Her mother turned forward again, stiff-necked and rigid with disapproval.

Years of suffering through the war were in that church. People had lost loved ones, homes, dignity—even faith. Suddenly, Charlotte wanted to turn and run, but instead spotted enough room for the two of them a few rows up. She nodded to Isaac, but he was frozen. She had to give him a little push to get him moving. Seconds later, they slipped into the pew as the pastor talked on. An older woman who was seated in front of Charlotte half turned in her seat to offer a little nod and a smile. It was a brief moment of relief. Charlotte glanced sideways at Isaac and could see the boy taking everything in: the pastor's robes, the ornate cross on the wall, the mural of Jesus behind the altar. Though the church was lovely, Charlotte couldn't help but think about the service she'd just seen at the colored camp. The giant oak, and the songs of people who didn't seem like they had much to sing about—all under a blue cathedral sky.

Suzanne didn't hear one word the pastor said. She fumed through the rest of the service and prepared the speech she was going to give Charlotte the minute they walked outside the church doors. She'd always had a lot of nerve, would do things just to get a rise out of her—but this was going too far. Dragging that little darky into the house of the Lord! It was a slap in the face of the entire congregation—for that matter, the entire town. And worst of all, she'd made the family out as fools. Now, when the service was over, she'd have to find excuses for what Charlotte had done. Or would she?

Suzanne was relieved to hear Pastor Brady begin the final liturgy.

"The Lord bless you and keep you. The Lord make His face to shine upon you and give you peace."

Ginny Watson, at the piano, launched into "Amazing Grace" and the congregants sang while the pastor made his way down the aisle to take his customary place at the door. Grace was the last thing Suzanne felt like giving. The hymn ended, hymnals closed, and they all started to file out of the church.

With Beau and Victoria trailing her, Suzanne tried to make her way to the door, but was waylaid time and time again by shocked members of the congregation who couldn't believe what had just transpired.

"I don't even know what to say about it," Suzanne said to anyone who stopped her. "Just between us, I'm sorry to say my Charlotte really never came back to me. This woman—imposter, really—who's taken her place is a stranger. A stranger in our home and we never know what she's going to say or do next. Please … pray for us."

Charlotte and Isaac were in line behind a few other parishioners and were doing their best to ignore the pointed looks and whispered comments directed their way. It was her turn to greet the pastor.

"I'm sorry we were late, Pastor," she said.

He flicked his eyes from her to Isaac, then nodded at her. "Charlotte, I'm just glad to see you made it back to church."

"Yes, well …"

"I think it might be wise for us to meet about your spiritual needs now that you're home." He looked her straight in the eye. "In the meantime, I'd like you to read John 1:11. It will provide a good place for us to begin our discussion."

Before she could even respond, he turned and thrust his hand out to the next parishioners in line. "Jeremy, Sally, good to see you," he said.

Charlotte and Isaac made their way from the church. She looked over her shoulder at the pastor and could see he was looking in her direction. *John 1:11.*

CHAPTER FORTY-ONE

She had done something purely on heart and instinct, and now her thoughts were turning faster than the wheels on the wagon. She remembered a conversation with Elijah. *"You're a strong, capable woman, with good instincts."* She'd laughed at his comment and listed her litany of mistakes. Then his amended advice: *"Whatever your instincts tell you—do the opposite."* Too late! *Why didn't I heed his words, heed my own history of blunders and stay home? I brought Isaac into a white church. What was I thinking? What have I done?* The thought of facing Suzanne, her brother, and her sister was daunting. This latest action would certainly do nothing to repair a relationship still reeling from the attack of the bounty hunters and the revelation of Elijah's service in the Union army. *Should have thought of that before I marched a black boy into a room filled with*

Southerners still stinging from the war. Then there was the pastor. The long look and his request to talk about her spiritual needs. She had a feeling her spiritual needs would probably end up falling into the category of minding her own business and letting *him* worry about the diversity of his congregation. She didn't want to talk to him any more than she wanted to speak to her mother. *Will I ever learn to think before I act?*

Isaac, normally one of the most talkative people she knew, was silent on the ride back home. He hadn't said a word since climbing up into the wagon and sitting as far across the bench seat from her as he could. They arrived back at the plantation stables. Charlotte turned to Isaac.

"It was a good service," she said.

Isaac stared straight ahead, but nodded. "Yassum, it was." He jumped off the wagon and looked up at her. "I'll unhitch Lucky."

"No, it's fine. I can do it."

"Den I be headed back home," he said. "'Preciate you takin' me."

Charlotte started to reply, but he turned and ran in the direction of the colored camp. Preoccupied with the pastor's words to her, she set to work unhitching Lucky from the wagon and turned him loose in the corral. She made her way quickly to the house.

The only Bible Charlotte had seen in the house was on a bookshelf in the parlor. The book was big, heavy, with an ornate cover and gold-leaf pages. She brought it to the settee and put it in her lap. If the pastor was couching his judgment about her actions with chapter and verse, she wanted to know. She began to turn pages, and couldn't help but think about Elijah's well-used Bible, its pages dog-eared and passages marked. After some searching, she finally found the gospel of John. But before she could find the correct chapter and verse, a voice startled her.

"Jes what d'ya think you're doing?"

She looked up from the Bible to see Chessie had entered the parlor. Charlotte flushed, feeling guilty when she had nothing to feel guilty about.

"Nothing. I'm just looking up a chapter and verse," Charlotte said.

"I'm talkin' 'bout dat boy."

"You mean Isaac?"

"A course I mean Isaac," Chessie said. "I seen you with him earlier today. Den I hear you take him to da white church?"

"That's right, I did," Charlotte said, determined not to let Chessie see she was having serious second thoughts about her decision.

Chessie shook her head. "Tryin' to ease your conscience with him ain't gonna work."

"I just brought him to church with me," Charlotte said. "Is that a sin?"

Chessie shook her head. "You don't even know what you done."

"I'm sure you plan to tell me."

"You jes bought dat boy a whole lotta trouble," Chessie said. "He already got himself in a bad way by taking up for you ev'ry chance he get. Now you go and do this!"

"What do you mean?"

"Der gonna be a price to pay fo' this and it ain't gonna be out a' yo' hide," Chessie said.

The words hit Charlotte hard. "I won't allow anyone to touch Isaac," she said. "No one is going to harm that boy."

"That didn't stop 'em afore, 'did it?"

Charlotte had nothing to say. Her fingers curled around the edges of the Bible.

"You ever feel a whip split your skin?" Chessie asked. She waited a moment for a response from Charlotte, but when she didn't get one, she shook her head with obvious disgust. "Mm-hmm."

"I didn't want to make things harder for Isaac," Charlotte said. "I wanted to show him how much I care about him."

"You care? Den stay away from dat boy. Dat's da best thing you kin do for him."

Chessie turned abruptly and left. Charlotte turned back to the Bible—and braced herself for another reprimand—this one from the written Word. She found the right passage and read John 1:11: "*He came unto his own, and his own received him not.*"

Charlotte read the words again and again. She replayed in her mind the short conversation with the pastor at the church door, his expression—his admonishment for her to read the passage. What was he trying to tell her? Was he for her or against her? She needed to know.

Charlotte left before breakfast the next morning. After spending the rest of Sunday afternoon and evening in her room, she'd successfully managed to avoid her family and their opinions of her actions. After arriving in Darien, she made her way toward the church, but more specifically to the small house Victoria had pointed out to her on one of their trips to town. Charlotte tied Lucky to a post in front of the parsonage and knocked. Pastor Brady answered the door.

"Charlotte."

"I know it's early," she said. "And I'm sorry to come unannounced ..."

He studied her, then stepped back. "Come in."

The pastor's home, owned by his church flock, was tidy, but very sparsely furnished. He led Charlotte to a plain table in the small kitchen.

"I was having coffee," he said. "Would you like some?"

"No, thank you."

"Please, have a seat," he said.

He took a chair and wrapped his hand around a coffee cup. "You read the passage?"

"I did."

"What do you think it means?"

"That the people of Darien won't like me for what I did."

A small nod from him. "What you did—bringing that colored boy to an all-white church, was ... stunning. I can't imagine you doing such a thing before you went away."

"I wouldn't know about that," she said.

"The old Charlotte Chapman was a staunch supporter of slavery," he said. "Has losing your memory changed your views so much—you would take a risk like that for yourself—and for that boy?"

"I can't speak to what I believed before," she said. "So I can't answer your question."

"I've heard the stories about you, Charlotte. How you joined the Confederacy. You fought to maintain the Southern way of life. You fought to keep colored folks enslaved. That is a person who is passionate about her beliefs."

"I don't remember any of that."

"My point exactly," he said. "You don't remember life before; you don't remember how people here suffered during the war. How they lost a third of their sons, husbands, fathers, brothers. How an entire town was burned to the ground by a regiment of colored Union soldiers so filled with hate they set fire to things just for the pleasure of watching them burn."

"I didn't mean to stir up hurtful memories," she said. "That wasn't my intention at all."

"You brought Isaac to a church filled with people who remember every detail of what I just described. People who have lost the only way of life they've ever known. Many lost their homes, their ability to earn a living. You brought him into a congregation who've been so steeped in a way of life, they still can't see it was wrong."

He let his last statement settle between them. Charlotte frowned. "You're saying you believe slavery was wrong?"

He studied her. "From the time I was a very young man, I knew God was calling me to be a pastor. To use God's Word to influence others, soften their attitudes, and speak to their hearts. But if I were to make bold proclamations like the one you did, I would find myself without a pulpit and no longer able to fulfill my calling."

He stared into her eyes as if searching her very soul. "What has God called you to do, Charlotte? Fall in love? Marry? Have children?"

"Be a genteel Southern lady, isn't that what I'm supposed to do?"

"Yes, that's exactly what you're *supposed* to do."

"Maybe I *could* do that, if men like you would be bolder."

"You think I'm using my calling as a shroud—a place to hide a spine too weak to take a public stand?"

"I'm sorry. I should never have said what I did."

He took a moment, fought back his emotions. "I've wondered that myself and won't know the answer until I stand before my Maker on judgment day."

"I can tell you I already know how it feels to have others hate me so much they'd want to end my life," she said.

"And that's the reason for our visit … to make sure you fully comprehend the world you've returned to." He leaned toward her. "There's a group of men. They operate in secret and are very violent." The pastor rubbed worry lines from his forehead. "They won't like what you did. And they won't hesitate to kill you if you continue to undermine their way of life."

CHAPTER FORTY-TWO

After arriving home from town, Charlotte went into the parlor and studied the portrait of her father—the face that had brought her home. By all accounts he was a man who'd loved his family and Southern heritage. Greatly admired by people in town, called heroic, brave—apparently he had loved her with his whole heart. *But would you love the person I am right now, Father? Would you still be proud of me after what I did yesterday at church?* He was a man who'd owned slaves. As many as three hundred souls at one point, according to Beau. It was the way things were done. *Is that the lesson for me? Get along—do things the way they're done here. This is my home—the place I dreamed of before I could even picture it.*

"What do you think he would have thought of your grand entrance into church with that colored boy?" a cold voice said.

Charlotte turned to see her mother walking across the parlor toward her. She couldn't run and hide in her room from the conversation she knew they were about to have. She braced herself for the tirade she thought was coming.

"I don't imagine he would have been pleased," Charlotte said.

"So, will you be bringing a different Negro to church every week? Or is it just the one boy who interests you?"

Charlotte shook her head. "I won't be bringing any more Negroes to church."

Her mother studied her. "Your father would be disappointed in you—"

"I'm aware …"

"If you don't follow your heart."

"What do mean?"

Her mother sank gracefully onto the settee. "What he loved most about you was your spirit. He loved that you had the courage to stand up for the things you believed in. The two of you didn't always agree on everything, but he admired how passionate you were about your argument, whatever the cause."

Charlotte's eyes filled with tears at her words. "I appreciate you saying that."

"I'm only speaking the truth." Mother patted the seat next to her. "Come, sit."

Charlotte did as she asked.

Her mother smiled gently. "Now, tell me what's on your heart."

"Do you really want to know?"

"I asked," Suzanne said.

Charlotte tried hard to articulate her thoughts. "I believe the houses in the colored camp are deplorable. I'm surprised a strong gust of wind hasn't toppled every one of them. And then there's the issue of reading and writing. I think that's a huge problem. Maybe not so much when they were slaves, but now that they're trying to make a living and be responsible for their own families …"

She stopped, afraid to say the rest of what was on her mind. *He came unto his own, and his own received him not.*

Mother frowned. "What? What were you going to say?"

"I think I've already said more than enough," Charlotte said.

"I'm not completely closed-minded, Charlotte," her mother said. "Now that they're trying to make a living …?"

"I believe Negroes who have accounts in town are being cheated," Charlotte said. "I saw it myself at the feed store. I think it's easy to take advantage of a man who can't read his own ledger and add up what he's being charged."

Her mother nodded thoughtfully. "I've heard rumors about shenanigans with bookkeeping. It's disappointing, of course, but if Jackson is doing it, you can probably assume it's happening with other merchants as well as the plantation owners."

"If that *is* the case, the colored men who are trying to turn a profit from the small plots of land they have will never get out of debt."

Mother sighed. "You are probably right."

"Do we subscribe to this practice, Mother?"

"I'd like to think not. I don't handle the tedious task of numbers—Beau and Jonas take care of things …" She frowned. "Would you think me weak if I said I don't want to know?"

"Not at all," Charlotte said. "It's a difficult subject."

"And I imagine a difficult decision to make if you want to take any kind of action," her mother said.

Charlotte nodded. "I don't know what to do."

Mother sounded grim. "I think you do. You are John Chapman's daughter. You must act accordingly."

Charlotte couldn't believe her mother was basically giving her blessing to uncover the wrongs in town and on the plantation.

"The thought of trying to prove it seems daunting," Charlotte said. "I don't even know where to begin."

"Georgia is part of the Third Military District. I suppose you would take your concerns to the Bureau of Refugees, Freedmen, and Abandoned Lands. They're the ones who handle this kind of thing."

"In Darien?"

"No. The Freedmen's Bureau is in Savannah. I believe the agent who handles the complaints for McIntosh County is Lucius Akerman. Once you make a claim of an outrage that's been committed on colored people, he has no choice but to investigate."

"I'd have to go to Savannah?"

"That's to your advantage, dear. You certainly wouldn't want anyone in town getting wind of what you're doing—and to be brutally frank, neither would I."

"But if I go there, make a complaint, won't that expose me to ... everyone?"

"The Freedmen's Bureau will keep your identity confidential," her mother said. "They understand the implications of accusations better than most."

"I'll have to think about how to obtain proof," Charlotte said, more to herself now than to her mother. "I can't exactly steal their books …"

"You can't steal them, but you could *borrow* them for a bit."

Charlotte nodded thoughtfully, then said, "Thank you for letting me tell you all this. For helping me talk it through."

"It's what families do for one another," her mother said. "We are your safe place from the world. Always."

Charlotte entered Dooley's wearing a white blouse and a navy skirt adorned with a decorative white apron. The apron had deep pockets meant to be nothing more than design, but Charlotte had big plans for those pockets. Dooley was helping another customer, a young woman Charlotte hadn't met, who lingered at the counter hemming and hawing over the purchase of three skeins of wool yarn. Dooley slanted a helpless look at Charlotte. "I'll be with you in a minute, Miss Charlotte."

"All right," she said.

Finally, the young woman pushed two of the three skeins toward Dooley. "I'll take these two."

Dooley, smile frozen in place, nodded. "Very good, Mrs. Turner." He reached under his counter and brought out his ledger. He flipped it open and carefully recorded the cost of the yarn, then slipped the book back under the counter. "So, if that's all, then …"

Mrs. Turner turned and pointed to something in the recesses of the store. "I can't buy one today, but I was wondering if you might show me some of your frying pans?"

Dooley sighed. "Of course." He turned to Charlotte. "What can I ..."

Charlotte feigned a look of chagrin. "I can't believe it, but I left my list at home."

"It's just about closing time, Miss Charlotte." He looked pointedly at Mrs. Turner, who paid him no mind.

"I know. I'll come back in the morning," Charlotte said.

Mrs. Turner was already heading toward the back of the store. "Coming, Mr. Dooley?"

He shook his head and rolled his eyes at Charlotte. "Coming, Mrs. Turner. See you tomorrow then, Miss Charlotte."

Charlotte nodded, waited for him to follow Mrs. Turner, then hurried around the counter. In seconds, she had the ledger tucked into one of her pockets and strolled out the door.

That night, by the time she'd made copies of Dooley's ledger and had poured over all the numbers, the candle had burned down to a small plug of wax. She added up the figures over and over again. For the colored farmers, numbers were padded, inflated—flat-out wrong. For the white landowners and farmers, it was a fraction of the cost for the same goods and services. It was even worse than she'd feared. The scratch of the nib of her pen over the paper seemed to reverberate in the deep quiet of the house while everyone else slept. What she'd confirmed about Dooley made her sad. *"Dance with an old friend of your father's?"*

Charlotte was waiting in front of Dooley's the next morning when he arrived. He smiled broadly at her.

"Come back with your list, did you?"

"Yes," she said. "So silly of me to forget it yesterday."

"Well, come on in," Dooley said. "There's never a wait when you're the first one." He went behind the counter and held out his hand. "Let's see that list."

She handed it over, and he turned to the shelves behind him and began to pluck items from the shelves. Charlotte took the opportunity to pull the book from her pocket and slip it behind the big jar of penny candy sitting on the counter. Dooley lined the items up on the counter. "Let me just write 'em in the book."

He ducked under the counter, then stood and frowned.

"That's strange. My ledger. It's usually right there on the shelf …"

Charlotte made a show of sweeping her gaze around. She pointed toward the penny candy jar. "Is that it?"

Dooley grinned. "Yep. Think I'd lose my head if it weren't attached. Now, let's fill out your tab."

She almost wished it hadn't been so easy, because now she had no excuse not to continue.

The feed and livestock shop was next. Jackson smiled broadly when she entered, and told her she would be happy to learn the chickens would be in ahead of schedule. Charlotte thanked him and assured him her mother would be pleased. She asked if it would be too much trouble for Jackson to double check the amount of feed they ordered.

The incriminating book was out and on the counter when a bell in the back rang. Jackson apologized, said it was the delivery wagon. He needed to go compare his order to the goods delivered. She smiled and said she could check with him the next day about the feed. In fact, she might have another order to place. Jackson stuffed the ledger back in a drawer under his counter and said he'd see her in the morning. He hurried through the store and out the back door, almost as quickly as Charlotte hurried around the counter and pulled out the ledger. She slipped it into her apron pocket just as Sam came through with his broom.

A breeze came through her window that night and put out the flame on her candle at about the same time she put down her pen. The room darkened, and she closed the cover of Jackson's ledger and thought about the families who would never be out of debt if the practice continued. They'd traded one form of slavery for another.

Earl Jenkins at the sawmill was more than happy to show Charlotte how much lumber it would take to build onto the existing chicken coop at the plantation. He kept his ledger in a desk drawer that didn't have a lock.

Though he traded mostly in mules, harnesses, and plows, Zeke Prentiss complimented Charlotte on her keen eye for horses. He had a new saddle she might like to try. The intricate, tooled design on the leather would be perfect for a lady of her stature. She asked him to write down the cost, maybe include the bridle and a blanket as well. She'd need to talk it over with her mother, but she promised to let him know her decision within the day. Zeke's ledger had a string pulled through the cover and it dangled from a nail in the wall. While Zeke turned to write down the prices for Charlotte, she slipped that string right off that nail, and the ledger went into the pocket of that very handy apron.

Ironically, the easiest books to get were the hardest for Charlotte to look at, and she'd purposefully left them until last. While everyone slept, she'd slipped the ledgers out of Beau's desk drawer and carried them to her room. Mother had made it clear she didn't want to know, but Charlotte did. She had to know if Beau was conducting the family business in an honorable way. It didn't take long for her to see he was not. The charges for use of the mill were ten times higher for the black families than they were for the white neighbors. Rent costs for the plots of land were exorbitant, not even close to the contracts the Freedmen's Bureau had approved. She felt certain most of the colored farmers probably suspected they were being cheated but didn't know what to do about it.

Well after midnight, tired and heartsick over Beau's involvement, Charlotte opened the drawer where the nubs of nine candles, wicks burned to the core, were tucked inside. She blew out the tenth candle and added it to the others. Alone in the dark, she thought of what she had to do next.

CHAPTER FORTY-THREE

Charlotte and Lucky arrived in Savannah late in the morning, having left the plantation before dawn. The town was shrouded in gauzy clouds that did little to filter the sun's heat. Though she was apprehensive about what she was doing, she knew it was the right thing. With her precious evidence inside her saddlebags, she made her way down the main road of town bordered by towering oak trees whose highest branches shaded all those below. She spotted the landmark her mother told her to watch for right away—an American flag waved from a flagpole at least thirty feet high. *"The office of the bureau will be inside Oglethorpe Barracks, dear. The Yankees took it over during the war, and now they use the buildings to run state government."*

The flag was positioned in front of a ten-foot-high brick wall that surrounded a courtyard filled with buildings. She had no idea how to get inside. Riding Lucky around the wall, she turned east onto Drayton Street and continued until she came to a small guardhouse. The two-story frame building was only about thirty feet long and thirty feet wide. She dismounted at the same time a soldier exited.

"Something I can do for you, ma'am?" he asked.

"I'm trying to find the office of the Freedmen's Bureau," she said.

He nodded, then pointed. "Through here, third building on your left."

With her evidence in hand, she found the windowless office without a problem. It was nondescript, furnished with four wooden desks and straight-backed chairs. A map of the United States hung on the wall. The eleven Southern states that had seceded were colored gray. Two men behind desks looked up at her entrance. One of them stood and smiled.

"Morning," he said.

"Good morning," Charlotte answered. "I'm looking for Mr. Akerman?"

The man looked momentarily disappointed, then inclined his head to the other man at a desk behind him. "Right there."

Lucius Akerman was a timid-looking man. Slight of build, he wore round, wire-rimmed glasses that balanced on a nose seemingly too narrow to hold them up. He stood as Charlotte approached the desk.

"Mr. Akerman?"

He nodded. "That's right. What can I do for you?"

Charlotte looked around nervously. "I'm from Darien and was told you were the man to see about filing a ... a complaint."

Akerman gestured to a chair in front of his desk. "Have a seat, Miss …?"

She sat. "I'd rather not say."

"Don't worry. It's for our official use only." There was a stack of files on his desk that he pushed aside to find a pad of paper. He had a pencil stuck behind one ear, which he pulled free. "Anything you say to me today will be in the strictest of confidence."

"Charlotte Chapman," she said.

The man who'd greeted Charlotte turned and looked at Akerman. "Heading out for a smoke, Lucius."

Akerman nodded, then turned back to Charlotte. "What is the nature of your complaint, Miss Chapman? Rude behavior from the Negroes? Possible theft?"

She shook her head. "No, I'm not here to complain about them. I'm here to register a complaint on their behalf."

He raised his brows, put down his pencil, and looked at her. "Is that right?"

"Yes." She pushed the papers she had across the desk toward him. "I suspected some merchants in Darien were treating their colored customers differently than their white patrons. Charging them exorbitant interest on their purchases, doubling and sometimes tripling the prices of the goods."

"You mean they charge the white customers less for the same product or service?"

"That's right." She indicated the paperwork. "I've made copies of the transgressions and the stores in which they occurred. I also believe some of the landowners made arrangement to take too much of the profits from their sharecroppers, and are charging them outrageous prices to lease the land. They won't make any kind of a profit at all with the way things stand."

Akerman took his time perusing the figures in front of him. Charlotte fidgeted in her chair, nervous, wishing the whole thing were over. She wanted to bring the injustice to light without *standing* in the light herself. Finally, Akerman looked up from her evidence, took off his glasses and stared at her.

"May I ask how you obtained this?"

"I … borrowed the ledgers from the stores, copied their figures, then returned the books without the knowledge of the shopkeepers."

"You must feel very strongly about this," he noted.

"Strongly enough that you'll see I brought the figures from our own plantation, Mr. Akerman. I can't ask you to clean house at other plantations if I'm not willing to do the same thing at ours."

"And your family? Are they supportive in your … endeavors?"

"They don't know I'm here," she said. "And as I stated earlier, I'd like my name kept off the official paperwork."

He nodded. "I'll see to it. Now, when someone comes in with a complaint, we call them outrages. Outrages are generally filed by Negroes themselves when they feel as if they've been mistreated, cheated, are feeling threatened," he said. "Our job here at the bureau is to investigate the accusations, try to bring justice to the situation."

"Good. Yes. That's why I'm here."

"My point is it's rare to have a white woman come into this office and file an outrage on behalf of the black community."

"Are you saying I *can't* file the complaint?"

He shook his head. "Not at all. I applaud your willingness to bring such a terrible situation to our attention."

He frowned and tapped his pencil on the desk. "What to do … what's our best course of action here …?" He finally nodded as if to affirm his own decision. "I think we need a meeting. Get everyone affected—the Negroes—assembled in one place so I can talk to them and explain the situation. We want to warn them about what's going on, tell them how to protect themselves from such unfair business practices."

"We?"

"I think it would help to have you there, Miss Chapman. They could see someone of your place in the community is on their side."

"I really wanted to remain anonymous, Mr. Akerman," she said.

"And so you will. But I fear they won't assemble if you're too scared to be there."

She reluctantly agreed. "Makes sense."

"Good," he said. "Do you think you can get the word out about the meeting?"

"I suppose …"

"It has to be done quietly—we don't want any trouble. Let's say four days from today. Friday at midnight?"

"All right. Where?"

"That's a problem," he said. "We don't want to call attention to ourselves by meeting in a public place."

"There's an abandoned farm near our property," she said. "The Crowley place. Perhaps in the barn?"

"Yes. Sounds perfect for our situation," he said. "And may I say I applaud your courage and conscience, Miss Chapman. Not many young women would care so much about a subject that has little to do with their daily life."

"Thank you, Mr. Akerman. And thank you for your time. I feel so much better knowing I have the bureau behind me on this."

Charlotte walked out of the office, feeling considerably lighter than she did when she arrived.

Lucius Akerman watched Charlotte walk out the door. He looked down at the stack of papers on his desk and was astounded at all she'd uncovered.

Akerman's office mate walked back through the door with his cigarette planted in the corner of his mouth. A stocky man in his midthirties was with him.

Akerman looked up from the papers. "That was her."

The stocky man lifted a brow. "When?"

"Four days from today," Akerman said. "Give you enough time?"

"Yeah. I'll head to Darien directly," the stocky man said. And without another word he turned on his heel and left.

CHAPTER FORTY-FOUR

At six o'clock sharp, the family came together for supper. They settled themselves in chairs and made small talk about the warm weather and the sudden influx of fruit flies Juba had been battling in the kitchen of late.

"It's disgusting," Victoria said. "Bugs in the house means someone is not doing their job." She arched a brow at Biddy who was holding the tray for Rose as she slipped plates in front of the family. Biddy averted her gaze and Victoria continued. "It's not as if we're overrun with fresh fruit. Where on earth do they come from?"

"It doesn't have to be fruit," Beau said. "Any rotting vegetable will do."

Charlotte had no appetite at all. Her stomach was a nervous mess, and she was wishing away the evening so she could get her task over and done with. Hoping to maintain the much-needed secrecy about her plan, she'd journeyed in the dark to the colored camp a few nights before to tell the farmers what she'd learned about the practices of some landowners and merchants. The men she spoke to weren't surprised at her revelations—they'd long suspected they were being cheated—but they *were* surprised she wanted to help. Once they learned she'd be there, they'd promised to get the word out about the midnight meeting at the old Crowley barn. *In six hours I can put in an appearance at the meeting, and then let the bureau take over.*

"Charlotte? Are you even listening to me?" Victoria said.

Charlotte turned her attention to her sister. "I'm sorry. What did you say?"

"I want to go to Savannah with you and pick out fabric for next season's dresses," Victoria said. "We'll make a real trip out of it. Supper in a fancy hotel, a special fitting at Madame Boucher's Shop to see the latest fashions from Paris. It will be fun!"

Charlotte frowned. The last thing she could think about was dresses. "I don't know …"

"Oh, please, Char! We need some fun. We deserve some fun!"

Their mother caught Charlotte's eye and smiled. "She's right, dear. You should plan a trip to Savannah for nothing but fun."

Charlotte forced herself to smile at Victoria. "Fine. Plan the trip."

Victoria puffed up with delight. "A sisters' outing," she said. Then she immediately sobered and looked at Suzanne. "Of course, you're invited too, Mother."

Mother slipped her fork under a fluff of potatoes. "Thank you, darling, but I think I'll pass. There is always so much to do here."

Biddy and Rose entered with another tray, this one with dessert. Biddy slid the tray across the sideboard, knocking over a candlestick. The noise startled Charlotte and she dropped her fork, which then clattered noisily onto her plate.

"Sorry, missus," Biddy said.

Their mother waved a dismissive hand at Biddy. Beau looked at Charlotte. "You seem a little edgy this evening, Char. Everything all right?"

Charlotte picked up her fork and lied to her brother. "Everything is fine. Absolutely fine." *At least I pray it will be fine ... and maybe this time tomorrow evening, I'll have nothing on my mind but new dresses.* She started to eat as if she actually had an appetite.

The hours ticked by so slowly Charlotte thought she'd go mad from waiting. Finally, at half past eleven, while the rest of the house slept, she crept down the back stairs in the kitchen and let herself out. She made her way around the house, and then started toward the stables. She was sure Lucky would be excited to go on a midnight ride.

The night air was warm but pleasant. The humidity that plagued the days seemed kinder in the dark, and she moved along at a fairly brisk pace. She hoped to get to the barn a little early. Go over with Mr. Akerman how he planned to present the evidence, and how they would substantiate her claims. Then she'd have done what she set out to do. It was now up to the Freedmen's bureau to confiscate and comb over all the books of the merchants and the plantation owners.

She walked along the red clay road lined by massive trees on either side. Gossamer bits of moss floated down from the thick canopy of branches above, and the glow from the full moon cast dappled shadows across the ground. The hem of her skirt swept over the packed earth with a quiet *swish, swish, swish.* Halfway to the stables now, she picked up the pace, anxious to get in the saddle and share the rest of the journey with Lucky.

The men came out from between the trees, on either side of her, appearing like ghostly apparitions in white hoods and robes. She stopped walking, more transfixed by the sight than frightened. But it didn't take long for the fear to take hold as she scanned their garish outfits, the holes in the masks where faceless men looked upon her in the moon wash. *They operate in secret and are very violent ...*

One of them stepped toward her. "Late for a stroll, ain't it, Miss Chapman?" His voice had purposely been made low, forced into a baritone that sounded unnatural.

Charlotte swallowed, prayed her own voice wouldn't betray how frightened she was. "I like to walk at night."

"Goin' someplace special?"

"No," she said. "Just walking on my own property. Property you are all trespassing on. Please leave."

With an unspoken cue, the men converged on her. So close she could see their eyes in the recesses of the hideous white cloth they had over their heads. She swiveled her head to look behind and could see they'd closed ranks. She was enclosed in a circle.

"What do you want?"

"What d'ya think?" one of them asked.

She shook her head. "I have no idea …"

Another white-robed figure took a step toward her. He lifted his finger and pointed in rage.

"We know about your little meeting," the man with the baritone voice said. "We know what you been doing in town."

His voice was familiar, but she couldn't quite place it. She felt chilled in spite of the warm air.

"Let me pass," Charlotte said with conviction emanating from pure fear.

"This ain't no place for you."

"I said, let me pass."

"You need to disappear like you did before—only this time don't come back."

"You can't force me to leave," she said.

"You need to understand, if you don't do what we say, we'll hang you till you're dead, dead, dead."

There was low chuckling all around the circle. Charlotte felt sick.

"Please. Please let me go home," she said.

"You go home," the baritone voice said. "Pack your bags and get out of Darien before sunrise. Otherwise, all hell's gonna break loose."

They turned and moved back through the trees. Charlotte had to remind herself to breathe as she turned and headed back toward the house.

Charlotte was packing when her mother knocked on the door and entered. She was wearing a robe, and her eyes looked sleepy and confused. "What are you doing?"

"I have to leave," she said.

Mother looked at a few dresses folded on the bed, the jewelry box. She moved toward Charlotte. "What are you talking about?"

"I was supposed to go to a meeting last night at the Crowley farm," she said. "Agent Akerman from the Freedmen's Bureau was going to be there, and … several of the Negro farmers …"

"What happened?"

"Some men were waiting for me." She shuddered. "They wore hoods over their faces, white robes."

Mother looked shocked. "The Klan … here. On our property." She touched Charlotte's arm. "They didn't hurt you, did they?"

"No, but they threatened me." Charlotte shook her head. "How did they know? Who could have told them?"

"It's been said they have eyes and ears everywhere," her mother said.

"Once I leave, things can go back to the way they were. Everyone will be safe then."

"We can't let them win, Charlotte. We need to take a stand."

Charlotte raised her brows, and studied her mother. "I appreciate your … sentiment, more than I can say, but my mind is made up. I just need to go."

Charlotte's mother pressed a handkerchief to her nose, sniffing back the tears that threatened. "What can I do to help?"

"Tell Beau and Victoria how sorry I am. That I'll miss them dearly."

Her mother wrapped her arms around Charlotte. "I'm so sorry it's ended like this," she said.

Charlotte held tight to her. "Me, too, Mother."

Charlotte made her way, one last time, to the colored camp. She climbed the broken steps that led to the house where Isaac lived. She knocked on the door and then entered. It was the first time she'd ever stepped inside. The room was dimly lit, cramped, and very musty. Isaac stood across the room as if he were expecting her.

"I knew you'd come," Isaac said.

"How did you know …?" But as she moved toward the boy, she noticed a woman sitting in the corner of the room.

"Chessie?"

Chessie's hands rested on a dirty tin box in her lap. "Me and you need to have a talk."

"There's no time. I have to leave."

"Isaac, hurry an' git Biddy for me."

With a nod, Isaac hurried out the door. Chessie looked at Charlotte. "You might wanna sit."

There was something in her tone, her demeanor, that made Charlotte do as she said. She found a chair across from Chessie, trying to still her panic over the ticking clock.

"You done changed. I didn't believe it. Maybe I didn't wanna believe it 'cause I been nursin' my anger so long it felt good to hold it. But I seen what'choo been up to. I know 'bout the meetin'. And I know some bad men stopped you from gettin' dere."

"How?"

"It ain't pleasant to tell you, but Miss Suzanne never cared much for you. Hated the way yo' daddy doted on you. Hated that yo' daddy never got over Miss Marie. She had her chil'ren siding with her. They was jes plain mean to you whenever yo' daddy was away."

Charlotte frowned. "It doesn't matter. It's all in the past now."

Chessie was adamant. "No. It's in da here and now. One day yo' daddy come home unexpected an' he heard 'em being real ugly to you. The longer he been gone wit da war, da more dat ugliness grew. He heard and seen enough dat day to tell 'em all to git out of his house."

"*What?*"

"He tell Miss Suzanne she and her chil'ren better be gone when he get back. He say Chessie will stay here with Charlotte. She stays—you go."

"And then he died," Charlotte said.

Chessie nodded. "Dat's right. And you left."

"But they were so happy when I came home," Charlotte said.

"I believe Miss Victoria be happy to see you," Chessie said. "The others been like me. Waitin' and watchin' and wonderin' who came home. Dey think since you don't 'member dey's s'posed to leave da house, dey don't hafta say a word as long as yo' memory stays gone."

"So the whole thing has been a lie? The concern, the welcome-home party?"

"Yassum," Chessie said as Isaac came back into the house with Biddy. "And dat ain't all of it."

Isaac had to give the young colored girl a little push to get her to move into the room. Nervously chewing a fingernail, she stopped near Chessie.

"Biddy came to me too and say somethin' you need to know," Chessie said. "But she's worried da way she find out is gonna get her fired from da big house."

"Just tell me what you have to say, Biddy," Charlotte said. "You won't be in trouble."

Biddy glanced at Chessie, who nodded her encouragement. "Well, Miss Charlotte, I like me some peach rum and da place I kin find it is in da wine cellar." Biddy stopped and put her thumbnail back in her mouth and started to chew.

"Get on with it," Chessie said.

"I be in da wine cellar a few nights ago, not exactly hidin', mind you, jes sitting behind one of da big casks and havin' myself a little nip of da peach rum … and I hear Mr. Beau and Miss Suzanne come into da room, and now I'm scairt, because if dey catch me, I'm in big, big trouble." Biddy's eyes widened as she spoke. "So I keep quiet and I hear 'em talkin' 'bout … you. Dey's talkin' 'bout books and numbers and a meetin' in a barn. But Miss Suzanne say you never gonna get to dat meetin' 'cause she gots a friend in da Klan whose gonna make sure you get the sweet Jesus scairt right outta you and you be runnin' so hard away from dis place they ain't never gonna hafta worry 'bout you again."

Charlotte felt the world tilt with all of the truth. She shook her head at the revelations, then turned hurt eyes on Chessie. "They planned the whole thing just to get me to leave. Why?"

"'Cause dey know'd da truth." Chessie looked down at the dirty tin box on her lap. "Dey jes didn't know where to find it."

Charlotte frowned. "People I thought loved me ... betrayed me."

Chessie studied her, her face impassive. "Makes for a bad pain, don't it?"

Charlotte heard the meaning behind the words, and in spite of Chessie's effort not to reveal her pain it was there all over her face. She crossed the few steps to Chessie and knelt in front of her.

"I am so sorry for the bad pain I caused you, Chessie," Charlotte said. "I don't know how I could have been so cruel. Forgive me."

Chessie's eyes hardened, her mouth a thin line of denial.

"Forgive me."

Chessie's lip began to quiver.

"Please ...," Charlotte begged.

Chessie's eyes filled with tears, but she stubbornly shook her head. Charlotte covered Chessie's hands with her own. The hard lines of Chessie's face began to relax. Tears slipped down her ebony cheeks. She released a pent-up breath and barely dipped her head in acquiescence. Charlotte rose to her knees and leaned in to hug her. Chessie reached out and ran her hand along Charlotte's hair, her eyes closed for one moment of peace. Charlotte pulled back, her face washed in relief.

Biddy and Isaac, forgotten in the moment, stood, staring at the two women. Chessie fixed a look on both of them. "Y'all act like you never seen a proper 'pology between two fine women 'afore."

Biddy shook her head. "Not like this one I ain't."

Chessie looked back at Charlotte, still kneeling in front of her. "Now, 'bout yer family and what dey done ..."

Charlotte shook her head. "I don't know what to do ... how to even respond."

Chessie patted the tin box. "Had this buried in a special place till jes today."

"What is it?" Charlotte asked.

"I believe dis be your future."

Chapter Forty-Five

The people would have questions when they found out John's daughter—the darling of Darien—was gone again. *And I need to have answers,* Suzanne thought, sitting at her writing desk in the parlor the next morning. She dipped her pen in ink and began to write her thoughts. *She couldn't handle our Southern ways. The North had won her over.* She paused, scratched through the last three words and added, *prevailed in their ignorance.* A satisfied nod and she continued: *We tried explaining to my dear daughter that slavery has done more to elevate a degraded race in the scale of humanity; to tame the savage; to civilize the barbarous; to soften the ferocious; to enlighten the ignorant, and to spread the blessings of Christianity among the heathen. But she would not hear any of it. And chose to leave, breaking our hearts once more.* Suzanne's thoughts were interrupted by the strains of the pianoforte coming through the house. Victoria playing a waltz. *How do I tell her Charlotte has left home?* Suzanne wondered. *And yet again without saying good-bye. I want to spare her the pain of her sister's actions, but how can I?*

Somewhere in her consciousness, she was aware of a faint knock on the front door. *I just want to keep Victoria safe here with me; how awful would it be if it were Victoria and not Charlotte who left … Unimaginable.*

Another knock and Victoria continued to play in the other room. Suzanne sighed. "Rose?" she called out. "The door?"

But Rose didn't materialize, and whoever was at the door was very insistent. With a sigh, Suzanne pushed back from her desk and made her way into the foyer. She pulled open the door at the fourth knock. Her brows lifted at the visitor standing there.

"Adam? This is a lovely surprise."

The family attorney frowned. "Surprise? I don't understand. One of your field hands came to town to fetch me. He said it was urgent I get here immediately."

A brief frown creased her brow, but she smiled and stepped back so he could enter. "Come in."

She was vaguely aware the music had stopped as he entered and swept the hat from his head. Suzanne closed the door behind him.

"I honestly don't know what this is about, Adam," Suzanne said. "If it was Beau who had you summoned, then he hasn't shared the reason with me."

"It was me," came a voice from behind them.

Suzanne whirled around to see Charlotte standing just inside the foyer.

"Good morning, Mr. Harper," Charlotte said. She looked tired, a little disheveled.

"Miss Charlotte. Is everything all right?" His brows furrowed with concern.

"It will be." She smiled. "Thank you for coming."

Suzanne stared at her stepdaughter. "Charlotte? What are you doing here?" She tried not to sound as shocked as she felt.

"I live here," Charlotte said.

Suzanne shot a look at Adam and saw the quizzical look on his face. She hurried toward Charlotte and tried to embrace her. But Charlotte stood rigidly in the embrace.

"Darling, I'm so happy you didn't leave," Suzanne said quietly.

Charlotte took a step back. "Where is Beau?"

"I'm sure he's in the fields," Suzanne said. "Why?"

Victoria entered the foyer. "Hello, Mr. Harper. I thought I heard someone at the door."

Charlotte looked at Suzanne. "Go get Beau."

Suzanne balked. "I'm not going to trot out to the fields to retrieve your brother, Charlotte, and everyone else is too busy with their duties."

"I have something to say that affects all of you," Charlotte said, including Victoria in her glance. "If you want to know what that is—I suggest you *do* trot out to the fields to get him. We'll wait for you in Father's study."

"Mr. Harper? Will you join me?" Charlotte said. He nodded, and the two of them crossed the foyer.

Victoria frowned, then started after them, but Suzanne grabbed her arm. "Oh no, you're coming with me to find Beau."

"What's the matter with Charlotte?"

"I have no idea," Suzanne said. She took her daughter's arm, giving Victoria no choice but to go with her out the door.

John Chapman's study had been spared any vandalism by the Yankees that had occupied the house simply because the commanding officer of the regiment had decided to use the space as his own. The trappings of the study were very masculine. There was a massive mahogany desk, a wooden floor covered with a thick rug, leather chairs, and heavy velvet drapes framing two windows that offered a view of the trees in the distance. A very faint odor of fine cigars still lingered in the air.

Charlotte tried to still her roiling emotions as her stepmother entered with Victoria and Beau. She stood with Mr. Parker and Chessie by the desk. An immediate frown creased her stepmother's face.

"Chessie? Why are you here?"

"Because I asked her to be," Charlotte said.

"I'm sure whatever you have to say is for family ears only," Beau said. "She doesn't belong in here. You're excused, Chessie."

"She's staying," Charlotte said in a tone that brooked no argument.

"What is all this, Char?" Beau asked. "Mother comes to tell me you're staying and I rush here to tell you how happy I am, and ..."

"Happy?"

Beau nodded. "Yes, of course I'm happy. I thought we'd lost you all over again after last night. I hated to see my big sister leave under such *un*happy circumstances."

Mr. Harper looked at Charlotte. "You planned to leave home again?"

"I considered it," Charlotte said, "but that was before I had all the facts."

"That sounds like good news," Beau said. "It must mean you don't believe the Klan will make good on their threats?"

Victoria gasped. "What do those awful men have to do with anything, Charlotte?"

"So you don't know?" Charlotte asked, but she needn't have asked the question. She could see the truth on Victoria's face.

Victoria shook her head.

"Who wants to tell her? Mother? Beau?" Charlotte turned to them.

"Really, Char … always so dramatic," Beau said, softening his words with a smile. "I think we all just need to calm down and have a reasonable conversation …"

"There is nothing reasonable about the two of you plotting to get me out of the house," Charlotte said. "There is nothing reasonable about telling the most hideous men in the South to frighten me within an inch of my life and threaten me like they did."

"Who is filling your head with such nonsense?" her stepmother asked, cutting a look toward Chessie. Chessie gave a shake of her head.

"I stood in my room, shaking in my shoes, and asked how the Klan would know where and when to find me, and all along it was you!"

"You want to blame someone for your own irresponsible actions, and you've chosen your own family," her stepmother said. "I find that reprehensible."

"I find *you* and your actions reprehensible," Charlotte said, glaring at her.

Charlotte caught the glint of steel in her stepmother's eyes before she softened her expression and looked at Mr. Harper.

"I'm sorry you're here to witness this, Adam," Mother said. "I can't even begin to imagine how John would feel to hear these lies coming out of Charlotte's mouth."

"Someone—not Chessie—overheard you and Beau talking," Charlotte said. "About the books, and the meeting at Crowley's."

Charlotte took a step toward them. "You said I'd never make it to the meeting. You've got a friend in the Klan who'll make sure I'm scared out of my wits and leave this place so fast you'll never have to worry about me again!"

Victoria looked at her mother and brother. "Is that true?"

Charlotte shot her sister a look. "Not too hard to believe, is it, Victoria?"

Mother turned to Mr. Parker. "We did it for her—for her own good."

"Mother," Beau said.

"We may as well confess, Beau." She looked at Charlotte. "Yes, I asked those men to be on our property and to scare you … but only because I knew if someone didn't put the fear of God into you, you'd keep doing reckless things."

She turned back to Adam. "You can see my reasoning, can't you, Adam? I was worried for her very life. Bringing a black boy to church! Stirring up trouble with the Freedmen's Bureau. Where was it going to stop? With Charlotte hanging from the branch of a tree?"

"So it was out of your concern for me?" Charlotte asked.

"Yes, dear. Out of concern. We didn't want to see you get hurt."

"I may have believed you if I didn't know you never liked me—let alone loved me."

"That's not true, dear!" Suzanne said.

Charlotte nodded at Chessie. The old woman squared her rounded shoulders. "It is da truth, missus. Ever'body in dis room but Mr. Harper know it be true."

Charlotte's stepmother pointed a finger at Chessie. "You shut up, Chessie. You shut up right now …"

But Chessie ignored her and went on. "I knowed how much Master Chapman loved Miss Charlotte, knowed how he wanted da best fo' her. He trusted his wife and other chil'ren to treat her good while he be away."

Chessie bravely looked Suzanne in the eye. "Yo done a good job at first at hidin' the way you felt 'bout her when he was home. But he never knowed how you treat her when he was gone. He never knowed 'bout the meanness, 'cause Miss Charlotte never say a word to him. Didn't want him worryin' 'bout her."

"That's enough out of you!" Mother clapped her hands together.

Chessie shook her head. "No, ma'am, it ain't. I gonna say da rest." Charlotte saw Chessie look her way and gave her an encouraging nod.

"Dat time he come home unexpected, dat time he got to see and hear the ugliness fo' himself was da day he tell da three of you to git out a' his house. Git out and don't come back for da way you treat Miss Charlotte. He tells me 'bout it—and tells me to stay and look after her. He say she better off with me and no one else den with you, missus."

Adam Harper was silent but hanging on Chessie's every word. Charlotte could see her stepmother fuming, and, in spite of her anger, she was worried.

"Da morning Master John was gettin' ready to leave—he called me into dis room and shut da door and he hands me an envelope dat's sealed wit' wax. 'Chessie,' he says, 'I want you to guard dis wit' yo' life.'" She frowned. "He look nervous dat day. Look like a man who sees da end of his time comin' but can't do nothin' 'bout it. He tol' me what's in dat envelope but say not to let anyone see it. If he die, den I'm to give it to Miss Charlotte or Mr. Harper."

Another frown, another shake of Chessie's head. "I see da hurt from y'all ever time Master John favored Miss Charlotte. Everyone seen it—weren't no secret. What he did wasn't right, but what y'all did last night—turning those white devils loose on yer own kin—that's jes evil."

Mother purposely looked away from Chessie to Charlotte. "Where is the envelope?"

Charlotte lifted the lid of a humidor on the desk, took out an envelope, and handed it to Mr. Harper.

"I haven't opened it, as you can see by the seal," Charlotte said, "but I know what's inside."

"Well?" Suzanne demanded.

"It's Father's will," Charlotte said.

"Father's will was read right after his burial, Charlotte. Just because you don't remember it doesn't mean it didn't happen," Beau said.

"Father's *amended* will," Charlotte said. "He changed it the morning he planned to leave—and left the entire plantation and all his holdings to me."

Beau barked out a laugh. "That's ridiculous. Tell her, Mr. Harper—tell her you read the will right here in this office after he died. Tell her he left the plantation to Mother."

But Mr. Harper was breaking the seal on the envelope. He withdrew two sheets of linen paper and perused it. The silent tension in the room was palpable. Finally, he looked up.

"Beau is right, Charlotte. I read John's last will and testament after his death …"

Beau barked out a laugh. "See?"

"But according to this," Harper continued, "John revoked that will and drafted this new one." He looked down at the paper again. "This leaves all of John's holdings, property, land, and money to Charlotte Chapman. It makes her the sole owner of the plantation."

"It can't be legal," Mother said.

"It is," Mr. Harper said. "It's his signature. I was his lawyer and friend for twenty years." He looked at Charlotte's mother. "It's authentic. Binding."

Harper turned to Chessie. "Why didn't you come forward with this, Chessie? You knew what it said … you knew what it meant."

Chessie nodded. "Yassuh, I knew. I knew da person who'd jes sold my grandson would'a had dis place and all da slaves dat came wit' it." She shook her head. "Didn't want to see a person like dat gain so much."

"It wasn't your decision to make, Chessie," he said.

"I know dat," Chessie said. "Ain't offering no 'scuse, 'cept fo' what I jes said," Chessie told him. "I also know dat dis Miss Charlotte be different dan da woman who sold my Kitch."

Charlotte felt her eyes well up at her words. She looked at her stepmother, seething just a few feet away, and realized she owed as much forgiveness as she'd been given.

"Suzanne …"

"I will fight you on this," Suzanne said. "I was married to that pompous man. I put up with him and his warring ways for years! I gave him two children!"

"I was going to ask you to leave the house," Charlotte said, "but I've reconsidered. I think now that we know where everything stands, we should find a way to forge some new, honest relationships …"

Suzanne laughed harshly. "Don't patronize me, young lady. This is my home and …"

"Technically, Suzanne, it's hers," Mr. Harper said. "So I'd be careful here how you proceed …"

"I'm going to proceed right out the door!" Suzanne said.

"Mother …," Beau said. "I wouldn't be rash …"

"Get some things together, Beau, Victoria. We're leaving."

"You don't have to do that," Charlotte said. "You can stay."

"I won't spend another night under the roof you claim to own."

"If that's how you feel," Charlotte said.

"That's how it is," Suzanne said. "But mark my words, Charlotte, there will be repercussions. I will fight you for ownership of *my* home, *my* land, *my* fields. I will be mistress of this plantation again."

Suzanne stormed out of the study with Beau and Victoria on her heels.

Charlotte stood on the veranda and watched the wagon roll away with the family she had tried so hard to remember. There was no joy in the moment—just an empty, sad feeling. Mr. Harper came up beside her and settled his hat on his head.

"I'll head to Darien and file the will at the courthouse."

"Thank you."

"I probably don't have to tell you Suzanne doesn't like to lose," he said.

She shook her head.

"And she's not an indecisive woman," he went on. "It won't take her long to come up with a plan to regain the plantation."

"But if I'm the legal owner ..."

"We both know, especially after last night, she's not going to be concerned with legalities," he said. "You opened Pandora's box when you brought forth the will. Suzanne will use whatever—*whomever*—she can to prevail."

"You'd better get going, then."

Mr. Harper put on his hat and looked at her with concern. "Be careful."

Charlotte felt Chessie come to stand beside her, though she kept her eyes on the departing figure of Adam Harper.

"What we do now?" Chessie said.

"God only knows."

Charlotte saw the attorney ride past fields and dozens of workers. Sun glinted on the brass buttons on the Confederate tunics that a few of the Negroes still had from their time in the war. Charlotte turned to Chessie. "When the soldiers came home from war and stayed on here as free men ... what happened to their weapons?"

Chessie looked out at the field at the people working in hopes of someday having a better life. "Dat box I gave you wit' da will? It wasn't da only thing in dat hole."

CHAPTER FORTY-SIX

With Chessie by her side, Charlotte stood on a rickety porch in the colored camp and looked at the sea of dark faces studying her. Isaac was standing next to Moby. Rose, Juba and Biddy were there—as was Bram, the man she'd seen chasing after Moby the day she arrived.

"The sole ownership of this plantation was left to me by my father," Charlotte said. "There are people who are angry about that and angry with me because of things I've brought to light. Unfair practices where your rights are concerned. I believe men will come to try and make me leave. You know the Klan—what they're capable of. They'll come and try to force me to leave, but this is my home. I want to fight—and I can't do it alone."

Her eyes sought out those in their old uniforms, their slouch hats pushed back on foreheads.

"This *will* be a battle," she said.

"And what if we don't win?" someone shouted. "Or what if it come time for da fight and you ain't dere—jes like dat meetin'!"

"I can promise I'll be in the fight, but I can't promise we'll win."

A surly-looking older man shook his head. "Ain't getting myself kilt fo' land dat ain't mine." A few in the group voiced their agreement.

"It's true, the land isn't yours. If Beau and Suzanne come back, you'll be handing over half the money you earn from your crops, and if I'm here, I'll make sure you don't lose all your profits on leasing the land. Do you want to keep paying thirty percent interest on goods, when white farmers only pay two? You need safer homes—warm in the winter, dry when it rains. Clothes for your children, medical care. Things you don't have right now. Men are going to bring the fight to my door. I'm willing to take a stand on your behalf. It's up to you if you will stand with me."

Bram took a step away from the group, pulled the hat from his head, and held it against his chest. He addressed Charlotte. "You right 'bout all those things, ma'am. All my people need is to be treated fair." He looked at the faces around him. "I'm with you."

Charlotte smiled with relief. "Thank you, Bram."

Chessie nudged her and pointed to some other men on the fringe of the group who had raised their hands. She nodded at all of them. A few of the men in the old uniforms raised their hands. Two more traded long looks with their wives first, then put their hands in the air. Charlotte counted hands and felt a glimmer of hope that maybe they'd have a fighting chance.

Less than an hour later, Charlotte was at the stables. She put a hand over her eyes to shield them from the sun, and looked up at Isaac sitting astride Lucky.

"You're sure you're all right doing this?"

He nodded. "I be fine. You sure *you* gonna be fine?"

"I'm sure." She studied him for a moment longer, then finally handed him a folded note. "Don't give it to anyone other than Pastor Brady."

He nodded. "I'll git it to him."

"Promise me you'll be careful. Stay in the trees on the way to town. And don't go near anyone except the pastor—understand?"

"Yassum."

She stroked Lucky's nose, then looked up at Isaac. "Give him his head and he'll fly over the ground. Trust him. I know he trusts you."

Charlotte had never been to the overseer's house before that afternoon. With a pistol tucked into the waist of her skirt, she knocked—and waited. Knocked again. She had not seen him in the fields that day so she could talk to him—thus the visit. She knocked harder, one more time. Finally, Jonas opened the door. Reeking of whiskey, he squinted at her.

"G'day to you, Miss Chapman." His gaze went to her gun. "Expecting trouble?"

"Just like to be prepared."

He stepped out of the door and swung a hand wide to invite her in. "Welcome to my humble abode."

Charlotte entered the unkempt house but stopped just inside the door. "I'm assuming you've heard the news?"

"That you booted the family out of *your* house?" He smiled. "Yes, ma'am. Heard something about that."

"They were given the choice to stay, Jonas," she said. "Just as I'm giving you the choice to stay."

He rubbed a hand over his unshaven face. "You know this ain't over for you." He looked at her gun again. "Of course you do."

"I *am* aware," she said. "And I'm preparing to fight for what's lawfully mine. My question to you is, are you prepared to fight with me?"

A frown. "I'm 'fraid I'm a little too drunk to make any such decisions right now. Come back tomorrow and I'll think about giving you my answer then."

Charlotte looked around at the mess, then made her way to pick up a basin of water. Without breaking stride, she carried it back toward Jonas and tossed it right into his face. He sputtered, cursed, and lunged at her but nearly lost his balance in the process.

He glared at her. "You can count me—*out*. I ain't helping—ain't fighting."

She digested his answer, then nodded. "Fine. Then you aren't staying either. I want you gone by the end of the day." She covered her pistol with her hand. "And if you're not—don't forget, I *am* a woman who is prepared."

Charlotte pried open an old ammunition crate that Bram and the other sharecroppers had unearthed from Chessie's burying spot. Nestled inside a bed of straw were several rifles, a few pistols, and enough ammunition to see them through a small war. She carefully checked each weapon she pulled from the crate while men around her boarded up the downstairs windows.

Isaac came through the door, shaking his head at her questioning look. "No message from da pastor, Miss Charlotte. He didn't give me nothin' to bring back to you."

She felt her heart sink. "What did he say?"

"He say he pray for you," Isaac said. "Dat be it."

She issued a disappointed sigh. "I'm glad you're back safe and sound, Isaac."

"I tucked Lucky back into his stable," Isaac said. "Kin I help here?"

He looked around as he said it, then backed away when she pointed to the guns in the crate.

"You can help me distribute these," she said.

"No, ma'am, I cain't."

Understanding dawned. "Of course, it's all right, Isaac. You can help Bram and the others with the windows."

"Yassum." The boy quickly made his way to the far side of the parlor where two more men were hammering boards into place over another window.

They heard the sound of an approaching wagon just before dusk. Charlotte hurried to a still unboarded window and peered outside. "Men are coming," she said. "And they're armed!"

She grabbed a rifle. The others followed suit as she made her way to the front door, opening it a crack as the buckboard drew nearer.

"I can't tell who it is," Charlotte muttered. "Can't see ..."

The wagon kept rolling toward the house. Charlotte yelled outside. "Stop or I'll shoot!"

The driver stopped short in the gathering dusk, and a familiar figure popped up from the back of the wagon. "Don't shoot! We're here to help!"

Charlotte released a pent-up breath and opened the door, telling those behind her, "It's the pastor!"

She ran outside and saw Bobby Wilkes sitting on the buckboard with Shorty Smithson beside him. The pastor was jumping out of the wagon, as were two men Charlotte vaguely remembered seeing at her welcome-home party. Charlotte hurried to the pastor's side.

"I didn't think you were coming," she said.

Pastor Brady didn't look especially pleased to be there. "Nevertheless, here we are."

Bobby made his painstaking way off the buckboard and propped himself up with his crutches. Shorty had jumped off the wagon and started to pull out some rifles.

"We're here to lend a hand," Shorty said. "Pastor said you're in trouble and I wanted to help."

Charlotte pressed her palms together over her heart and smiled. "Thank you, Shorty."

Shorty gestured to a man in his early thirties with a balding pate, and another man who was as short as Shorty was tall. "That's Barney and Joe."

"I'm grateful you're all here," Charlotte said.

"You got a plan of defense?" Shorty asked. "'Cause if you don't—you're gonna need one."

"We're boarding up the lower level," she said. "Our best defense will be to take the second floor—hope they come in through the door and we'll get them as they head up the stairs."

Shorty nodded his approval. "Good plan. Looks like you still have some boards to put in place?"

She nodded and he made his way toward the house with Joe and Barney in trail. Bobby started past Charlotte on his crutches, then stopped. "Took a lot of nerve to bring that colored boy to church," he said. "Thought you were crazy."

"You and everyone else," Charlotte said.

"But then I watched that kid look at you with such admiration in his eyes. You did a brave thing for him. You did the right thing. I want my boy to be proud of me for doing something besides wasting my days feeling sorry for myself. I want him to look at me that way again."

Bobby headed toward the house. Charlotte turned to Pastor Brady, who stood clutching his Bible. "I don't know why you changed your mind about coming," Charlotte said. "But I'm thankful you did."

"After Isaac left, I tried to pray for your safety," he said. "But each time I prayed, the answer I got back from God was my praying wasn't enough. He told me to come and stand with you—so here I am."

CHAPTER FORTY-SEVEN

They stood behind a second-story window and peered out at the red-orange glow that wove in and out of the trees lining the road to the house. The streaks of orange grew brighter, flames licking at the black sky.

"Shouldn't a' done this. Lord, shouldn't a' done this," Bram said in a shaky voice.

Charlotte stared down into the darkness, the flames of torches high in the air as horses pounded their way closer and closer. White robes flowed behind the men and hoods covered their heads and the heads of their horses. She shivered at the macabre sight they made and had to remind herself they were just men under those sheets. Just *evil* men.

"Everyone to their places," Charlotte said.

Men scattered. Isaac stayed near Charlotte, and the pastor reluctantly took the pistol she pressed into his hand.

"Aim at anything in white, Pastor," she said.

"My best weapon is the Lord's Word, Charlotte," he said.

"But you can shoot?" she asked.

"In a pinch."

"I'd say we're in that pinch, Pastor," she said.

He nodded and hurried away. Charlotte watched the men dismount, torches sent sparks into the air. She counted thirteen men under those hoods. She had ten in the house with her.

From her vantage point, Charlotte could see one man had stepped in front of a line of men that had formed. "Come out of the house, Charlotte!" he bellowed.

It sounded like the baritone speaking—though he wasn't making as much of an effort to disguise his voice as he did during their first encounter.

"Come out or we're burning the whole place down!"

"Sweet Jesus, no," Isaac said. "He gonna burn us out."

Charlotte pulled the hammer back on her rifle and said a silent prayer of thanks that there was just enough moonlight to illuminate her targets.

Pastor Brady, trembling from being in the possible presence of violence, felt God nudge him to speak. He knew he could be the voice of reason before chaos ensued. He kept cover beside the window, but held his Bible in the air, the book lit from the lantern in the room so all could see he was a man of peace—a man of the cloth. "Stop! Stop your threats in the name of all that is holy and good. Evil acts only bring you to the gates of hell!"

A voice from below yelled out to him. "You joined forces with evil, Pastor. You're headed to your own lake of fire!"

Beside the house, six more hooded men moved through the darkness. There were no torches, no calling cards of fire to announce their arrival. They were silent as they made their way up to the house and began to look for a way inside.

Pastor Brady yelled out in his best sermonizing tone, "I am here as an ambassador of peace! I beseech you to leave …"

A bullet ripped through his Bible, tearing it from his hand. He dropped to the floor, trembling with the thought of how close he'd come to dying, then crawled across the room to retrieve the book. He stuck his finger into the hole in the center of the leather cover. "Truly a holy book."

Outside, he could hear the leader of the Klan continue to yell at Charlotte.

On the ground floor, a window in the kitchen slid up its sash and a white-hooded figure pressed through the space and into the room. To the sound of sporadic bursts of gunfire outside, the man strode across the kitchen, white robe flowing out behind him with his haste, and entered the walk-in pantry. He found a small door in the wall and pressed the mechanism to open it—then folded his large frame into a good-sized dumbwaiter. He disappeared into the wall, between the floors—until he arrived at his second-floor destination.

Outside, the baritone Klansman moved closer, continuing his tirade. He swiped his torch back and forth in the air as if he were waving a fiery wand. "I'm not fooling around here, you black-loving turncoat!"

Charlotte cocked her rifle with steady hands.

"I'm giving you to the count of three to show yourself at this front door," the man shouted. "Or I'm burning everything!"

"Isaac, you might want to move away," Charlotte said.

"One!" came the voice.

Charlotte eased the barrel of her rifle into position.

"Two!"

She settled her eye near the sight.

"Three!"

She fired on the man with the torch. He dropped and the other men scrambled for cover any place they could find it. Torches lay in the red clay of the circle drive like small pools of fire.

Shots rang out that skittered into a window frame of the house. Isaac yelped. And Charlotte heard sweet music to her ears: the pastor started to shout from the window again.

"Cowards! Heathen! Listen to the Word of the Lord! 'And hath made of *one* blood *all* nations of men for to dwell on all the face of the earth.' You are wrong! You are wrong in your thinking and wrong to be here!"

Charlotte could see the men below her fanning out. She took aim again and fired. Another man down and now two men sprinted around the house. She yelled out instructions. "Two men heading east. Someone stay on them!"

In the hallway, the door to the dumbwaiter opened a crack and the man in the hood peered out as two black men ran past. Silently, the hooded man pushed out of the dumbwaiter into the hall. He knew where she was now—knew where to go. When he entered the room, they were occupied—and unguarded.

"Here's more bullets, Miss Charlotte," Isaac said. He stood next to her, hand out with the ammunition. She was so intent on reloading her gun, she didn't see or hear the man behind her until his hand snaked around her mouth and he dragged her away from the window. She could see the white of his sleeve, the robe around his legs. She struggled, tried to scream, saw Isaac's terrified eyes. Then a voice in her ear said, "Charlotte. It's me."

Her own eyes widened with recognition. The hand eased the pressure over her mouth, and she spun around at the same time the man removed his hood.

"Elijah!"

He put a finger to his lips. "Shh."

It was the most natural thing in the world to throw herself into his arms. She felt his arms go around her, hold her close for a precious few seconds. Then he pulled back and looked into her eyes. "I leave you alone for two weeks …?"

She wanted to laugh and cry at the same time. Isaac was there then, awkward at first, but hugging Elijah. "Cap'n, I can't believe it. Jes can't believe it."

"There's talk in town," he said. "I became one of the enemy to find out their plan."

She couldn't get over it. "You're here."

"I'm here," he said with a reassuring nod. "Now where are the men who came with the pastor?"

"Shorty, Barney, and Joe are guarding the staircase that goes to the foyer," she said. "Bram and Bobby Wilkes are at the other end of the hall at the top of the kitchen steps. Our defense is the high ground—take out whoever tries to come up."

"Shorty and Barney are Klansmen. They planned to get in a place where they'd be able to do the most good …"

"Shorty? No!"

"They're going to let the Klan breech the stairs once they're through the front door," Elijah said. He pulled the hood down over his face. "They'll think I made it up the back steps. Gives me the advantage."

He was back out the door so fast that Charlotte and Isaac almost didn't believe he'd been there at all.

Elijah made his way to the top of the grand staircase. He could see Shorty and Barney positioned side by side, looking down on the floor below. Between them lay another man, motionless, presumably Joe—and almost certainly dead. Elijah reached down into his boot and withdrew his knife. He could hear the last of the boards being flung from the front door below as he got to within a few feet of the men.

"Sounds like they're almost through," he said.

The men turned, saw him in his robe and hood and nodded. Elijah squatted down between them and one of the men grinned. "Here comes the cavalry."

"Don't sully the name," Elijah said. In quick order, he dispatched both men with his knife. They slumped at the top of the stairs as the front door burst open. Hooded men poured inside and made straight for the stairs. Elijah began shooting, and men started falling.

Behind him, he heard the same kind of firefight ensuing at the opposite end of the hall. Klansmen, confused at first by the hooded man shooting at them, dropped down, tried to take cover, but the repeating action on Elijah's rifle let him pepper the bullets until the men were either dead or running.

From the window, Charlotte counted five hooded men run from the house toward their horses.

From the other end of the hall, Bobby could see the Klansman firing down the stairs. He made his way until he was midway down the hall, stopped, cocked his gun, and pointed right at Elijah. As his finger pulled the trigger, a feminine hand shoved the gun up and away from his target. The shot rang out and smashed into the wall.

"He's with us! He's one of us!" Charlotte yelled. "Shorty was in the Klan. So was Barney."

The sound of sporadic gunfire echoed while they stood there. And then Isaac was hollering. "They're leaving! They're running away!"

They could hear the shouts of victory coming from the other men in the house. "They're running scairt, now!" Bram shouted.

Elijah pulled off his hood, came striding down the hall. Bobby studied him.

"Wait. You're that Yankee ..."

Elijah shucked off the white robe and nodded. "Guilty as charged."

Bobby made his way closer to Elijah, stopping just a couple of feet away. "It was a Yankee who took my leg," he said.

"It was a rebel who took my brother," Elijah replied.

Bobby stuck out his hand. "Glad we're fighting on the same side now."

Charlotte watched the men shake hands. Isaac rushed up to Elijah and fired off questions without taking a breath.

"How'd you get here, Cap'n? Did you take the train again? Are you feeling all right? Did you find out who hired the bounty hunters that tried to get Miss Charlotte?"

"All great questions, Isaac," Elijah said, "and I'll answer them right after I have a few words with Miss Charlotte."

He took Charlotte's hand and pulled her into a room across the hall and closed the door. They could hear the muffled sounds of the men celebrating their victory. But standing alone with Elijah in the moonlit room, Charlotte could think of nothing but his nearness and the serious look in his eyes.

"I had a terrible fever from infection after I got to St. Louis," he said. "Would have died in the hotel basement if not for the kindness of an industrious janitor …"

"Elijah …"

He furrowed his brow. "There were dreams. Strange dreams of white horses stampeding toward you. Fire that streaked through the sky. I knew I needed to get to you—help you. But I couldn't and it nearly drove me crazy."

"I knew you shouldn't have gone. You could have died," she said.

"The fever broke and the terrifying dreams were gone and in their place—another dream. A hopeful dream."

"Tell me about it," she said.

Elijah shook his head. "I don't think I can …"

"That's not fair. Now you *have* to tell me," she said.

"I think I should just show you." He stared into her eyes, leaned down, and kissed her.

"Cap'n? Miss Charlotte?" Isaac's voice came through the door. "Dey's lookin' fo' you out here!"

Charlotte felt Elijah's smile against her lips. She tipped her head back to look at him. "I'll go talk to them, thank them. Once I do that, I'm all yours."

He smiled. "That's the rest of the dream."

CHAPTER FORTY-EIGHT

Charlotte gently swayed at a writing desk situated under a small round window. She dipped her pen into the inkwell, and began to compose another entry into a journal twelve months in the making.

September 5, 1867—Is today the day? Lord, I hope so. This unresolved feeling follows me—lingering in the back of my mind. It's not just me it affects but all of my relationships both present ...

She stopped for a moment and gently placed her other hand on her rounded belly.

... and future. Elijah keeps reminding me we can't undo the past, but we must always do our best to right our wrongs.

The floor beneath her rolled, and she swayed in her chair. She took hold of the desk with her left hand to wait it out. Once the motion stopped, she turned her attention back to the journal and continued ...

We are just over forty-eight hours into our journey following the latest information we've obtained. Please, Lord, don't let it be another dead end.

A knock on the door interrupted her thoughts, and she turned in her chair.

"Come in."

The door opened and Elijah poked his head inside. "We'll make landfall soon," he said.

"Good." She paused, concerned. "How is she doing?"

"Nervous," he said.

"I would imagine so."

"How are you doing?" he asked.

She offered a tremulous smile. "Nervous too."

His smile was reassuring. "I would imagine so. You'll want to join us soon."

"I will."

Elijah disappeared back out the door, closing it behind him. She turned back to her journal, saw her left hand splayed across the page, then after a moment's hesitation, slipped the gold wedding band off her ring finger. Lifting the mercy medallion from around her neck, she unhooked the clasp of the chain, threaded it through her ring and put the necklace back on. Charlotte tucked the chain under the bodice of her dress, then turned her focus back to the journal. A half smile played on her lips, and her eyes filled with amusement as her pen once again flew over the page …

I asked Elijah the other day if he had any regrets about resigning his commission to be my husband, and he didn't hesitate for a second. "Life with you has been much more dangerous and unsettling than

*any assignment I had in the army—including the Indians. Regret?
Never."*

Charlotte put down her pen, blew softly to dry the ink on the
page, then closed the journal. The floor continued to sway beneath
her. When she stood, she took a moment to get her bearings before
she made her way from the room.

The schooner deck was filled with activity. The vessel had been
rigged to carry both freight and passengers, and the crew had a
plethora of duties to carry out in preparation for docking. Charlotte
looked up at the voluminous sails that had caught the wind early
and carried them from the Georgia coast toward the small island in
front of them. The swell of the turquoise ocean gently rocked the
ship when the first mate began to lower the mainsail. There were a
few other passengers who had journeyed with them from the East
Coast, and they stood at the rail of the boat looking toward land.
Charlotte spotted Elijah and Chessie on the bow. Ever conscious of
the motion, she made her way toward them and put her arm behind
Chessie's back.

"Almost there."

Chessie nodded, her eyes on the land. "I got worries 'bout home."

Charlotte and Elijah traded a glance. "What kind of worries?"
Charlotte asked.

"Ain't none of us there if a problem happens," Chessie said. "Dat
ain't good."

"Bram is perfectly capable of handling problems that arise while
we're away," Elijah said. "He's proven himself to be an excellent
overseer."

"Dat's true. He has taken to da job," Chessie agreed.

"And you know what a taskmaster Isaac is," Charlotte added. "He'll make sure everyone is doing their job."

Chessie chuckled. "He a good boy. Loves you and Elijah like a son loves his ma and pa."

"You know that's how we think of him," Charlotte said. "No more worrying now, you hear?"

Chessie nodded and looked from Charlotte to Elijah. "I knows how hard you both been tryin'. Dat counts for a lot."

As they approached the island, they could see the tall palm trees dotting the landscape like sentries and the hot white glare of the sand against the azure blue of the water.

They came to anchor in the port of Nassau and disembarked the ship. There were dozens of locals looking to make money on the few tourists coming from the boats. Men hollering out prices for buggy rides, tours of the island, fresh shellfish. Elijah maneuvered through the hawkers, keeping Charlotte and Chessie close behind him. He went up to the one man who wasn't aggressively trying to get his business.

"Can you take us to the Royal Victoria?" he asked.

The black driver nodded, quoted a competitive price, and then gestured to his open-topped buggy.

The road was populated by a few pony carts and women in brightly colored dresses balancing large flat baskets on their heads. They passed a large swath of land edged by piles of debris.

Charlotte frowned at the devastation. "What happened here?"

"Had a bad hurricane blow through here last year, mum," the driver said. "Very scary for everybody."

"Any deaths?" Chessie asked.

"In the islands we lost over three hundred people."

Charlotte saw Chessie draw her arms over her chest and furrow her brow.

"It's gonna take a long time to put things back together again," the driver continued. "The place seen better days for sure. Lots of desperate people. Wind is mighty."

"How did the hotel fare?" Elijah asked.

"It was spared, but it's got its share of scars," the driver said. "They lost part of the roof and nearly all the gardens. Used to be folks would come just to see those gardens."

The driver pulled the buggy in front of the Royal Victoria Hotel, a white four-story building that seemed to be deserted.

Elijah helped both ladies from the buggy and tipped the driver. Chessie started toward the hotel entrance. "Let's go see."

The former grandness and glory of the hotel was visible behind the overall feeling of struggle. A young couple walked arm in arm through the lobby, and an older man sat with a cigar and a newspaper in a cluster of chairs near a window. They were the first white faces they'd seen since leaving the boat. The hotel was quiet. They went to the front desk and rang a bell.

A handsome black man appeared and smiled broadly. "Welcome to the Royal Victoria."

"Thank you," Elijah said.

"How many rooms, sir?"

"We're looking for some information first," Elijah said.

"What kind of information?"

"We believe there's a young man in your employ," Elijah said. "His name is Kitch."

The man barely gave it any thought at all before shaking his head. "No, I'm sorry. Never been a man named Kitch in my employ."

"Are you sure?"

"Unusual name," the man said. "I'm sure."

Charlotte looked at Chessie, but she had already turned her back on the counter and walked a few feet away.

"Have you worked here long?" Elijah asked.

"Since we opened in '61," the man said. "I have several young men on staff, but no one with that name. I have an Earl, a Washington, a Thomas. There's a Maxwell, Jordan, and Lincoln …"

Elijah held up a palm. "It's all right."

Elijah glanced at Charlotte, and she tried to put an accepting smile on her face, though she failed miserably. He turned back to the man behind the counter. "We'll be needing two rooms for the night."

"Good, very good, sir."

Charlotte looked over her shoulder to see about Chessie—but she was gone. She stepped away from the counter, gaze covering the lobby, but there was no sign of her.

Making her way to the double doors that led outside, Charlotte pushed through and stepped into the garden. It was filled with new plants and young trees, and she could see the effort that had been put in place to create a beautiful vision someday. She walked a few feet down the path, made a turn and stopped short when she saw Chessie and a young man in an embrace. Though Chessie's grandson, Kitch Washington, towered over her, he leaned low and she patted him over and over on the back. Her expression was one of bliss.

Charlotte's eyes filled with tears, and before she fully realized it was happening, she started to sob. Deep, racking sobs she couldn't stop, couldn't quiet. Even though the memory of how she'd wronged Kitch and Chessie was still missing, the relief of putting things right was greater than she could have ever imagined. She saw Chessie coming toward her, and she shook her head.

"I had no idea … no … idea."

Chessie reached out for Charlotte and gathered her close in a hug that calmed her, and she gave herself over to the warm embrace.

I always thought of my circumstance as entirely unique, but what I've come to realize is that I'm just like everyone else in that we all carry burdens. Many of them are tucked away, deep inside under lock and key. We go through life knowing there is something not quite right about ourselves but don't understand why. Today, I got to unlock the box—and release a burden. The music I discovered was a piece of my life; the song that played was about a girl who realized her mother is a seventy-year-old woman with ebony skin and deep brown eyes.

She raised me, loved me, and showed me Mercy.

... a little more ...

When a delightful concert comes to an end,

the orchestra might offer an encore.

When a fine meal comes to an end,

it's always nice to savor a bit of dessert.

When a great story comes to an end,

we think you may want to linger.

And so, we offer ...

AfterWords—just a little something more after you

have finished a David C Cook novel.

We invite you to stay awhile in the story.

Thanks for reading!

Turn the page for ...

- **Mercy's Real-Life Counterparts**

MERCY'S REAL-LIFE COUNTERPARTS

Thousands of women served as nurses during the American Civil War—risking life and limb to be angels of mercy to wounded and dying soldiers. Through personal diaries and eyewitness accounts, their stories have been recounted on the pages of history books and their bravery and sacrifices have been well documented.

Clara Barton, the most famous of those nurses and founder of the American Red Cross, was quoted as saying, "I'm well and strong and young—young enough to go to the front. If I can't be a soldier, I'll help soldiers." Barton, known as the Angel of the Battlefield, felt it was her Christian duty to help soldiers, a notion instilled in her by her father. She knew well the perils that faced her on the battlefield, recalling a time where she nearly died when administering to a soldier: "A ball had passed between my body and the right arm which supported him, cutting through the sleeve and passing through his chest from shoulder to shoulder. There was no more to be done for him and I left him to rest. I have never mended that hole in my sleeve. I wonder if a soldier ever does mend a bullet hole in his coat?"

Clara Barton exhibited patriotism, compassion, and bravery when she was on the battlefield tending to those soldiers who needed her. But there was another group of women, not as well documented as the nurses, who were driven by their own patriotism and bravery, and it is that group of women who served as part of the inspiration behind Mercy, our protagonist in *Traces of Mercy* and *Finding Mercy*.

Even though it was illegal at that time for a woman to enlist in the army, it is estimated by historians that over four hundred women disguised themselves as men and fought for both the Confederate and Union armies during the Civil War. Besides patriotism, women had a variety of reasons for going to such extreme measures to participate in the fighting. Some did it for love—to remain close to a husband, fiancé, father, or brother. Some did it for the money. An army private during the war made thirteen dollars a month for soldiering, an amount nearly double what a housekeeper, cook, or seamstress would have made at that time. Most of the women went undetected in their disguises—living, sleeping, and fighting next to their fellow soldiers. They were skilled and brave; they could shoot as well as the men and ride a horse with equal expertise; and they suffered the same hunger, fear, and dread as anyone else in the company to which they were assigned.

The documented cases of discovery among the female soldiers are small. Seven were found out because they were wounded and required medical care (as was the case with Mercy), seven were taken to prisoner-of-war camps, at least six disguised female soldiers shocked everyone and gave birth in the field, and nine more lost their lives during battle. Teenager Lizzie Compton, who was known as Jack to fellow soldiers, was discovered to be a woman after she was wounded during a battle. When a military doctor treated her, he discovered her secret and she was sent home. Not to be dissuaded, Lizzie went on to reenlist in six more regiments. Each time she was discovered to be a woman, she was discharged and she reenlisted with a different regiment. Lizzie served in the Union army for eighteen months of the war.

Some of the women who donned men's clothes and fought actually had permanent changes to their personalities. Frances Clayton joined the cause with her husband in 1861. She enlisted with the name Jack Williams and served in the Missouri artillery and cavalry units. It's been reported that before her time in the army was over, Frances (aka Jack) took up gambling, cursing, and cigar smoking.

New Orleans resident Loreta Velázquez is another woman who couldn't seem to endure sending her husband off to fight in the war alone. It is reported Loreta dressed as Lieutenant Harry T Buford to accompany her husband and served briefly as a company commander under Confederate Brigadier General Barnard Bee at Manassas. She kept her secret for nearly a year and wrote in her own memoirs that once discovered by her fellow soldiers, she left the company and became a secret agent.

Jennie Hodgers, known in the military as Albert Cashier, enlisted in the Ninety-fifth Illinois Regiment and fought at Vicksburg, Nashville, and Mobile. She spent the duration of the war in disguise without being discovered, and then after the war, she went on to live as Albert Cashier for fifty more years. Some accounts say it was an automobile accident that Cashier was involved in that led to the discovery that the Civil War veteran known as Albert Cashier was actually Jennie Hodgers. The 1913 revelation made newspaper headlines across the country.

Union soldier Private Franklin Thompson enlisted in the Second Michigan Infantry on May 14, 1861. He was for all intents and purposes a soldier like anyone else, but in actuality Franklin Thompson was Sarah Edmonds. While Sarah survived the battle of Antietam, she was unfortunately struck with a case of malaria a few months later. She knew that a doctor's care and hospitalization would lead to the discovery of her secret identity, so she deserted her company. When she was once again in good health, Sarah donned another disguise—this one as a male Negro slave—and worked as a spy, delivering dispatches under enemy fire for Union General Orlando Poe. In 1884 Sarah attended a regimental reunion as Franklin Thompson and told her old comrades her story. Those same fellow soldiers are said to have helped her persuade the government to drop her conviction as a deserter and file for a veteran's pension. It is widely held that she was successful on both counts because in some records she is the only recorded female member of the Grand Army of the Republic.

While their reasons for disguising themselves as men and fighting during the Civil War were varied, these women, who fought in one of the most tumultuous wars in American history, were brave, showed remarkable courage and gumption, and in many cases, demonstrated grace under fire.

Speaking about the war, President Lincoln said:

> The will of God prevails. In great contests each party claims to act in accordance with the will of God. Both *may* be, and one *must* be, wrong. God cannot be *for* and *against* the same thing at the same time. In the present civil war it is quite possible that God's purpose is something different from the purpose of either party—and yet the human instrumentalities, working just as they do, are of

the best adaptation to effect His purpose. I am almost ready to say that this is probably true—that God wills this contest, and wills that it shall not end yet. By His mere great power, on the minds of the now contestants, He could have either *saved* or *destroyed* the Union without human contest. Yet the contest began. And, having begun, He could give the final victory to either side any day. Yet the contest proceeds.

Although Abraham Lincoln was most certainly referring to the men who were fighting, his words ring just as true for the women who fought right by their side.

The contest lasted four agonizing years, and during it all, the women who enlisted in disguise sought neither recognition nor medals, and they were right there until the very end.

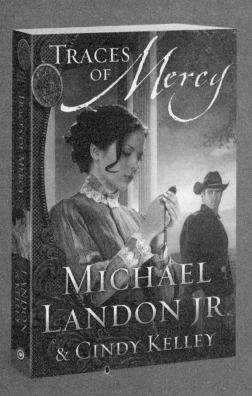

Some Things Are
Best Left Forgotten

At the end of the Civil War, they found her wounded and suffering from amnesia. Unable to remember anything of her past, she takes the name Mercy and begins life anew. But what's in her past, once uncovered, could destroy her.